THE other ONE

JIFFY KATE

The Other One
Copyright © 2016 Jiffy Kate
Published by Enchanted Publications
First Edition: October 2016
ISBN 978-0-692-77674-2

This book is a work of fiction. Names, characters, places, and incidents are the product of the authors' imaginations and are used fictitiously. Any resemblance of actual events, locales, or persons, living or dead, is coincidental.

All rights reserved. Except as permitted under the U.S. Copyright Act of 1976, no part of this publication may be reproduced, distributed, or transmitted in any form or by any means, including photocopying, recording, or other electronic or mechanical methods, without the prior written permission of the author.

Enchanted Publications
www.enchantedpublications.com
enchantedpublications@gmail.com

Visit the author's website at *www.jiffykate.com*

Edited by:
Nichole Strauss, Perfectly Publishable
www.perfectlypublishable.com

Cover Design by:
Jada D'Lee Designs
www.jadadleedesigns.com

Cover images by:
Dreamstime.com (stock photo)

Interior Design & Formatting by:
Christine Borgford, Perfectly Publishable
www.perfectlypublishable.com

prologue

THE SOUND OF TIRES SCREECHING and metal crunching catches my attention, and I look over Evan's shoulder just in time to see another car coming straight for us.

There's no bracing for impact, no time to prepare.

The words "Oh, God" barely leave my mouth before the collision.

Glass explodes around me as my head slams into the windshield.

The loud horn blaring keeps me alert long enough to register that something very bad has happened, but too soon, the bright flashing lights overwhelm, and my brain does what it can to protect itself: it shuts down.

one

"SO, TELL ME, TRIPP. WHY do you want to work here?" Mr. Dubois asks.

I keep my gaze on my fingers, willing my nerves to settle. I've been practicing and preparing for this interview for days. I know what I need to say, but making the words come out is hard. It's one of the things I hate about myself right now. My brain is like a landmine of knowledge. Sometimes, I fall into the massive holes, and I can't climb out. Where the old me would speak freely with confidence, the new me overthinks each word for fear of saying the wrong thing or sounding stupid.

I can do this.

Taking a deep breath, I slowly look up and find Mr. Dubois watching me, waiting patiently. I'm still not comfortable with a lot of eye contact, so even though I know I should look him straight in the eye, I can't, and I avert my gaze, focusing on his pale-blue bow tie instead.

He's maybe five years older than me but dresses like the southern gentlemen of my grandparents' childhood. The seersucker suit he's wearing matches his bow tie and suspenders, with the only oddity to his outfit being the scuffed-up cowboy boots on his feet.

I can do this.

"I . . . I like the atmosphere here," I begin, swallowing down my nerves. "It's busy, but not overwhelming." Maybe I should clarify that bright lights and loud noises sometimes mess with my head?

No.

I'd rather not elaborate. I don't want him to think I'm crazy or that I can't do this job.

I can.

I will.

I need this.

I can do this.

"The location is great," I continue, clearing my throat and trying to sound confident. "I attend Loyola, which is just around the corner . . ." My words trickle off because, of course, he knows Loyola is nearby.

I let out a huff through my nose and continue with my rehearsed replies. "The business hours work well with my class schedule . . . Oh, and I like the food."

"Oh, yeah?" he asks as he smiles at me, and I think that last part might've scored me a few brownie points. It never hurts to compliment your maybe-future employer, right?

"What's your favorite dish here?" he asks, and this question could trip me up because it's not something I planned, but it doesn't. This time my answer needs no rehearsing.

"The shrimp and grits, hands down," I say with a slight smile.

"Excellent," he says slyly, leaning in and looking around as if to prevent anyone from listening in on our conversation. "That's my favorite, too. Just don't go tellin' my wife I said that. It was her idea to start sellin' that dish. I didn't want to because we've got a restaurant around the corner that sells nothin' but grits and gumbo. I didn't think it'd have a snowball's chance in hell to succeed. Turns out, it's one of our top sellers. We're using her late aunt's recipe, some secret ingredient that keeps the folks comin' back for more. She loves to rub it in that she was right and I was wrong, and believe me, I give her plenty of reasons to gloat."

My body slowly relaxes as he goes on about different items on the menu and how they came about. The way he's talking with me so casually helps put me at ease. I get the feeling the interview is going well, and about half-way through his spiel, I'm finally able to give an easy, natural smile.

I can do this.

"Well, Tripp, I think you'll do just fine here at The Crescent Moon," he says, standing from his chair. "Follow me. We'll go see Dixie. She's who keeps this place runnin' smoothly and is in charge of the schedules. You'll wanna kiss her ass a little," he says, winking back at me as we walk out of his office. "Come see me in the kitchen before you leave; I'll introduce you to the staff."

"Does this mean you're hiring me, Mr. Dubois?"

"Damn straight it does. And please, call me Wyatt. You're part of the family now!"

Mr. Dubois—er, Wyatt—gives a hearty slap on my back before continuing his way down the hall.

I can do this.

No, wait. I did it.

Holy shit, I did it!

Dixie is a nice, older lady with thickly drawn eyebrows and the longest fingernails I've ever seen. I don't know how she's able to type my information into the café's computer system so quickly with those things, but she does, and I'm grateful.

I'm starting to feel tired. The stress of the day is catching up with me. Between my anxiety and nerves and rush of adrenaline, it's the perfect storm for a migraine, and I don't want to be here if one hits. I don't get them as often as I did a few months ago, but when I do, they come on strong. And I'm pretty much useless for the rest of the day, confined to my apartment with the shades drawn and a blanket over my head.

I hate them and try to avoid them at all cost.

Handing my pre-written class schedule to Dixie, she smiles at me reassuringly. "How are you, darlin'?"

"Good," I reply.

She asks me a few more questions about my schedule and days off, and I answer them as calmly and evenly as possible. And I'm glad I don't have to make much eye contact. Most of her focus is on the screen in front of her, instead of me.

When I meet new people, I'm always worried they'll see the scar before they see *me*, and that always leads to questions. The last thing I want to do is answer more questions, especially about my scar or how I got it, but Dixie doesn't seem to notice, or if she does, she doesn't mention it.

She sets up a time for me to come in tomorrow after my classes for training and tells me I'll have my work schedule by then as well.

When she's finished with me, I meet Wyatt in the kitchen.

He introduces me to the cooks and servers, who are preparing for the dinner shift. They all look up and say hello, but continue doing whatever it is they're doing. I try to concentrate and think of something that'll help me remember their names, but I know it's futile, so I give everyone a small wave as each of them glances up from their work, hoping somehow, I'll eventually fit in here.

"Tripp, I'll see you tomorrow at two for your training," Wyatt says, officially dismissing me.

"Yes, sir. I'll be here."

His smile is genuine as he nods his head my way before turning and addressing the rest of the staff. "Alright, team. Let's look alive out there. It's dinner time, and the fine people of New Orleans are ready to be fed! Y'all have a great shift and work your asses off because that's what I'm payin' you for."

For a second, I'm reminded of how it used to feel to get pep talks from my high school coach in the locker room. I guess working in a restaurant is a lot like playing football, or any sport. You have to work together as a team to reach your goal. It's been awhile since I've been on a team, and suddenly I'm filled with dread at the thought of letting people down.

"When you get out there, remember you're a team," Coach Smith begins. "And there's no 'I' in team! We win together, and we lose together! If we want it bad enough, we're gonna get it! So, you get out there and play like the champions I know you are! I want your best! You got me?" he yells, his voice getting louder and louder with each statement until the vein in his forehead is about to pop out with the last question.

"WE GOT YOU!" we all reply in unison.

"WHO ARE WE?" he yells.

"WARRIORS!"

"WHO ARE WE?"

"WARRIORS!"

"WHAT ARE WE GONNA DO?"

"WIN!"

Before that last word is out of our mouths, I take off running, leading the guys down the tunnel. The moment the door opens, the blinding lights from the stadium are all I can see until I set my focus on the fifty-yard line. The crowd is chanting.

WARR-IORS!

WARR-IORS!

I'm acutely aware that this is the game—the one that will determine my future. There are scouts here from several colleges, including Tulane, and depending on our performance tonight, a few of us may get scholarship offers. We have to do this for us, for our school, and for Coach Smith. He's always been there for us, and we can't let him down now.

"Alexander?"

"Yes, Coach?"

"This is your game, son. This is where a boy becomes a man. I know you've got it in you, so let's bring it home." He nods with confidence, adjusts his headset, and walks away. He's always had confidence in me. Since the day I stepped onto his field as a sophomore, he's made me feel like I can accomplish anything.

Jogging up and down the sidelines to warm my muscles up, I squint my eyes, trying to see past the bright Friday night lights. I glance up to the middle section and see my mom and dad sitting in their usual spots. My mom gives a little wave, not wanting to embarrass me, and my dad gives me the nod, similar to Coach Smith's, letting me know I've got this, because he believes in me, too.

From the belly of the kitchen, the chime on the front door can be heard, signaling a customer's arrival. It's then I realize I'm still standing in the spot Wyatt left me. Everyone else is busy with their jobs, zipping around, oblivious to my presence. So, I turn my gaze to my feet and walk back through the swinging doors.

As I pass through to the dining area, movement catches my attention. Wanting a glimpse at what my job will be like, I pause; thinking a waiter or waitress will be coming any second. Turning my head just a little, I watch as a young woman slides into a booth, all the way to the inside as if she's making room for someone to sit next to her. Her eyes are focused on the window, never looking down or at a menu, and I can't help but stand there and stare at her.

A throat clears, making me jump, and I don't know if I should feel relieved or embarrassed to see Wyatt standing behind me.

"She's a regular," he tells me, looking over at the same girl. "She comes in every Thursday and sits in that same booth, but she doesn't order or say much. We just leave her be."

"Okay," I say as Wyatt leaves me standing. For some reason, my eyes are still on the girl. It seems like a strange thing for someone to do—come and sit at a café, but never order anything—but I'm sure she has her reasons, and to be honest, I'm happy to know I'll have at least one easy customer.

I can do this.

As I head for the front door, I give my future non-customer one last glance. I expect her to continue staring out the window, so when she turns around and our eyes meet, it catches me off guard. My body freezes—not just because she makes eye contact or for the fact that she's beautiful, but also because I don't think I've ever seen eyes quite as sad as hers. They're dark and deep and full of unshed emotion. Something about them—her—makes my heart clench. I haven't had a reaction like this to a girl in a long time. The feeling practically levels me.

Quickly, I turn away, averting my gaze back to the floor and forcing my feet forward. The second my hand is on the doorknob, my pulse begins to race, and beads of sweat break out on my forehead, sure signs of a panic attack looming over me like a ticking time bomb.

The panic attacks are worse than the migraines because they come without warning.

First, it's my heart beating out of rhythm.

That's followed by tightness in my throat, like someone has me in a vice grip.

Then, it's the lightheaded feeling, and I can no longer breathe.

I've got to get out of here before I make a total fool of myself.

I can't do this.

Pushing my way out of the door, I walk quickly in the direction of my house, willing myself to calm the fuck down.

I force myself to breathe.

Eventually, I fall into a familiar trance as I count my steps to focus on something besides myself and the feeling of imploding. Ten steps turn into a hundred. I'm so focused on taking deep breaths and steps that I don't hear my phone ring in my pocket. It's the vibration from the voicemail that pulls me out of my stupor, causing my steps to halt for the first time since I left the cafe.

When I finally dig the phone out of my pocket, I take a second to get a grip on my surroundings. And then, I hit redial, not waiting to listen to the message first, because I know who it is. She has a sixth sense. It's like a beacon goes out to her when I'm in distress.

"Tripp?" she asks, forgoing a normal greeting. And I can hear the edge of concern in her voice, even though she's trying to keep it under wraps. "Is this a bad time? Did I interrupt your interview?"

"Hey, Mama," I say, cracking a smile as her familiar voice helps ground me. "No, I'm done and on my way home. What's up?"

"Oh, nothing's up. I was just wondering how your day is going . . ." she hedges.

I love my mother. She's my biggest supporter and fiercely protective. I know she babies me more than she should, but I allow it because it makes her happy. I can tell she's dying to know how my interview went, but she's trying to respect my boundaries and let me do things my way. And I appreciate that—it's progress.

"My day's been great. I finished my homework for the week, got my hair cut earlier, and got a job. You know, same ol' same ol'," I say, waiting to see how long it takes her to realize what I've just said. Of course, it doesn't take her long.

"You got the job," she says, trying to hide her excitement. "Oh, Tripp. I knew you could do it. I'm so proud of you."

Even though we're speaking on the phone, her words still make me blush.

"Thanks, Mom."

"This calls for a celebration! Would you like to go out or eat in?" she asks.

"Let's stay in tonight, if that's okay." Part of me wants to celebrate—not just because of my new job, but also to thank my family for everything they've done to help me get to this milestone. But there's this other part of me who can't stop thinking about the girl at the café with sad eyes.

"Of course. I'm sure Liza won't mind us getting together over there. Now, what about the food? Is there something special you'd like for me to cook, or would you rather I pick something up?"

It only takes me a few seconds before I know what I want: Louisiana Pizza Kitchen. Best pizza in New Orleans, no doubt about it.

"Do you want a fried oyster pizza or a jambalaya pizza?" she asks with a giggle.

"Both, please."

"I don't know why I asked. I knew you'd say that. I'll call your sister and let her know we'll be eating over there. I'll pick up the pizzas on my way. Are you walking, or do you have your bike?"

"I'm walking," I answer.

"Well, be careful. If you get tired, hop on a streetcar."

"I'm fine, Mama. I'm almost home. I'll see you when you get here."

As soon as I hang up and slide my phone back into my pocket, my thoughts are immediately back on the sad girl again.

Somehow it doesn't seem fair that I should have fun when she's sitting there all alone. And a very small part of me, a part that's been buried for quite a while, thinks about going back to the café and talking to her. But, of course, I won't do that. I *can't* do that.

And as I continue walking, I wonder why she had an effect on me. What's different about her? Why is she so sad?

It hasn't been that long since I left the restaurant and her face has popped into my mind at least a dozen times. It's pretty obvious I'll be thinking about her a lot. So, I need a nickname—something other than *the sad girl from the café*, because that's too long and annoying. And, whoever she is, I doubt she'd like that.

I rack my brain for a name that suits her, but nothing comes to mind. And once again, I'm annoyed with my lack of control over my brain. I constantly feel like it betrays me these days. But instead of allowing myself to get worked up, I breathe.

Leaning up against the street sign at the corner, I inhale deeply and hold it for a few seconds, before exhaling.

I try to forget everything except the movement of my chest.

In through the nose.
Out through the mouth.
In through my nose.
Out through my mouth.

When I open my eyes back up, I realize I've probably been leaning against this post for a while, because my body feels much more relaxed. The technique seemed to do the trick, and thankfully, I didn't attract an audience. I do the sign of the cross in thanks that Mrs. Devereaux isn't out in her garden. If she saw me, she'd be out her gate and across the street, praying for me.

Hell, maybe that's what I need.

With that thought, inspiration hits and forces my brain into submission. I begin thinking of as many saints as possible. One of them might be suitable as a nickname for the girl at the café. I'm not saying she's a saint, but something about her seems otherworldly, so maybe one will work. I know Mary is often referred to as *Our Lady of Sorrow* . . .

Should I call her Mary?
No, too common.
No offense, Blessed Mother.

As I cross the street and continue to walk down the sidewalk to my sister's house, I resign myself to the fact that I'll never think of the perfect name, when suddenly one of my favorite subjects comes to mind: mythology.

What about a Greek goddess?
She *is* beautiful.
But that might be too cliché.
What about the Algea?

It's funny—not in a ha-ha kind of way, but in an

I'd-like-to-remove-my-brain-and-trade-it-in-for-a-new-one kind of way—that I can remember something as complex as mythology, but I can't remember events from less than a year ago. The information is still a struggle to recall, but once I do, it usually flows out.

I remember that the Algea are goddesses of sorrow and grief.

That kind of fits and it could work.

But which one?

What are their names?

I pause in the middle of the sidewalk and pinch the bridge of my nose until the information finally comes to me.

Lupe, Achus, and . . .

A smile splits my face as I recall the last one—*Ania.*

It's perfect—unique and beautiful, just like the girl.

two

NOW THAT I'VE DECIDED ON a nickname for the girl, I feel a sense of relief. These days, the smallest successes make me happy and hopeful, like maybe I will get back to normal eventually.

With the weight of the interview off my shoulders and the pride I feel from landing a job, I'm ready to celebrate with my family.

As I walk in through the back door of my sister and brother-in-law's house, I spot two of my most favorite people in the whole world: Emmie and Jack Walker.

"Uncle Tripp!" they both scream as I squat down to their level as they make a beeline for me and knock me flat on my ass.

My niece and nephew are the coolest three-year-olds, and the fact they're twins only makes them more special. It amazes me how Emmie is the spitting image of her dad, Benjamin, with dark wavy hair and dimples so big they could hold a marble inside, while Jack looks exactly like my sister, Eliza. Well, he looks more like Liza did before she started dying her hair blonde, but they share the same ice-blue eyes, courtesy of my dad. Jack's hair is more of a dark brown like mine and my mom's. Genetics are fascinating.

"You're here!" Liza exclaims, clapping her hands together. "A little birdie told me you have some exciting news." Her sing-songy voice makes me smile. I look at Emmie and Jack, who are also smiling. For little people, they're very perceptive.

"I know Mama's already called and told you I got the job, Liza. It's not that big of a deal," I say, knowing how false my words are, but trying to downplay it, because I hate the attention. It makes my skin feel crawly.

"Tripp Alexander, it *is* a big deal," Liza scolds.

"Well, I wouldn't have gotten the job if you hadn't helped," I tell her, pushing myself off the floor and onto my feet. Emmie and Jack run into the living room, onto their next adventure.

"I merely made a phone call and suggested to Wyatt that he should interview you; I didn't force him to hire you. But, in all honesty, I know too many embarrassing stories involving Wyatt Dubois." She winks. My sister is a bit evil but in the best way. "There's no way he'd ever go against me," she says with a laugh before pulling me into a fierce hug and whispering, "I'm so damn proud of you."

Like my mother, Eliza's very protective—almost to the point of smothering me and she'd do anything for me: make calls, blackmail old college friends to get their brother a job . . . hover, meddle, tell little white lies when need be.

That's what families do, right?

"Tripp Alexander," my mom says in shock, standing in the darkness of the kitchen. "What on earth are you doing out at this time of night?"

"He wasn't," Liza says, walking in the door behind me, scaring the shit out of me in the process. "I called him and asked if he would come and walk me in. There was this creepy car following me on my way home, and I knew Daddy would be asleep, so I called Tripp instead." She looks up at me nodding, urging me with her eyes to agree with her and go along with it.

Man, she's good . . . or bad, but regardless, mom seems to be going for it. I turn my gaze from Liza back to my mom and nod in agreement, afraid to say anything because I'm a horrible liar. Had Liza not been behind me, my ass would be grounded for the next week, if not longer.

"Well . . . then, I guess that's good," my mom says, wrapping her robe around her tighter as she walks into the dim light of the foyer. "I'm glad you didn't take any risks, baby. There are crazy people in this world." She cups Liza's cheek, planting a kiss on it, before turning to me and doing the same.

After locking the door behind us, she makes her way up the stairs. "You both need to get straight to bed. It's late."

I let out a huge breath, relief finally flooding my body.

"What the hell, Liza?" I whisper.

"I saw you turning down Chartres and followed you home. I was hoping I'd pull in the same time as you, but I got caught by the light, and you didn't."

"I can't believe you lied to Mom." I quietly laugh under my breath, realizing she's had a lot more practice than me.

"Oh, hush. You would've done the same for me. That's what family is for." *She pats my cheek, similar to what my mom had done minutes before, but without the kiss. Thank God.*

Liza might be a typical older sister, sometimes ratting me out or giving me shit, but ultimately, I know she'll always have my back.

After Ben comes home from work and my mom walks in with the pizzas, we all gather in my sister's formal dining room. The table is set with my sister's "special occasion" dinnerware because she insists that today is a "special occasion."

"Does Wyatt still wear those crazy bow ties?" Ben asks, bringing me back to the conversation.

"Yeah, he was wearing one today for my interview." I chuckle, remembering his crazy get-up.

Liza giggles. "That boy has been a contradiction in fashion since the day I met him. Bow ties and cowboy boots have always been his signature look, along with his shaggy hair. He's a great guy, though. You'll like working for him, I'm sure."

I nod my agreement as I finish the last bite of my fried oyster pizza. Working for Wyatt won't be a problem, but taking care of customers while staring at *Ania* all day might be. Over two hours later and I still can't stop thinking about her.

After dinner is over, I hug everyone and tell them good night. Tomorrow is a school day, and I have to spend some time preparing before I go to sleep. Besides, this day has taken everything out of me, and the quietness of my space and my bed are calling my name.

Once in my apartment, I make sure the door is locked and the kitchen sink is empty before I head to my room and lay out my shorts and T-shirt for the next day. It's a month into the fall semester, but that doesn't mean the weather's getting any cooler in Louisiana. It's pretty much flip-flop weather year-round down here, for which I'm grateful.

All of my classes are on Mondays, Wednesdays, and Fridays. I was anxious to get back to my studies this semester, but knowing I needed to ease back into the student lifestyle made me cut back from my usual six classes a term to only three. I'm trying not to push myself too hard, too fast, but I just want to be . . . *normal* again. I want it so fucking bad, I can taste it.

I double-check that my textbooks and binder are in my backpack, along with plenty of pens and pencils, before placing it by my door. While my shower heats up, I make sure my watch has the start times of my classes set up as alerts. I have the same alerts set on my cell phone because you can never be too careful.

Being late one time back in August was enough to set me straight. I swear everyone was staring and laughing at me as I tried to sneak to a seat in the back of the class. Embarrassment permeated my body to the point I couldn't concentrate on what the professor was saying—it was paralyzing—but there was no way I was going to risk sneaking back out of the room. So, I stayed in my seat until the last person was gone, then promptly rushed home to lick my wounds.

Something that used to come so easy to me, like school, is now my own personal Everest. Every day, I plan and prepare so I don't make the mistakes of the day before. And every night, I go through ritualistic habits to ensure the success of tomorrow. Sometimes, it's exhausting, but I can't give up. Not now.

Steam begins to fill the bathroom, signaling that my shower is hot, so I undress and step under the spray, letting the water wash away the day.

When I'm out of the shower with minty-fresh teeth, I attempt to control the hair on my head. I swear it doesn't matter what direction I brush it; it still looks like I didn't even try. It'll just stand straight up or curl in the opposite direction. It used to drive the girls I dated crazy. I threatened to cut it once and my girlfriend at the time threatened to break up with me if I did. I guess I could cut it now. I haven't been with a girl in over seven months, so there's no one to protest, and I don't see that changing anytime soon. But, the longer hair has a different purpose now.

Now, it's camouflage, something to hide behind.

Anytime I have to look at myself in a mirror, my eyes automatically zoom in on the scar that cuts just above my right eye and down onto my cheek. It looks so different than it used to. The color has faded to a faint shade of pinkish-purple, almost iridescent in the right light. It's smooth, and now that my eyebrow has almost grown back, it's not *as* noticeable. But it's still there. I still see it. And I know other people do too. I see their looks of curiosity, and sometimes I hear them whispering. I hate the whispers the most. I hate people making assumptions about me because they don't know anything.

With that thought, a wave of guilt washes over me, because I think I've done that to the girl at the cafe. I've spent the afternoon guessing about her situation and making up different reasons about what makes her so sad, but I don't know anything about her . . . I don't even know her name.

Wyatt told me that *Ania* doesn't talk to anyone when she's in the café.

I can't help wonder if she noticed me.

Did my hair cover my scar?

If not, did she notice it?

I double-check the alarm on my clock on the nightstand and then turn the lamp off.

Sometimes, right before I drift off to sleep, I get anxious thinking about what the next day will bring, but not tonight. Tonight, my thoughts are filled with dark brown hair and sad eyes.

⚜

AFTER GRABBING A PROTEIN BAR and bottle of water, I make my

way downstairs to my bike, setting my bottle into the holder and hopping on. The morning is less humid and less busy. I always enjoy my ride to campus.

When I arrive at the bike rack in front of the Student Union, I hop off and lock up my bike.

While walking into my building, I spot several people I know from class, but we don't acknowledge each other. They're all merely acquaintances, not friends. I had friends when I was at Tulane, but they've all moved on. Most of them have probably graduated by now. Loyola is a much smaller campus, just under a third of the size of Tulane, which is why I switched after the accident. The smaller classes and the fact I don't have to see familiar faces are my favorite things about this school.

As I sit down in my Intro to Courts class, I make sure to set my recorder. Without it, I would fail most of my classes. It's hard for me to keep up with the handwritten notes, and I often forget what one class was about by the time I make it to the next. Liza helped me set up my schedule, and I'm glad I listened to her advice and only took classes every other day. It takes me the rest of the day to transcribe the recordings onto paper and go through my notes, committing to memory as much of the information as I can before the next class.

I'm grateful for the distraction of sitting in lectures today. If I had the day off, I would've spent the entire day worrying about training. With this being a new experience, I would've come up with a million ways to fail, given the chance.

Before I know it, I'm saddled back up on my bike and headed to The Crescent Moon.

As I walk in the front door, Wyatt is the only one in the dining room.

"Tripp! It's great to see you. You ready to learn the ropes?" he asks reaching his hand out to shake mine and I can't help but smile when I notice the polka dot suspenders and matching bow tie he's sporting today.

"Yes, sir," I answer, feeling a sudden onslaught of nerves. Since I have trouble remembering things, I wonder if I might need to take notes, but I don't want Wyatt to think I'm incompetent. So, I'll just do the best I can, and I guess, if I need help remembering, I'll have to ask for help, even though I hate it.

After spending a couple of hours giving me the dime tour, going over policies and procedures and showing me my basic duties, Wyatt tells me to take a break at one of the tables closest to the kitchen.

Sliding a bowl of gumbo toward me, he asks, "So, what do you think so far?"

My stomach growls as I inhale the delicious aroma . . . hints of cayenne and oregano hitting my nose and making my mouth water. My granola bar from this morning is long gone. Then I remember, he asked me a question.

"I'm sorry?" I ask, looking up from the steaming bowl.

He chuckles and shakes his head, sliding into the seat across from me. "What do you think so far? About the job?"

"Oh, right. Well, it doesn't seem *too* complicated, which is good . . . for me." I take a quick bite, wincing at the temperature, but not caring, because it's so damn good. "I think if I focus on the main tasks, keeping them in order—greeting the guests, taking their orders, bringing their food, and then the check—it seems manageable. I just worry about having more than one or two tables at a time and getting things mixed up."

"It can take a few days to get the hang of things, but don't worry. No one here wants you to fail. If you fail, then we all fail, and that's just not good business. We're all here to help, so don't be too shy or too proud to ask, alright?"

I nod, taking another bite of gumbo.

Wyatt and I talk a bit more about what's expected of me before he sends me to see Dixie and get my work schedule. My first real day of work is next Tuesday. It's such a mixed bag of emotions that I'm feeling—scared, excited, hopeful . . . anxious. I always have some level of anxiety, but knowing I'm going to be thrown into a new situation with new people only makes it worse . . . especially when I think of seeing *her*.

Ania.

For some reason, I still can't get her out of my head.

I can't remember what I had for dinner two nights ago, but I can remember her face as plain as day.

three

Shoving off my covers, frantically trying to untangle my legs, I wipe the sweat from my forehead and take deep breaths.

The nightmares started Friday night after I got home from the café, and got progressively worse all weekend. I tossed and turned all night. Images of failure were flashing through my mind—breaking dishes, customers yelling at me, a look of disappointment on Wyatt's face.

Yesterday, during my classes, all I could think about was greeting customers and taking orders, going over menial tasks until it's all I could think about. And I'm starting to think this job wasn't a good idea.

Maybe it's too soon?

Maybe I'm not ready?

I honestly have no idea how I'll survive today.

But one thing I do know is that I *can't* fail.

Failing at this job would mean letting down my family and I've done enough of that to last a lifetime. I'd also let down Wyatt, and even though we just met, I don't want to do that, because his opinion already means a lot. And it would mean I might never see *Ania* again, and I might never know her real name or what her voice sounds like or why she hides behind her curtain of long dark hair.

These are the thoughts that put me on edge.

But I'm hoping they'll also be what keep me from messing everything up.

I've done enough of that. It's time for me to start pulling my weight and getting on with my life.

Dr. Abernathy always says, "If you're not busy living, you're dying." I've been close enough to dying to know that I want to be busy living.

Just as my hand rests on the handle of the back door of the café, my phone rings in my pocket. Looking at my watch, I see I'm still early for my shift. So, I take the phone out of my pocket and answer it.

"Hello, Mama." I let out a deep breath, as if I'm annoyed, but I can't help the small smile that creeps up on my face. Closing my eyes, I let her voice do its job.

"Hey, baby. Just wanted to say good luck today and I'm so proud of you."

"Thanks."

"I'll see ya at dinner tonight."

"Yep, see ya tonight."

"You're gonna do great, Tripp." Hearing her confidence in me and knowing that she's there for me, no matter what, is just the push I need.

"I hope so."

When I finally put the phone back in my pocket and walk through the door, there are a few people milling around in the kitchen. Two of them I recognize from the day of my interview. All three of them nod their head and greet me with a "hey" like I belong here. I'm not sure I do just yet, but it's nice to know they don't look at me like the freak I feel like sometimes.

The melodic tone from the saxophone player who stands at the corner of the street is filtering through the partially opened window over a large stainless steel sink, and a guy at the counter in the middle of the kitchen is humming along. Everyone seems to work together like a finely tuned orchestra, and the fear of failure hits me again.

What if I mess up their orchestra?

What if I can't do this?

A girl with a curly blonde ponytail walks through the swinging doors with a tray full of partially empty glasses. She pauses to pin an order slip on the wire hanging over the counter with one hand, while balancing the tray precariously with the other.

What if I drop a tray and break all of the glasses?

Do you get fired for that?

Self-doubt is eating me from the inside out, but just before I can tuck tail and run back out the door, Wyatt's voice fills the room, handing out instructions and saving me from myself.

"Julie, the couple at table four changed their mind about dessert."

He sets a stack of plates in the steamy sink before practically dancing over to the big stove, where a muscular guy with floppy brown hair is whisking with one hand and flipping with the other.

"Shawn, I was instructed to give compliments to the chef on the butter sauce today," he says, tipping his imaginary hat, and then he turns his attention to me. "Tripp, it's good to see you again. Are you ready to get your feet wet?"

He can probably tell from the scared-as-shit look on my face that I'm having second thoughts. His smile and a firm hand on my back are all that's keeping me in place.

"You're going to do just fine," he assures me, gripping my shoulder and easing me toward the door that leads to the main part of the café. I peek out as the doors part and see a few tables with customers, but for the most part, the place is pretty empty. My shoulders sag with relief, and I take a deep breath, trying to convince myself *I can* do this.

"You can do this," Wyatt says, eyeing me from the side as if he can hear the war going on in my mind. "I have faith in you."

I nod my head in response and begin following him around the room, shadowing his every move. He allows me to watch and learn without pushing me into the lion's den. Gradually, I begin to feel more comfortable, moving easily between the crowded tables and knowing when to duck or scoot out of the way.

"See ya next time, darlin'." Wyatt waves as one of the last customers leaves. It's not the end of the day, just the end of the lunch rush, and as he explained to me earlier, a time to get everything back in order before the evening crowd descends.

I think the time between lunch and dinner will be my favorite time at work. The crowd is gone, the café is quiet, and I'm left to monotonous chores like folding napkins and wrapping silverware. It's calming, ritualistic like some of my coping techniques, and it's exactly what I need in the midst of all the newness.

The bell above the door chimes, signaling a customer. Wyatt opens the swinging doors wide, greeting them as they come in, offering a table by the window and announcing their server will be right with them. Then, he looks over at me with a wink.

Oh, shit.

Is that me?

Am I their server?

I don't think I'm ready to fly solo.

What if I forget the specials?

"Table five is all yours," he says, hitting me lightly with his towel as he passes by.

Slowly, I stand from my spot at the table in the back and place the unused napkins next to the shiny forks I've been rolling into a neat pile. Rubbing my now sweaty hands down the front of my slacks, I take a step toward the table. The people aren't paying me any attention, and looking at them, they seem nice enough. I clear my throat and swallow hard, willing my feet to move in their direction.

"Welcome to The Crescent Moon," I say mechanically, walking up to the edge of the table, but not making eye contact. "What can I get you to drink?"

Out of habit, I sweep my hair to the side to cover my scar.

The couple takes what feels like minutes to look over their menus as I wait with pencil and pad in hand. My heart is beating fast, but I manage to keep my hand from shaking. Both of them order a rose mint tea, our house specialty, which seems easy enough until I start thinking about delivering two piping hot cups of tea. Without saying another word, I stumble over my own two feet as I turn and head for the safety of the kitchen.

"Two rose mint teas," I mumble, internally berating myself.

"Two rose mint teas," Sarah repeats, leaning over to meet my eyes with a smile. "Everything going okay?"

"If you consider being a moron and almost knocking over two

tables *okay*, then yeah." I can't help but give her a small smile in return, because something about her big round eyes remind me of my niece Emmie and thoughts of Emmie always make me smile.

"Don't let the first-day jitters get to ya. Trust me; we've all been there. I'm sure you'll break a few plates before it's all over with," she says, laughing as I turn around and head back out the door, nearly running over Julie and a full tray of dirty dishes.

"Sorry."

"No problem."

As I struggle through my first day—forgetting orders, spilling soups, and nearly dumping an entire pitcher of ice water on a lady—my mind occasionally drifts to *her* . . . Ania. I wonder why she only comes here on Thursdays.

When Wyatt approaches me and starts making small talk, it's on the tip of my tongue to ask about her, but he seemed so closed off about the subject the first day I was here, I'm afraid to bring it up. So, I wait.

Thursday seems like a year away.

⚜

"SO, ARE YOU READY FOR your second day at work?" Liza asks as she pours coffee into two mugs, one for her and one for me. "Wyatt said you did well for a newbie." She smiles as she looks back at me over her shoulder. I knew she would check up on me.

"I can't believe he didn't fire me."

"Oh, please. You're not the first new employee to make a few mistakes on your first day. Besides, it's a lot to take in and . . ." She drifts off, and I know what she wants to say. She wants to make excuses for me and blame my incompetence on something that's out of my control. But she can't make excuses for me the rest of my life.

"Liza," I warn.

She turns around and gives me her concerned look—mouth twisted, worried eyes—making her look just like Mama. "It's going to take time. You can't expect to be back at full speed right away."

"I know." I pinch my nose and release a deep breath of air.

"Just do your best. That's all you can do. Take it one day at a time, just like the doctor said."

"Thanks, Liza."

"Anytime." She kisses me on my cheek as she pushes the cup of coffee into my hand. "Have a good day. I can't wait to hear about how the second day goes," she says, closing the front door behind her on her way out.

The highlight of today is that I'm finally going to see *Ania* again. My mind races with questions and curiosities, but more than anything, I just want to see her and have a chance to commit more of her to memory—the color of her eyes, what her smile looks like, and the sound of her voice. I'm hoping I get a chance to talk to her . . . *if* I have enough nerve to talk to her.

Today is similar to Tuesday. I check in with Dixie when I arrive, and she gives me my time card and a smile that boosts my confidence. Wyatt allows me to shadow him through half of the day, and then he puts me in charge of a couple of tables toward the front. I try not to watch the door and the clock, but the longer I have to wait and anticipate seeing *her*, the more worked up I feel inside. Somehow, I have to get a grip before I cause myself to have a migraine and am forced to leave before she even gets here. *That* would be horrible.

I ask Wyatt for a five-minute break, and he tells me to go ahead, but not before asking me if everything is okay. I nod my head, telling him nonverbally that it is. But the truth is all of the anticipation of wanting to see *Ania* has me feeling anxious, and I need a few quiet minutes to take some deep breaths and get myself in check.

As I lean back against the brick on the outside of the café, I inhale deeply through my nose, taking in the delicious, rich aromas from the kitchen, and attempting to clear my mind, only concentrating on my diaphragm going up and down.

"Care for a smoke?" someone asks, startling me.

I turn to look at the dark-haired girl from the kitchen, Julie. She's holding a half pack of cigarettes in my direction.

"Sometimes it helps when I'm having a stressful day. You look like you could use it."

"I'm fine. I just needed a few minutes alone." As soon as the word leaves my mouth, I feel like an asshole. I didn't mean it like that, but sometimes I say things without thinking.

I turn to her to apologize for sounding so rude, but she waves me off.

"No worries. We all need a break from time to time."

"Well, I didn't mean it like that. Sometimes I say stupid shit." My hair falls into my eyes as I turn my head to look over at her.

She laughs, blowing out a puff of smoke over her shoulder in the other direction. "I like you."

"Thanks," I say, giving her the first genuine smile I've had all day.

There was a time when a lot of people liked me and wanted to be my friend, but that time seems like a lifetime ago.

"Hey, Alexander," Evan hollers down the corridor, running to catch up with me.

I stop and wait for him. "Hey."

"So," he begins, throwing an arm around my shoulder, "you comin' to the party tonight at Amanda's house? I hear her parents are gonna be gone, and Whitney's supposed to be spending the night." The last part comes out suggestively, and I can't keep myself from laughing at him.

"I don't need Amanda's parents to be gone to get Whitney alone," I reply confidently because it's the truth. Whitney and I have been together for the last two years, and we're perfectly capable of finding time to be alone. "But the party sounds fun. I've got dinner with my family tonight, but I'm sure I can make my way over there later."

"Dude! You have to! It won't be a party if you're not there."

"I said I'll be there."

"Cool!" He slaps my back before running back in the direction from which he came. I roll my eyes, because that kid is always on the run, even on the football field, which is why he's my number one go-to for passes. He and I make a great team. I wish he were interested in signing for Tulane. He'd be a great asset to my future team.

"Have a good weekend, Mr. Alexander," Mr. Brown says as we pass in the hall.

"You too, Mr. Brown."

It's going to be weird not being here next school year. Most kids are counting down the days until they get to college, but I've loved every second of high school. As much as I'm ready to take the next step in life, I'm going to miss this place.

"There you are." Whitney reaches around and slides her hand into my back pocket. "I've been looking everywhere for you."

"Hey." I kiss the top of her head, looking behind us to make sure no one is looking before I move my attention to her lips. "Ready for the weekend?"

"Ready for some alone time with you," she says, pulling me closer as she leans into me. "You're coming over to Amanda's tonight, right?"

"Yes, I already promised Evan . . . and Trey . . . and Marcus, earlier at lunch," I tell her.

"Good. It wouldn't be a party without you." She looks up at me with her big blue eyes, and I can't resist placing another kiss on her lips.

"So I've been told."

"You got a new table, Tripp," Sarah calls out as soon as I walk back into the building.

I nod at her before I take in a deep breath and slowly let it out. A quick glance at my watch tells me I only have an hour left in my shift, so I straighten my shoulders and walk to the front, determined to end my work day on a positive note.

My new table is a nice older couple, who are very laid-back and easy to please. After their hot teas and appetizers are served, they settle into effortless conversation. It's clear they've been in love for a long time and are perfectly suited. They remind me of my parents in that respect, and I can't help but wonder if I'll ever find my soul mate one of these days. I used to think it was a given for me, but now, I'm not so sure.

Barely paying attention to my surroundings, I nearly trip over my own two feet as I turn around to head back to the kitchen, because sitting at table six is the long dark hair I've been waiting for all day. Thankfully, she's turned toward the window and doesn't see me stumbling around like a drunk. I manage to stay upright the rest of the way into the kitchen, where I brace myself on the wall and take deep breaths.

Opening my eyes, I see Julie and Sarah both watching me but trying to look busy at the same time. Neither of them says anything, but they exchange a glance across the counter as they finish garnishing plates that are ready to be taken to the customers—*my* customers.

"Two specials are up for table five," Julie says loudly over the roar of the busy kitchen.

After I compose myself and feel like my hands are steady enough to carry the plates to the table without dropping them, I pick them up and head back out through the kitchen doors. Setting the plates in front of the older couple, I politely ask them if there's anything else I can get them before turning around and stealing a glance at *Ania*.

Part of me is internally begging for her to look up, but the other part is saying no. If she looks at me, I'll probably make a fool out of myself, but I'd love to know if her eyes are as sad as they were last week.

What color are they?

Are they brown?

Blue? Green? Gray?

Does she ever smile?

Is the sadness always on her face?

Technically, her table is in my section, and even though I know Wyatt told me not to bother her, I'm fighting the urge to offer her some water or ask if she needs anything.

I wonder how long she stays. Glancing down at my watch, I notice it's just a little after six, which means she must come here right at six o'clock, or at least she did today. I make a mental note so that I can be more prepared next time. I'm tempted to set a timer in my watch like I do for everything else, but that would be weird.

As I continue walking between my few tables, checking on the customers, I keep an eye on her, waiting for her to look up and notice me, but she never does. When I have the older couple's table cleared, I intentionally walk by hers. Slowly. She's wearing a black long-sleeve T-shirt that she has pulled over her hands as if she's cold and her tattered brown leather backpack is sitting beside her like a placeholder. A journal or notebook of some sort is laid out in front of her, but from what I can tell, the pages are empty. She hasn't budged much since she got here. If I didn't know better, I'd think she was a statue, but I hear her clear her throat as her hand comes up and brushes at her face.

Is she crying?

That's probably a stupid question. If her face looks anything like it did last week, I'm sure she is. I think that's what bothered me the most. She looked like she could shed tears at any moment, and for whatever reason, it resonated in my chest.

I guess the better question is: *Why is she crying?*

And why do I care?

The lump in my throat is unexpected, and I try to ignore it as I continue walking to the kitchen to drop off the tray of dirty dishes.

Something deep inside pulls me to her, and I can't explain it. I've never felt drawn to another person like this, and it's startling.

"Don't try to figure her out," a voice whispers beside me, as I watch *Ania* from afar.

I turn to see Sarah beside me, following my line of sight to the table where she sits. "She's never said a word to any of us. Well, besides Wyatt. Apparently, they go way back. She's been coming here for a few years, but I guess she hasn't always been like that," she says, motioning to her still form now staring down at the blank pages in front of her. "Sometimes she just sits, and sometimes she writes in that book. She always comes on Thursdays at six o'clock and stays until at least seven, sometimes longer. There's something mechanic about the things she does, but I've never been able to figure her out."

I look over to see Sarah in deep thought, shrugging her shoulders as she stands, perplexed over the girl with the long dark hair.

four

THE FACT THAT I DIDN'T even get to see a glimpse of *Ania's* face yesterday is plaguing me.

I dreamed about her again last night. It was nothing specific, just a girl in a long white dress standing in a pool of water. I never saw her face, but I know it was her. She was standing there, her dress floating around her, making her appear ethereal, while her dark hair hung down to her waist, much like it has the two times I've seen her. Grey skies opened up above her, and rain poured from the clouds, dripping off the ends of her hair.

I think what bothers me the most is that I know I have an entire week to wait for my next chance to see her. I had hoped, at the very least, to see her face yesterday. Of course, I'm not a big fan of eye contact, but I want to see hers. What if the next time I see her, she still stays hidden behind her veil of hair? What then? Do I wait another week? *Can* I wait another week? The longer I wait, the more invested I feel, and I don't even know why or what I'm seeking.

When I can't comprehend something or remember something from my past, my therapist always tells me to start with the truth I know and go from there. My truths about *Ania* are a short list. All I know is that she goes to the café every Thursday, and she intrigues me. Other than that, I'm left with a bunch of questions and unplaced emotions.

Liza sensed something was bothering me when I came in from work yesterday evening, but I tried to convince her it was the pressure of having a job and adjusting to something new. She gave me the one eyebrow look that says she doesn't quite believe me, but she let it rest.

If I'm not mistaken, later that night, I overheard her on the phone talking to Wyatt. I'm sure she was checking up on me, and I know she thinks I don't like that, but, honestly, it doesn't bother me. I feel indebted to my family, so if they need to check up on me or keep tabs on me to feel better, then I'll let them. We all have things to cope with, and I can't begrudge them their mechanisms. If I were in their shoes, if I had almost lost them, I'd probably be overly protective and somewhat irrational from time to time, too.

⚜

AS I ROLL OUT OF bed, I begin my normal morning routine: make my bed, eat breakfast, brush my teeth, get dressed, then grab my backpack and leave. Performing these tasks in the same order allows my day to start in a calm manner, and I need as much calm as I can get, especially after my dream.

Biking to campus, I'm still struggling with what to do about *Ania*. I'm so curious about her, and I know I won't get any answers until I talk to her, but I just don't know if I *can*. I stutter and trip over my words while having a conversation with my family members. What makes me think I won't do the same or worse if I try to speak to *her*? And I get the feeling she doesn't want anyone to speak to her, which makes it even harder.

Part of me thinks I should give up before I crash and burn, save myself from the embarrassment of rejection, but I don't think I can.

What I'd love more than anything is to be able to talk this over with my dad.

If he were here, he'd know what I should do. He always did. He always had the best advice, even when I didn't want it.

"Tripp, how was your study session tonight?" my dad asks as I walk in the back door a little after curfew.

"Fine." I shrug as I let my backpack drop off my shoulder and to the floor

with a loud thud.

Both of my parents have a signature expression when dealing with my sister and me. My mom cocks her left eyebrow and purses her lips together. This particular look is usually paired with her hands firm on her hips while her right foot taps a demanding rhythm. My dad, though. His "look" isn't as dramatic as my mom's. He simply focuses on my eyes with both of his brows raised expectantly while the words "I know you're full of shit. Now, 'fess up" are practically written across his forehead.

That's the look he's giving me right now.

I learned a long time ago; it doesn't do me any good to try to bullshit my way out of a conversation with either of my parents, so I let out a long sigh and tell the truth.

"I wasn't studying; I was with Whitney," I admit, deciding full-disclosure is my best bet.

My dad doesn't look surprised, and I'm not sure if that's good or bad.

"Son, we've discussed priorities before, isn't that right?" he asks.

"Yes, sir."

"I understand that your girlfriend is a priority to you, as she should be, but you have other things to focus on, too. Mainly, your grades. Unlike the football field, where you play as a team, your test scores are all on you."

"Dad, I don't know why you're so concerned with that. I'll get into college because of football. What I score on the SATs doesn't matter."

"What happens if you get hurt and can't play football anymore? Your mother and I will always help you if you need it, but I'm not going to pay your tuition so that you can party your way through college. It's very simple. If you want a career that pays well, you'll need a degree, and to get that degree, you have to pass your classes. You're a very bright young man, but don't take things that come easily to you for granted."

No one, not even my dad, could've predicted just how right his advice to me was that day. Football did get me into Tulane, but it didn't keep me there, and it most definitely didn't get me into Loyola. I've learned some hard lessons these last few months, but I'll be damned if I ever take anything for granted again.

I have a lot of regrets about the past few years and I refuse to add to the list.

I know talking to a girl might not seem like a big deal to a lot of people. It wouldn't have been a big deal to me seven months ago. But now, it is. It's something I want almost as much as I want to feel normal again.

I *want* to know her.

Unlike last week, this week I'm grateful for the seven days I have to wait between her visits to the café. Hopefully, I'll be able to work up the courage to say something, anything.

I spend most of the time during my classes on Friday daydreaming about what it'd be like to talk to *her*. Several scenarios flit through my mind.

In one vision, I can see the old me walking right up to her with the confidence I was born with and saying hello. She'd return my easy smile. That Tripp would slide into the seat across from her and tell her he's noticed her, and he'd like to get to know her better.

But that Tripp is in the past. I no longer have that kind of confidence in myself or in my ability to walk up to a girl and start talking.

From there, my mind drifts to more likely first interactions, like walking up to talk to her and then forgetting everything I'd rehearsed, stumbling over a chair and falling into her table, spilling water on her—each scenario more embarrassing than the one before.

I hate this version of me. I hate that I can't just snap my fingers and go back to what I was seven months ago. The frustration brings tears to my eyes, and I hate that too. I don't want to feel weak or incompetent, but the more I try to push forward, the more I feel like I'm going backward.

⚜

"WHAT'S GOT YOU LOOKIN' LIKE someone ran over your puppy?" Liza asks, nudging me with her hip as she dries the dishes I'm washing.

"Nothing." I look down at the suds in the sink. My mind obviously has been adrift with thoughts of *Ania* for a while. I thought of her as I picked up the first plate and now I'm down to my last fork.

"Everything okay?" she asks.

"Yeah, everything's fine," I say, making sure to keep my tone even.

"Classes going okay?" she continues.

"Yes, Liza," I reply, trying not to let annoyance seep into my words.

I know she's going to push until she gets her answers. The worst part is I know what's bothering me, but I don't know how to say it. And even if I were able just to spit it out, I'm not sure how Liza would handle it.

"Have you been feeling okay? No migraines or panic attacks?"

"No. Not in the last few weeks." There was that moment at the café last week, but I don't feel like elaborating, and since I was able to get through it on my own, I don't see any reason to bring it up.

"Have you been having nightmares again?"

"Not recently," I lie.

"Keeping your appointments with your therapist?"

I let out an exasperated breath as I dry my hands on her towel. "Yes, Liza. I'm doing everything I'm supposed to be doing—therapist appointments, getting enough sleep, going to class." My chin falls to my chest, and I drape my arms over the sink.

"Then what's bothering you?" She crosses her arms over her chest as she leans against the cabinet beside me. "I'm worried about you. You seemed like you were doing so well, and now this week, I feel like you've taken a few steps back. If work is adding too much pressure, then maybe we jumped the gun on that. Maybe you just need to focus on your classes for this semester."

"No!" My head pops up, and I realize I probably answered too abruptly, but there's no way I'm quitting work. I like my job, and if I don't work, I don't see *Ania*, and that's out of the question.

Liza raises her eyebrow at my tone of voice.

I laugh, breathing heavily out of my nose, releasing the tension that felt trapped inside.

"What's so funny?" she asks, her lips turning up into a curious, but still slightly worried, smile.

"You gave me the mom brow," I tell her with a teasing smirk.

"I did not!" She whacks me with the dish towel, and it stings a little, so I dip my hand in the dishwater and flick it at her.

"Oh, you're so gonna pay for that," she says, her voice playful, but the mom brow comes out again, and it makes me laugh.

"You started it."

Liza sighs and leans back against the counter. "So, are you going to tell me, or am I going to have to beat it out of you?"

"A girl," I say, simply because I don't know what else to say, and I know she's not going to let this go until I give her some answers.

"A girl?" Liza repeats, questioning with her tone and her expression. I see the twitch of her lips, and I know this conversation isn't over. "What's her name?"

I push another laugh out through my nose, gripping the back of my neck. "I don't even know." The admission makes me feel foolish—stupid. How have I let a girl, whose name I don't even know, get so far under my skin?

"Hmmm," she says, grinning at the floor. "But you *want* to know her name?"

"Yes."

"So, you're going to ask her?"

"Yes—No . . . I don't know." I groan, resuming my position against the sink and burying my head in my arms. "I feel like if I say anything I'm gonna mess it all up and scare her off."

"You're not gonna scare her off," Liza says softly. Her hand comes up to rub my shoulder because she thinks I'm making this about me, and although it is, in part, it's more about *Ania*. "She'd be crazy to run away from you."

"What if I've forgotten how to be with a girl?" I feel my cheeks get hot with my admission, but I can't deny that it's a real fear.

"You haven't. It's like riding a bike."

"What if it's not like that for me? What if I never get back to normal?"

"Who says you're not normal?" Liza asks defensively.

I know I shouldn't go here with her because it pisses her off. I should save this for one of my appointments with Dr. Abernathy, but I can't help the words that spill out. "Lately, I feel like the more I push myself to get back to where I was, the more I get further and further away."

"Is that a bad thing?"

Her question hits me right in my gut.

Maybe she's right? Maybe it's not such a bad thing?

Over the past seven months, I've been forced to see who and what matters. The friends I thought were always going to be there bailed on me. The girl I thought would always be there dumped me. The life I thought I was going to have took a hard left turn . . . or maybe it was right.

"And if this girl is anything special, she'll see what we see. She won't stop at the obvious. She'll look deeper."

"I already feel things for her, and I don't even know her name," I confess, liking that my chest feels lighter getting that out in the open. "Is that weird?"

"Not necessarily. What is it about her that makes you want to get to know her?"

"She's just sad," I say, letting my thoughts drift to *Ania*. "Her eyes always look like she's been crying or like she could at any second. And if she notices someone looking at her, she lets her hair fall across her face as a shield. You can tell she doesn't want to be seen. But I see her. And I want to see more. The more she denies me that, the more I want it."

I wish I could talk to *Ania* as easily and comfortably as I talk to Liza.

"Have you ever stopped to think maybe you see some of yourself in her?"

"No, I—I don't know," I pause for a second, wondering if that's it. "The only thing I can think of when I look at her is that I'd like to help her . . . make her not so sad."

"Well," Liza says thoughtfully. "The next time you see her, just walk up to her, count to three, and say hello. Just do it. Don't overthink it." She pushes off the counter and places her hands on my shoulders, forcing me to look her in the eye. "Most of all, just be you, because you're good enough."

five

"THE NEXT TIME YOU SEE *her, just walk up to her, count to three, and say hello. Just do it. Don't overthink it."*

Liza's words from last week have been on a constant replay since I walked into work this afternoon. Somehow, I managed to make it to Thursday without losing my mind or having a panic attack. Tuesday, when I was working, I kept trying to imagine myself talking to *Ania*. I tried to see myself doing just what Liza said—walking up to her, counting to three, and saying hello—but now that the time is getting closer, I'm not sure I can follow through. I also don't want to torture myself by thinking about it for another week. I wish there was another place I could see her, some place where other people wouldn't be watching, but until I grow a pair and introduce myself, that will never happen.

Taking a deep breath, I glance at the watch on my wrist for the millionth time in the last two hours.

"Got a hot date?" Wyatt asks, startling me, and I nearly drop the tray of glasses I'm currently carrying back to the kitchen. Thank goodness they're empty.

"Whoa, didn't mean to spook ya." He laughs, flashing me a wide smile and helping me steady the tray.

"Sorry," I say, my voice coming out shaky, like the tray, and I can feel my heart pounding. I hate that Wyatt caught me watching the clock. The last thing I want is for my boss to think I don't want to be here, because I do. I want this job. If nothing else, it makes me feel more normal.

"Don't be sorry, man. It's all good!" He rests his hand on my back as we walk to the kitchen together. "So, *do* you have a hot date?" he asks, waggling his eyebrows suggestively.

"No—I was just, uh . . ." He's the last person I want to admit this to, so I try to think quick, which isn't an option for me, so I wing it. "I just have, uh—studying. I have a lot of studying to do . . . when I get off work." My face feels hot from the lies coming out of my mouth, but I can't stop them.

"Did you need the night off?" he asks, sincerity written all over his face. "You know, we're always willing to work with you on your schedule. All you have to do is let Dixie know. School always comes first."

"No! No." I swallow, trying to relieve the tightness in my throat. It's not like Wyatt is one of those dick bosses who thinks his shit is way more important than yours. He cares about his employees. So, standing here making up a stupid lie feels wrong. "It's fine. I'll have plenty of time."

"Well, you let me know if I can help in any way," Wyatt says before patting my shoulder and walking toward his office. When he's gone, I take a deep breath, forcing myself to relax.

I hate that I lied to him, but what else was I supposed to do? He's already told me to leave *Ania* alone, so what would he have said if I had admitted to wanting to talk to her? Would he think I'm defiant or just stupid? I don't want him to think either of those things about me.

I'm so lost in my thoughts that I'm on autopilot as I go to greet my new customer. Not registering which table I'm headed for, I walk until my thighs bump into the rounded corner of wood, making the entire surface shake. As I reach my hand out, startled eyes flash to my horrified ones, but there's something familiar about them. I know these eyes.

Ania.

She scowls briefly before turning away, back toward the window, letting her hair fall forward. Naturally, I'm speechless and embarrassed, so I make quick strides to the hallway leading to the kitchen, pressing my back against the wall when I'm hidden from everyone, trying to mold myself into the plaster. Squeezing my eyes shut, I pound my fists against the wall a few times and let out an aggravated growl.

This is one of those times when I wouldn't mind having at least some of the old Tripp back.

"Hey, brah, when are you gonna buck up and ask Whitney out?"

I inhale deeply, finishing my cigarette before tossing it to the ground and smashing it with the toe of my boot. Rolling my eyes, I laugh while blowing the smoke out of my mouth.

"Why are you so curious about Whitney and me? I've already told you; I'll ask her when I'm good and ready."

My buddy, Tyler, and I are hanging outside, smoking, while the rest of our classmates are inside, celebrating the first football game and win of our junior year.

"Speak of the devil," Tyler murmurs. The sound of a screen door slamming catches my attention, and I look up just in time to lock eyes with Whitney Greene.

Whitney and I have known each other forever, attending the same schools since kindergarten. We've always been friendly toward each other but never hung with the same crowd until high school. This past summer was particularly good to her, maturing her body from an awkward teen to a beautiful young woman, and every hard-leg around here has been drooling over her since the first day of school. I was more than pleased to hear she was interested in me, but it hasn't made me rush to ask her out.

She gives me a shy smile that blooms bigger after I wink at her. I watch as her friend whispers something in her ear, making her giggle before she glances at me again.

We've been tip-toeing around each other for the past three weeks, teasing each other with smiles and playful eyes, and suddenly, I don't want to play anymore. Bits and pieces of a conversation I had a month or so ago with my dad come to mind, but I pay them little attention. There is nothing gentlemanly about the thoughts I'm having for the blonde-haired beauty standing in front of me.

I want her.

When her eyes land on mine again, I hold her stare for a good five seconds before raising my index finger and beckoning her to me. Whitney walks slowly, yet confidently, toward me as I sit on the open tailgate of Evan's truck and light another cigarette. I watch her long legs get closer, forcing my eyes to travel up her slim hips and narrow waist, landing on her full tits when she steps in between my legs.

"I thought athletes weren't supposed to smoke," are the first words out of her mouth, and I love that she speaks her mind without apology. Most girls around here say what they think I want them to say and never show their true selves. What's the point in that?

"We're not supposed to; I just needed something to keep my mouth busy. You know of any other ways to keep my lips occupied?"

Our mouths are only a couple of inches apart, and her sweet cinnamon breath blows over me when she laughs and answers, "I have some ideas."

"So, you and me, huh?" I ask, playing it cool. Yeah, this is definitely not from the Sid Alexander Book of Courtship. I think about adding something to it, being more romantic, but the way her eyes are shining in the moonlight makes me stupid.

"Yeah, you and me," she says.

And, it *was* Whitney and me—for a long time, but not anymore.

I mentally force my mind not to repeat the list of things I've lost recently like a broken record. If I fall into that pit again, I might not be able to crawl out.

"We gotta stop meeting here like this."

Looking up, I see Julie leaned up against the opposite wall, watching me with a small smirk on her face.

Great.

"You okay?" she asks.

"Yeah, I'm fine. I just needed a break." I tilt my head down, letting my long hair cover my scar and also my face because I feel like she's judging me. Every time I'm at my weakest, she seems to be around for the shit show.

"You know, you shouldn't over think things out there," she says, nodding her head toward the front of the café. "It's not rocket science. No harm done if you screw up. Just relax and you'll be fine. And, if all else fails, just remember this is New Orleans, and it's not called The Big Easy for nothin'."

She gives me a wink before pushing off the wall and heading back toward the dining area.

I *wish* it were that easy. I wish my problems ended at those tables out there. I also wish I could talk to *Ania* as easily as I can Julie, but I can't. I guess it's because I'm not interested in her the way I am in the girl with the sad eyes. One thing's for sure. I'll never get to know *Ania* if I don't talk to her first, and I won't talk to her if I keep hiding like I'm doing right now.

Frustrated with myself for even more reasons than before, I force myself from my place of hiding and head to the front of the café to check on my customers. I briefly let myself glance over at *Ania's* table, and I'm surprised to see her still sitting there.

At least I didn't scare her off.

For the next hour, I wait on tables while secretly watching *Ania*. She makes it easy for me by only staring out the window and ignoring me. She's so good at blocking out her surroundings, never moving her gaze, not even when a plate hits the floor in the kitchen. I've never seen someone so lost in their thoughts.

Well, except for me.

I find a tiny bit of solace in the fact that she obviously has her own issues.

The more I watch her, the more my confidence starts to grow.

I'm going to talk to her tonight.

Every time I look at her, I repeat those words in my head.

I'm going to talk to her tonight.

Checking my watch, I realize she's been here for two hours, just sitting and staring out the window. She hasn't spoken or had anything to eat or drink, and my heart cracks a little as it registers how much she must be hurting. I could be wrong, but everything I've observed from her screams heartache.

Now's the time.

I'm going to talk to her.

I bring two glasses of water to a nearby table, but only place one down in front of the gentleman who is dining alone. I'm still holding the second glass as I head toward *Ania's* table. Like the cup of water shaking in the Jeep with every step the T-Rex makes in the movie, *Jurassic Park*, the water in my glass threatens to splash out the closer I get to her. Quivering hands be damned, *I can do this.*

My feet feel like they're made of lead as I take the last two steps to stand next to her booth. I'm so close; I can see the few wispy strands of hair blowing around her face, courtesy of the ceiling fans above us. She's so beautiful.

I can do this.

My mouth opens, but no sound comes out. When I close my mouth and try again, the same thing happens. *Ania* must sense me invading her personal space because during my third attempt to speak, she turns her body and looks at me. Her eyes are dull, still filled with sadness, but I search past that for more, and I see the brown . . . the beautiful, rich brown. At least I'll go home tonight knowing what color her eyes are. But past that, there's nothing. I was hoping for a spark of curiosity or a touch of friendliness, but instead, I see guilt, pain, and warning—her silently pleading with me to stay away.

Words are still not forming in my brain, and I realize I'm standing at *Ania's* table with my mouth open, staring at her.

I'm an idiot.

I'm an idiot who's reached his limit for the day. I can't take any more self-doubt or loathing or disappointment. If I do, I might explode.

I carefully place the glass of water on her table, and then turn toward the front door.

I turn the handle forcefully and run, needing to feel the burn in my lungs and my legs . . . needing to feel something besides failure.

I don't pause to take off my apron or leave behind my pad and pencil.

I just run.

I don't stop to get my bike from the rack out front.

I run.

I don't even stop when I hear my name being called loudly behind me.

I keep running.

I run until my lungs hurt so bad that I'm forced to stop, bracing myself on my knees and inhaling so deeply, but still unable to catch a full breath. My eyes sting, and when I finally look up, I have no idea where I am. The stench from the gutter at my feet is what finally pulls me out of my head.

"Hey, sugar. I could show you a real nice time," a sugary-sweet voice says from my side as foreign hands rake through my damp hair, and my feet take flight again.

My breath is so labored; the struggle to get oxygen to my brain is causing my head to throb. Pressing my back against a brick wall in a dark alley, I try hard to block the noise and focus on my diaphragm, but it doesn't work.

Nothing's working.

The deep breaths, the diaphragm thing, nothing.

Slowly, uncontrollable fear creeps in, and I feel the heat in the tips of my ears, my throat closing in on me. Beads of sweat are dripping down my cheeks.

Fumbling in my pocket, I'm relieved to find one thing going right for me today. My phone is there. As quickly as my shaking hands will allow, I press the speed dial.

"Tripp, my main man. How's it hangin'?" Ben's voice comes through the phone, and I squeeze my eyes, hating that I'm doing this to him, but having no other choice.

"C–can you come get me?" My voice stutters as my heart tries to beat its way out of my chest, and my head feels like someone has it in a death grip, my eyes bulging from the pressure.

I'm going to die.

After everything, this is how my life is going to end. In a disgusting back alley.

"Yeah, yeah, I can," he says calmly, but I can hear the underlying concern. "You gotta stay with me, though. Where are you?"

I'm pretty sure I know where I am, but I look up at the street sign for confirmation.

"Bourbon."

"What the hell are you doing there?"

"Long story," I say, still panting between each word.

"Can you make it to the corner at Canal?"

"I think so."

Somehow I do. I make it down to the corner of Bourbon and Canal and slide down the wall of a store that sells luggage for twenty dollars, waiting for Ben. I see him when he gets off the bus, his eyes scanning the crowd of people until he spots me sitting on the ground.

"This ground is disgusting, you know? There's a reason they wash the street every morning," he says, leaning down with an examining look on his face.

He's being Ben and doing what Ben does best—defuse and downplay the situation.

I grimace at the thoughts his words provoke, but can't find it in me to care about the condition of New Orleans' streets at this moment.

"I'm gonna need a full disclosure as soon as you feel better," he says, helping me off the ground and to the corner to wait for the light. As soon as we make it across, we hop on the first bus that'll get us close to the house, and Ben hands me a white pill and a bottle of water. The fact that I can now ride the city bus or streetcar without a full-blown panic attack is another small victory, but I'm feeling not so victorious today.

The ride home is horrible for more reasons than one. I feel like a failure. I didn't talk to *Ania*. I made a fool out of myself trying. Ending up in this situation, needing Ben's help—it all feels like a huge setback. I feel the tightness in my throat reappear, but this time, it's not because of my anxiety, it's defeat, and it's so heavy that my chest might cave under the weight.

I manage to keep it together until I'm lying in my dark, cool apartment. Liza tried to insist on staying over, but Ben convinced her that I just needed a little rest and some alone time. I'll have to remember to buy him a case of Abita for saving my ass. Again.

The hammering in my head continues through the night, only allowing me intermittent moments of unrestful sleep. The nightmares are back, but mixed in with the recurring sights and sounds are images of a girl submerged in a dark body of water, and the feeling of panic as I watch helplessly.

six

"Rough night?" Ben asks, his eyes peeking over the top of his coffee cup before he slowly takes a sip.

My reply is nothing more than a moan and a nod. It's all I can muster this morning after the night I had. I just recently started feeling like my head is going to stay in one piece. The threat of an explosion or it splitting down the middle has passed, but it's left me with a major migraine hangover.

The remnants after an attack or a migraine are similar to what I used to feel after a drinking binge at the Sig house, but without the fun of the night before. At least when you're sick from drinking, you only have yourself to blame.

Glancing over at the clock on the wall, I see it's now a little after ten o'clock, and it dawns on me that Ben should be at work, but he's not, which can only mean he took the day off to be here for me. The lump in my throat that I've been trying to push down since last night is back. I feel weak and helpless and I hate it. All the emotions I've worked hard to suppress are forcing themselves to the surface.

"I'm sorry," I croak out because I don't know what else to say.

"No need for apologies. We've been over this before."

His reminder should soothe some of the ache, but it doesn't make me feel any better. If anything, I feel worse. I hate continuously putting my family through turmoil. We've all been through enough. The worst part is I thought I was getting better. I haven't had an episode like that in a while.

"Don't do that, Tripp," Ben warns. "Don't go getting lost in your head and bottling all that shit up." He sighs, setting his mug down on the table and leaning back in his chair. "Why don't you tell me what happened? Maybe you'll feel better if you talk it out."

I let out a deep breath, raking my hand through my hair, undoubtedly making it look worse than it already did. "It's embarrassing," I admit. My eyes focus on the tiny nick in the wooden table in front of me. My finger runs over the ridge, over and over, until I finally open my mouth and start talking.

"I was trying to get up the nerve to talk to a girl." Seems like a good place to begin.

Ben sits quietly, arms crossed, and lets me tell my story, leading up to the moment I called him.

"Well, at least you tried," he says when I'm finished and completely spent, resting my head on my folded arms. "Listen, Tripp. A couple of months ago, you wouldn't have even considered it. So the fact you were willing to even to try is a huge step in the right direction. I mean, yeah, it sucks things didn't work out, and I'm sorry you suffered the consequences, but you handled everything the best way you know how."

"I totally fucked everything up." I want to say that I always fuck everything up, but that statement doesn't usually go over so well.

"No, you didn't."

My silence is the only answer he needs because I feel like I did. There are so many *what ifs* playing through my already cluttered mind right now.

What if Wyatt is pissed at me?
What if he fires me?
What if I'm missing something really important in class today?
What if she doesn't come back?
What if I never see her again?

With the mental onslaught of worst-case scenarios, my heart is pounding out of my chest and my hands grip the edge of the table, searching for a way to ground myself.

"Deep breaths, Tripp." Ben's voice is close, and his hand rests on my shoulder. "It's not as bad as it seems. We'll work through this."

His tone is calm and even, just like it always is. There's never judgment or pity.

Maybe that's why I've always trusted and depended on him?

Well, maybe not *always*.

"Mom. Dad. This is my boyfriend, Ben Walker," Liza says, beaming as she stands beside the Neanderthal she brought to dinner tonight. The last douche bag she brought home ended up breaking her heart, and I'll be damned if I'm going to sit back and watch this prick do the same.

Up until Bishop Lambert, heir to the Lambert Hotels, Liza hadn't ever really brought boyfriends around. He was her first serious relationship, and it ended shitty. I thought I was going to have to hunt him down and beat his ass, or else Dad was going to get thrown in jail for shooting the son of a bitch. Every time Liza came home crying, the chance of one of us ending up in jail increased. Which would've been seriously ironic, seeing as Dad was one of the best attorneys in the state of Louisiana.

"Mr. and Mrs. Alexander, it's a pleasure to meet you." Wow. The Neanderthal speaks in complete sentences. "Tripp," he says, nodding in my direction. "I've heard a lot about you."

"Mhmmpf." I grunt out my response, and now I sound like the Neanderthal. Liza's icy glare over the big burly guy's right shoulder is enough to send me into hypothermic shock.

"Liza tells me you're a stud football player," he says, still trying to break the ice. "I played back in the day."

"Yeah, Tripp is planning on playing at Tulane when he graduates," my dad says, puffing his chest out a little.

We all sit down at the dining room table. The conversation from there on out is a lot less stuffy. Ben charms the pants off of my mom with his "yes, ma'ams" and complimenting her cooking over and over. It's a bit overkill if you ask me.

"I hear you love to fish, Mr. Alexander," Ben says, as he helps my mom clear the table. "My grandparents have a nice pond about an hour or so out of town. It's great for catching some catfish. I'd love to take you some time."

Football know-it-all.

Cleaning off tables.
Bringing up fishing.
What an ass-kisser.

I blindly flip through the channels on the TV in the den as they all talk. Ben and my dad plan a fishing trip for the weekend after Labor Day.

I'm pretty sure my mom is mentally planning their wedding already.

"Hey, Tripp. I hear you like fast cars. Wanna come out and see my Camaro?"

Twenty minutes later, I've decided that Ben isn't such a bad guy after all. The fact that he's going to help me finish overhauling the Impala doesn't hurt, either. I want to be able to drive it the day I turn sixteen, but if I don't get a move on, it'll still be sitting in the garage covered with a tarp, and I'll be taking my driver's test in my mom's old Subaru.

It was my dad's first car, and he saved it for me. A beautiful 1967 Chevy Impala. There're a few scratches here and there, but for the most part, the exterior is perfect. Under the hood is where all the work needs to be done. My dad helps me when he has time, but his caseload has been really heavy lately, so I've been doing most of the work myself. Ben offering to come over and give me a hand is pretty cool of him . . . for a Neanderthal.

⚜

"SO, WHAT DO YOU WANT to talk about today?" Dr. Abernathy asks from across the room.

Exhaling loudly, I feel my frustration rise again, not because I'm talking with Dr. Abernathy, because she's one of the people who's been there for me through my darkest days, but because I'm forced to deal with all of this in the first place. It's getting old, revisiting the same demons over and over.

"Why the long face?" she asks as she rests back in her chair.

"I guess it's because I felt like I'd been making progress, and now . . ." I pause, searching for the right feeling. "I don't know. Seems like I'm going backward."

"What makes you feel that way?"

Suddenly, the fray at the bottom of my khaki shorts is very

interesting. I pick at the loose threads, trying to avoid the question at hand. I know, after all this time, she's not going to judge me. She's never made me feel bad about anything I've told her, and I've told her a lot of shit. I just don't know how to put *Ania* into words. Because it's definitely *her*. She's why I'm so twisted up inside . . . why I ran from the restaurant . . . why I abandoned my responsibilities and why I didn't look back.

But she's *not* to blame. That's all on me. If I weren't so messed up, none of this would be happening in the first place.

"Tripp, we've been through this before. I'm not a mind reader. If you want me to help you figure out how to fix it, you have to tell me the problem."

I do want to fix *it*. I want to fix *me* so that I can talk to *her*.

"Have you ever liked someone you don't even know?" I ask as I continue to pick at the edge of my shorts, not wanting to make eye contact.

There's a long pause before Dr. Abernathy says, "Tell me about her."

I look up and I'm not sure what I expect to see, but it's not the slight smile that's on her face. It's been a long time since we've discussed the opposite sex in one of these sessions. It feels so foreign; I don't know where to start.

"Well, I don't even know her name," I admit.

"Okay, but you know something about her. You must want to know her for a reason. Let's start with the facts. What is it about her that makes you want to know her?"

"I—I don't know. I told Liza it was because she has these sad eyes, but that's not all of it. The sad eyes just make me want to take it away . . . whatever *it* is that makes her look so hopeless. I feel drawn to her and my heart kind of hurts when she's close by."

"What happened at the restaurant yesterday?"

I take a deep breath before I begin. "I had a talk with Liza about wanting to talk to this girl, and she told me just to go for it. I wanted to *so* badly. Something about talking to her made me feel normal, because this time last year, had I not been with Whitney, I would've just walked up to her and said hello. So, I'd prepared myself, rehearsed, pictured myself walking up to the table . . . all the things you've told me to do when approaching a new situation. But the minute I saw her walk in, I panicked."

Breathe.

"I almost fell right into her table. I hid in the hallway for a few minutes and tried to get myself back under control, but the second I made up my mind that I was going to do it finally—talk to her—I just . . . freaked. My hands were shaking so bad. I tried to put a glass of water on her table, and when she looked up at me, like *really* looked at me, I didn't know what to do. So, I ran." My hands go to my hair, and I dip my chin to my chest. "I just fucking ran."

"And then what happened?" Dr. Abernathy asks, always encouraging me to get it all out.

"I got lost, like in my head. All I could think about was how much I hate that I can't change this," I say, pointing to my head. "I want to think normal and act normal and the fact that I couldn't make myself do something so simple . . . I couldn't take it anymore. Pushing my body felt good. It felt like I was getting rid of all the shit I had built up. I ran for so long and so hard that, when I finally noticed how bad my chest hurt and I slowed down, it took me a minute to figure out where I was."

"Were you scared?"

"Yeah," I admit, because this is my safe place. "Especially when I realized I was on Bourbon Street. The smells and the noise and all the people." I pause as a groan leaves my mouth and I grip my hair. "I already felt a migraine coming on. It was a nightmare. I hid in an alley and called Ben."

"Good. That's good, Tripp. That's what you should've done."

I laugh, but there's no humor behind it because it doesn't feel *good* . . . I don't feel *good*.

"It's not about controlling the situations; it's about handling them appropriately. You didn't have any control over how you responded to the stresses of the day. What you were feeling was probably the culmination of a series of stressful situations, and you finally snapped. It happens to everyone, not just people with brain injuries. It could've been worse. You didn't harm yourself or anyone else. We're calling that success."

I nod and try to let her words sink in, but it's hard.

"What about the nightmares?" she asks. "Have you had any recently?"

"I hadn't had one in a while, probably since the week before school started back. But I had one last night."

"Same scenario or something different?"

"Same thing—it's dark, and all I can hear are these eerie, piercing noises. It shouldn't even be scary. I mean, I can't see a damn thing. It's just this bad, ominous feeling I get, and the next thing I know, I'm waking up in a cold sweat, breathing like I just ran a marathon."

She takes a second to make some notes, and I try not to let my body react to the memory of the dream.

"So, what about your work?" she asks, changing the subject. "Have you contacted them since the incident?"

"Yeah, Wyatt, my boss, he came to the house to check on me."

"How did that go?"

"I explained what I could. I mean, I apologized for my behavior and promised that I wouldn't let anything like that happen again."

"Tripp," she says, in a calm, but firm tone. "What have we discussed about setting yourself up for failure? I'm not saying that you *will* have another episode like that, and I hope that you don't, but don't put unnecessary pressure on yourself. Don't promise things you can't guarantee."

"I was afraid he wouldn't let me come back to work."

"Well, what did he say?"

"He's a cool guy, so he was more concerned about me, making sure I was okay."

"That's good to hear. Do you want to go back to work? Do you feel like it's too much, too soon?"

"Have you been talking to Liza?" I ask sarcastically because I know she hasn't. She's like Fort Knox; anything I tell her stays right here. I know that. It's why I trust her so much and can easily confide in her.

She smiles and quirks an eyebrow at me. "Stop deflecting."

"Well, I like my job. It's challenging, but I don't feel like it's too much or too soon." I have to go back. I have to see *her*. I'm not sure how Dr. Abernathy feels about that, but I don't feel like I have any other choice but to go back and try again. Maybe one of these days I'll be able to talk to her, and maybe she'll talk back to me.

Maybe I won't panic.

Maybe she won't look so sad.

Maybe I can make her smile.

Dr. Abernathy and I sit in comfortable silence for a few minutes while she writes on her notepad, and I think of *Ania*.

⚜

TODAY IS THE FIRST DAY I've felt somewhat back to normal since last week, and I'm pretty sure it has everything to do with the fact I'm going to see *Ania*. The nerves are there and the underlying anxiety, but I'm also . . . happy.

I guess that might be what I'm feeling.

All I know is I want to see her. Even though the last time I saw her was a disaster of epic proportions, she's all I've thought about. And I've thought about every scenario and all the possibilities, and the worst thing I can come up with is that she doesn't show. Everything else, I can deal with. I can even deal with her looking at me weird or whispering about me, as long as she's there.

I park my bike out in front of the café on the rack before walking around to the back door. I guess I could walk in the front, but I like coming in this way. It makes me feel like I belong here. I'm slowly getting the hang of things. Except for the setback last week, I've done fairly well. I've broken a few dishes and messed up some orders, but nothing that's gotten me fired so far. And that feels good.

At the end of our session on Friday, Dr. Abernathy pointed out my accomplishments and different milestones I've achieved, reminding me I'm doing better than I think I am. She also told me that, while *Ania* is a distraction, she's a welcomed one.

It's a pretty slow day, and I'm glad. My head has been in the clouds since I got here. I find myself watching the clock and counting down the minutes until *she's* supposed to be here. When the big hand finally inches toward the six, my attention switches to the front door instead of the clock.

An elderly couple, who have become my regulars, show up, and as I'm taking their drink orders, I feel like a shot of electricity hits my insides when I hear the bell above the door chime. I don't even have to turn around to know she's here.

When I walk back to the kitchen to turn in an order, I want to look at her, but I can't. I'm suddenly stricken with the fear of what I might see.

What if I ruined my chances of ever talking to her?
What if she looks at me with disgust?

My new resolve I had just moments ago is already fading fast, so I walk faster, nearly running into Sarah when I barge through the kitchen doors in search of safety.

"Sorry," I mutter, never looking up at her, but I can feel her eyes on me.

"No problem," she says as she takes the slip of paper out of my hand and calls out my order for me.

In a few minutes, the drinks magically appear on the tray in front of me. "Thank you," I tell her, partially lifting my head so she can hear me.

"You're welcome."

I manage to get through the next hour without any incidents. I allow myself glances in *Ania's* direction, but I try to stay focused on my tasks at hand.

The shirt she's wearing today is a light blue, I have noticed that, and her dark hair is a lovely contrast. And today, instead of staring out the window, she's been writing in the book she always brings. For a good thirty minutes, every time I look over at her, her head is bent down and her hand is flying swiftly across the page. I wonder what she writes about in that book. I want to know all her stories—the sad ones, the happy ones. I want to know what she's thinking about when she closes her eyes and takes in a deep breath as if she's retrieving a memory that's trying to escape. I want to know everything.

When I make another trip to the kitchen to dump a tray of dirty dishes, the clock on the wall confirms that it's half past seven, which means she'll be leaving soon. I wish she would stay longer. We haven't talked, and I still don't know anything more than I did the last time she was here, but I just like being near her . . . in the same room as her.

As I walk back through the doors, she's standing from the booth and adjusting the brown backpack on her shoulders. She pulls her long hair out and allows it to cascade back down, covering her shoulders and the bag. Just when I think she's going to leave without even a backward glance, she turns her head toward me.

For a brief moment, our eyes lock.

No words are exchanged, and her expression hardly shifts, but right before she looks away, the corner of her mouth turns slightly upward.

And my heart skips a beat, or fifty.

To most people, that wouldn't have seemed like anything.

They wouldn't have even noticed.

But to me, it's everything.

seven

"WHERE'S THE FIRE?" LIZA TEASES as I'm hurrying around the dining room, gathering up my books and notes I've been using to study.

"Fire! Fire!" Jack yells, running from the living room, through the dining room, and into the kitchen.

"Stop, drop, and roll!" Emmie instructs in her adorable three-year-old voice that sounds more and more like my sister every day.

"See what you started?" I laugh, cocking an eyebrow at her as I slide the last textbook into my backpack.

"Well, at least they're properly trained in fire emergencies."

We both laugh as the two midgets run from the kitchen back into the living room and then back around, making another lap. Jack is now imitating a fire truck, and Emmie is following behind with an armful of stuffed kittens she's rescued. "I'll save you, Mr. Goldfish," she assures the orange-colored tabby she's clutching by the neck. All of Emmie's stuffed animals are named after her favorite foods.

"I should get going. I have to be at work by three," I explain.

"That's not for another hour. Sure you don't want to stick around and have a late lunch?"

"No, thanks. I had some of Jack and Emmie's mac and cheese that Ben made for them earlier . . . and I, uh, just want to make sure I'm not late for work." I smile over at her, hoping the lame excuse I just gave sounds legit.

"Oh, okay," Liza says slowly, nodding as a small smile grows on her face. "Well, you better get going then. We wouldn't want you to miss any of your favorite customers."

"I'm not. It's not like the—never mind." I can't argue with her. I want to tell her she's wrong, and this has nothing to do with what she's thinking, but it does. It has everything to do with what she's thinking. Somewhere in my mixed up brain, I feel the need to be at work as early as possible, especially on Thursdays. Even though I know *she* won't be at the café before exactly six o'clock . . . but she *will* be there, and I have to make sure I'm there, the earlier, the better.

When I get to work, since I'm early, I busy myself with wrapping silverware and helping Dixie post the new schedules in the kitchen.

"You're fitting in here just right," she says to me with a thoughtful look as I tack up the last of the papers she's been handing me.

"Thanks," I tell her, giving her an easy smile back. Normally, I don't handle compliments well, but no one is around right now besides the two of us, and her words are just what I need to hear today.

As customers start to trickle in, I try hard to stay focused, making it my goal for the evening not to spill anything or get an order wrong. They're lofty goals, but I like challenging myself. And so far, I'm succeeding.

I also try not to watch the clock, but I can only do so much. Tonight, it's either don't drop plates or stop watching the clock. I choose to save the dishes. It's a noble effort.

When six o'clock rolls around, every inch of me is on high alert.

She'll be here soon.

Surprisingly, I almost feel calm . . . still a bit anxious, but not as bad as last week and certainly not as bad as the week before.

Perhaps it's because of the almost-smile she gave me last Thursday. I haven't stopped thinking about her lips making that slight turn since then. And when I allow myself to think about what a full smile from her would feel like, I practically break into a sweat.

In the midst of my daydreaming about Ania's smile, I don't hear the chime on the door, but I do feel an immediate shift in the atmosphere. And I know she's here. My entire body is driven by an unknown force as it turns toward her, like a ship following a beacon in the night.

It's not until Wyatt clears his throat behind me that I realize I'm standing in the middle of the café, holding an empty tray, and staring at her.

For a second, I'm afraid he might be upset he caught me slacking on the job, but as he continues toward the kitchen, his deep chuckle sets me at ease.

After putting the tray in the kitchen and busying myself with refilling water glasses, I take a chance and look over at *Ania*. Her face is red, almost like she's flushed, which immediately makes me worried that she might not be feeling well.

It's always bothered me that *Ania* never eats or drinks while she's here. And I realize I've obviously inherited my mama's intense disdain for anyone going hungry in her presence.

If she's sick, she might not want to eat anything, and I know when I don't feel well, water is the last thing I want. When I'm sick, my mama always brings me a cup of hot tea. It doesn't matter what ails me; she thinks tea will help. Maybe she's right? Without letting myself think about it too much, I walk into the kitchen and request a cup, gathering normal condiments while Shawn pours the steeping hot water.

I briefly question myself on my way back out to the dining room but shut it down as fast as it pops into my head.

Later.

I'll think later.

As I reach her table, I'm momentarily distracted by the late evening sun shining through the window reflecting off of something hanging from *Ania's* neck. I squeeze my eyes shut for a brief moment before slowly opening them and focusing on the offending gleam distracting me from delivering the tea.

Recognition dawns and hope seeps out of my body, deflating me like a balloon with a pinhole leak.

If I'm not mistaken, it looks like an engagement ring. It's not on her finger, where most people wear them. It's hanging from a chain around her neck, but still, it's a single large diamond, and she's wearing it. It must mean something to her, and I can't think of any other reason, except that she belongs to someone.

I set the mug down and mumble something about her not needing to pay for the tea and then pointing to the milk, sugar, and lemon I also brought because I didn't know how she likes her tea.

My spirits lift a bit as she gives me another half-smile, slightly bigger than the one I got last week. When I return it, her cheeks flush again.

She must be coming down with something.

In some weird way, thinking she might be sick bothers me more than the idea of her being engaged.

And I *hate* that she might be engaged. That makes me feel like I'm going to be sick.

"I hope you feel better soon," I mumble, nodding my head toward her tea, and then walking away, through the kitchen and out the backdoor.

I'm not running, not this time, but I do need a second to process.

I don't know why I'm so surprised to see her wearing an engagement ring, even if it's dangling from a chain and not on her finger. Of course, she'd have a boyfriend or fiancé or whatever. She's easily the most beautiful girl I've ever seen. Just because I've never seen her in the café with anyone, doesn't mean she's not someone's . . . *someone*.

But I'm so confused. I know my brain doesn't work right these days, but I wouldn't think someone in love would look so sad and hopeless.

Love is supposed to make you happy.

I must be the biggest idiot in the world.

I don't look at *Ania* for the rest of my shift, and I don't watch her leave as I'm bringing the bill to my last table. The pull I feel toward her is still there, though. The recent knowledge I've gained hasn't changed that one bit.

She still looks like she could use a friend, and Lord knows I could too, so if that's all I can be to her, then that's what I'll be.

⚜

THE NEXT SIX DAYS ARE torturous. My mind is spread thin with scattered thoughts of what I should be thinking about—work, school, and my daily routine—competing with thoughts of *Ania*.

Is she engaged?

Is she married?

If she were married, wouldn't she wear that large sparkly ring on her finger instead of on a chain around her neck?

Why didn't I notice it before last Thursday?

Wyatt could tell I was distracted at work on Tuesday, more than normal. He pulled me to the side and asked me if everything was okay. I told him it was and that I just had a lot on my mind. The look he gave me made me think that he didn't quite believe the line I was feeding him, but he didn't push.

Wednesday, during my classes, I was so lost in thought about *Ania*, I didn't even notice when one of my professors had ended class. It wasn't until someone bumped into me with their bag that I was pulled out of my haze and realized I was the last one sitting in the classroom.

Today, going through my normal routine of getting ready for work, I'm seriously contemplating asking Wyatt about *Ania*. I know that seems crazy, but *if* she's married or engaged, if she's technically someone else's, he'd be the most likely person to know. And I know he instructed me to leave her alone, but my mind won't rest until I know more facts about her . . . until I know what I can let myself hope for when it comes to her. So, I'm going to find a way to talk to him.

As I poke my head inside the back door of Liza and Ben's, I give the door a knock to let them know I'm there.

"Hey, Tripp."

"Hey, Liza. Where's Jack and Emmie?"

It doesn't escape me that the house is too quiet.

"Ben had the afternoon free, so he took the kids to the zoo."

"Sounds fun."

"So, how's your week going?" she asks. "Any progress with your favorite customer?" This has become a normal conversation between the two of us. I almost confessed the nickname I've given her, so she'll quit calling her my "favorite customer", but I decided I didn't want to share it . . . or her. I don't want to share *Ania*.

"I think she's engaged."

Liza's head whips around and her eyes are large and questioning. "Really? Did you talk to her? Did she tell you that?"

"No, I still haven't had the nerve to talk to her, well, not like a real conversation. But last week, I noticed a ring hanging around her neck. It *looked* like an engagement ring. Maybe she's married? I mean, would she wear it around her neck if she's married?" My nerves start getting the best of me as I verbalize my fears, and I find myself pacing as I'm talking.

"Tripp, stop. You're going to worry yourself right into the ground . . . or wear out my wood floors." She places both hands on my shoulders, forcing me to stay in one spot. "Listen, quit making assumptions. Remember what Dad always said?"

"Yes, *ass* . . . you . . . me . . . I remember."

"Right. So, stop assuming. Wait and find out for yourself. I know it seems scary, but if this girl means that much to you and you don't even know her name yet . . ." She pauses, her blue eyes staring at me pointedly. "You owe it to yourself to be patient and find out more about her."

"I'm not giving up," I confess, remembering how I felt last week when I first saw the ring—resolved. No matter what, I still want to be her friend. I want to know her. I can't just walk away and forget she exists.

At this moment, I realize my life has been sectioned off by so many events, and the day *Ania* and I walked into the same café is one of them. There will always be before *her* and after *her* . . . It's up to me to make a move and let her know how I feel, then let her decide the rest.

But, none of that can happen unless I talk to her.

"I'm glad you're not giving up," Liza says with a soft smile. "It's good to see there's still some fight left in you. I like it." By *it*, she means *Ania*. I can see it in Liza's eyes every time she brings her up. It's funny how a girl I don't even know has already woven her way into my life.

Later that evening, while I'm at work, *Ania* slides into her booth at just a minute or two after six. We're having our first few days of cooler temperatures, and she's dressed accordingly, wearing a light gray sweater with a thin scarf wrapped around her neck. It may still be seventy degrees outside, but to us southerners, that's cold.

The few times I walk past her table, I try to see if I can catch a glimpse of the ring again, but she must have it tucked into her sweater. I also notice there's nothing on the ring finger of her left hand, which is something I've been thinking about since last week. I thought maybe I had been so distracted by her sad eyes that I overlooked it.

The wanting to know is starting to gnaw at my insides. I feel questions on the tip of my tongue, and it's killing me that I can't slide into the booth across from her and say, *"Hi. My name is Tripp. Is this seat taken?"*

The old me would've done that.

At almost eight o'clock, I notice *Ania* is still sitting in her booth. My shift will be ending in a few minutes, and normally, she'd already be packing up her things and leaving. But the journal she usually has in front of her has been replaced with an actual book tonight. She's been preoccupied with the words on the pages all night, hardly glancing up for more than a second and that's usually between page turns. So, I guess she's so wrapped up in the story, she's lost track of time.

As I walk back toward the kitchen to put my apron up, I notice Wyatt walk from the opposite side of the dining room and slide into the booth across from her, casually, without any fanfare—just like I had thought of doing only moments earlier. She lifts her head from her book to look at him, and he smiles. And I can only guess that she's smiling back at him, and that makes my insides twist. And my chest ache.

Bringing my hand up to rub the tightness away, I feel a flash of something else surge through me as Wyatt reaches across the table and puts his hand on hers.

I know this feeling.

It's been a while, but there's no denying what's coursing through my body this very moment—pure, unadulterated jealousy.

Not trusting my restraint and afraid I'll make a scene, I walk quickly through the kitchen doors, slamming my apron down on the counter, before exiting out the back door.

I can't get my bike unlocked fast enough, my hands fumbling with the chain. As soon as it's free, I start peddling before my ass is even in the seat. I ride so hard and fast that I'm pulling into the long drive of

Liza and Ben's house in half the time. My chest is heaving and my hands are shaking, partly from the exertion and partly from the incredible amount of jealousy I can still feel pumping through me along with the adrenaline from my ride.

Normally, I'd go into the main part of the house and warm up leftovers Liza always leaves for me, but tonight, I head straight up the stairs to my apartment. The need to be alone and release the pent-up emotions is stronger than the growl in the pit of my stomach.

I want for just once to feel like the universe isn't completely against me.

I'd like to handle situations like a normal fucking person for once.

I want to scream.

I'd love to hit something.

Fuck.

I slam my fist down on the counter in my bathroom, hard enough to feel the shooting pain up into my elbow. If I stand here and look at myself, things could get really ugly. So, instead, I skip my normal nightly routines and walk to my bed. Falling face first into my pillow, I muffle the scream that comes from the pit of my stomach. It's attached to every emotion I've been feeling, practically making my toes curl on its way out. And it doesn't stop until my throat feels raw and the tension in my chest eases.

At some point, after endlessly berating myself, I drift off into an unrestful sleep, accompanied by the unsettling dreams that I can't seem to shake.

⚜

THE NEXT MORNING, WHEN I wake up, my head is throbbing, and I consider skipping class. But, since I've already missed a couple of days, thanks to my last episode on Bourbon Street, I know I can't afford to.

Fortunately, this feels like a regular, run-of-the-mill headache, so hopefully a hefty dose of Tylenol and coffee will do the trick.

After my normal morning routine, I walk out of my apartment and down the stairs, inhaling deeply as I try to continue to clear my head. Last night got to me. I don't know why I thought I could talk to her, and now I think that maybe I can't.

Liza and Ben have already left for work when I let myself in the back door, which means the kids are with my mom. I normally rush around so I can spend at least a few minutes with them, but after the night I had, I'm sure I look like shit, and I don't feel like fielding a bunch of questions, especially regarding *Ania*.

Seeing her interact with Wyatt last night was too much.

After spending the last few weeks wanting nothing more than a casual conversation with her, watching someone else get that instead of me pissed me off, pure and simple.

Now that I'm thinking more rationally, I know their chat was platonic. I should be grateful that someone can talk to her and check up on her.

Wyatt is a good guy and a married one, and he doesn't seem like the type who would cheat on his wife, especially in his restaurant. But my mind is an irrational place sometimes.

⚜

FOR THE NEXT FEW DAYS, I try to put all of my focus on my classes and catch up on my school work. Finals will be here before I know it and I want to be prepared. Being so caught up in *Ania* has put me a little behind, and if I'm ever going to do more than attend school and work, I've got to learn how to balance everything. Prioritize, as Dr. Abernathy would say.

By Tuesday, I don't feel as worked up as I did when I left work last Thursday. When I walk through the back door of the cafe, Shawn tells me Wyatt is up front and wants to speak to me. My stomach feels like it's going to fall out of my ass. It's never a good sign when your boss wants to speak to you first thing through the door.

Oh, shit.

"Hey," I say, finding him at a table and trying to sound as casual as possible.

"Hey," Wyatt says, looking up and acknowledging me.

He gathers some papers and stacks them into a neat pile, setting them to the side.

"It's been a pretty slow day. Thought I'd get caught up on some of the less-fun parts of this job," he adds with a smile as he casually drapes his arm over the back of the seat, pulling at the yellow suspenders with his thumb.

I smile awkwardly, unsure if he's expecting me to say something or if I'm just here to listen. So, I just wait, nervously.

"So, what's up? How's life?" he asks, his demeanor calm, but I don't feel calm. I feel like I'm walking in front of a firing squad. I'm afraid he's going to put me on blast for the few almost-incidents regarding a long-haired brunette who often sits at the booth behind him, and my nerves are about to get the best of me.

Maybe I should just come clean and confess my sins?

No, stupid idea.

"Uh, good, I guess." I finally respond as I fidget with my apron, re-tying the string around my waist, trying not to panic.

Wyatt motions for me to have a seat across from him, so I do, taking a deep breath in and exhaling, putting Dr. Abernathy's techniques into practice.

So not working.

"So, you've been here for what, a little over a month now?" he asks but doesn't wait for a response. "How do you like it so far?"

"I like it." I nod my head, but my eyes stay focused on the table in front of me. When I realize I'm not making eye contact, I quickly look up and try again. Not looking at people can also be a sign of lying. But I'm not. "I *really* like my job," I tell him with all the sincerity I can muster, making sure to look him directly in the eyes as I say it.

"Good, good," he says, tapping his hand on the back of the bench. "Well, we really like having you on board, and I wanted to tell you I think you're catching on pretty well. But I also want to make sure you feel the same and to see how you're handling balancing work and school. Are you keeping your grades up?"

"Did Liza call you?" I question because I'm trying to figure out exactly what's going on. He did say I'm doing a pretty good job, so I'm guessing he's not firing me. *Hopefully.* And he hasn't brought up

Ania . . . yet.

Wyatt laughs as he leans forward, resting his elbows on the table, similar to how he was the other night when he was talking to *Ania*.

Not now.

I can't think about that right now.

"No. Surprisingly, she hasn't called to check up on you in a while," he says with a wink and a chuckle. "I just wanted to check in with you and make sure everything is going well and that you like your job. I like my employees to be happy."

"Well, I finally feel like I'm not messing up every order," I tell him, trying to relax. "So, there's that."

"We all make mistakes," he says, waving off my comment. "Don't sweat the small stuff, Tripp. I haven't fired you yet, have I?"

I swallow hard, wondering if this is where he answers his own punch line and gives me a pink slip.

"You're doin' great," he says, smiling.

"Thanks," I reply, letting out a nervous laugh.

"Do you have any questions or concerns?"

"Uh, no. I don't guess so."

"And, your grades, they're good?" he asks, following up on his original question.

"Yeah, pretty good."

"That's what I like to hear." He stands from his seat and pats my shoulder as he passes by, and I let out a deep sigh of relief.

That was a close one.

And even though I know this would be a prime opportunity to ask him about *Ania*, I can't do it. It's on the tip of my tongue, but I can't. Because that conversation might not be so easy and after nearly pissing myself, just thinking I was in trouble. I can't go there, not today.

⚜

AS I WALK BACK FROM my Wednesday afternoon class, I'm already thinking about *her* and the fact I'll see her again tomorrow. Deep in thoughts of long brown hair, I nearly run over the lady who sells flowers on the street corner.

"Flowers for your lady?" she asks, holding a long-stemmed bloom in my direction.

Its petals are exotic, branching out in every direction. I notice the unique flower matches her—covered in bright reds, blues, and oranges.

"I—I don't have a *lady*," I say, attempting to walk around her.

"A handsome fella like you doesn't have a lady?" she asks, her pale gray eyes doubling in size with surprise. "Maybe you don't have a lady because you haven't given her one of these."

Her tone is suggestive as she twirls the flower between us.

My dad climbs into the front seat of the Impala, with three bottles of beer.

"I figured now'd be a good time for you to have your first beer," he says, popping the top of one of the bottles before handing it to me. "Besides, it wouldn't be fair for Ben and me to drink one in front of you, and Lord knows we need one after all the hard work we've done today. Just don't tell your mama."

I guess now would also be a bad time to tell him I've had my fair share of beer . . . among other things.

"Uh, thanks, Dad." I try to make my words sound grateful and privileged, like this is a really big deal because it is. I'm sitting in the front seat of my dad's Impala, and if I turned that shiny key over in the ignition, this baby would purr to life. The three of us have been working practically every weekend over the last few months to get her running.

Two years late, but who's counting?

Me, that's who.

This car means everything. It's a dream come true, for my dad and me. And it's freedom because now I won't have to ask to borrow anyone's car.

"She's a beauty," Ben says from the backseat.

"Hey, don't spill your beer in my car." I see him in my rearview mirror. His lips smirk around the mouth of his beer bottle before his hand comes up to slap the back of my head.

"I think your old man and I have just as much right to this thing as you do!"

"Whatever, dude! This baby is mine!"

My dad is chuckling from the passenger seat. "Was it worth the wait?"

"Hell, yes," I tell him, running my hands along the steering wheel, soaking it in.

"So, who's gonna be the first lucky girl?"

"Oh, she's already gotten lucky," I say with a smirk, earning me a low five from Ben, so my dad doesn't see.

"I hope you're not being a manwhore," my dad says, sipping his beer. "Please tell me you're at least using good manners . . . and protection."

Manwhore? Has he been reading Liza's Cosmo or something?

"Dad," I groan, rolling my eyes.

"I'm just making sure. And you know, Tripp . . . it's not all about sex. If you really wanna get a girl's attention, you should try a little courtship from time to time."

"Courtship?" Now I'm the one falling over laughing. "Dad, seriously. That's so 1950!"

"Tripp, courtship is a lost art, and trust me, if you can master it, girls—and their parents—will be eating out of the palm of your hand." His voice gets lower as he continues like he's giving me the directions to the Holy Grail. "It's all about wooing a girl. You can't just ask a girl out; you've gotta sweep her off her feet."

"Well, I don't know how to do any of that."

"Which is why I'm going to tell you."

I notice Ben leaning up against the back of the seat. He's suddenly all ears like he needs any of this. My sister is already eating out of the palm of his hand. Ben Walker can do no wrong in her book. It's disgusting.

"First, always be yourself. Anything else is second rate," he begins, talking low and slow like we're on an undercover mission. "Second, make her laugh. Girls love to laugh, and it puts them at ease. Always dress to impress. I'm not saying you have to wear shirts and ties or any of that bullshit, but don't look like you just rolled outta bed. Always compliment her. But not just any compliment. Make them specific to her. Which brings me to my next topic: listen. You've gotta listen to the girl, Tripp. Make her feel like she's the only girl in the world. Like you only have eyes for her . . . and you should only have eyes for her," he says seriously, giving me the look.

"Got it."

"I'm not kidding. None of this funny business. And that especially goes for you, Walker!"

"Sir, yes, sir," Ben says, saluting.

I start to snicker, but my dad levels me with another glare, and I immediately get in line.

"Be confident when you're around her. Even if you don't feel confident, act confident. Girls like it when a guy is sure of himself. It makes them feel safe."

Ben and I both nod.

"Be honest, always look her in the eyes, and find a way to make her smile on a daily basis."

"How?"

"Anything. Write her a poem, or give her a compliment."

"I am not writing a poem," I tell him. That Shakespeare shit is for the birds.

"Well, then buy her flowers. Girls love flowers. But," he says, pausing, holding up a finger. "You can't just buy any flower. You do that, and the girl will know you're taking the easy way out. You've gotta find out what her favorite flower is, and if you don't know, then you need to guess . . . Try to find one that makes you think of her, something that's unique to her. Whatever you do, don't overuse the flowers. Give them to her when she's least expecting it. That's when they'll have the biggest impact."

We sit there for a few minutes, soaking in all of my dad's wisdom. The pale light of the moon is the only thing lighting up the garage.

"Start this baby up. We never did check to see if the eight-track still works."

I turn over the engine as he pulls a box of cassettes out from under his seat. He pulls one out of its case and pops it in. The soulful blues of Otis Redding flow through the speakers as we sit back and listen to him croon about trying a little tenderness.

On my way to work the next morning, I make a point to stop where the lady who sells the flowers always stands. Instead of the vibrant, multi-colored flower she pushed in my face on Wednesday, I purchase a single blue iris.

"Such a thoughtful choice," she muses, handing me the flower as

I hand her my five dollars. The wink she gives me in exchange tells me she remembers me. Smiling, I silently thank her.

Last night after I got home, I spent some time researching the meaning of different flowers and found that the iris has a significant history in Greek mythology, acting as a link between heaven and earth. It also symbolizes faith and hope.

It's perfect for *Ania*.

eight

WALKING IN THE BACK DOOR of the café, I'm relieved when I see the only person in the kitchen is Shawn, the cook, and he has his back to me. I slip *Ania*'s flower in a glass of water and tuck it behind a large stack of plates on the shelf. I'm a few minutes early but decide to get to work. The busier I stay, the faster the next three hours will pass. It's going to be hard to keep my nerves in check, but I have the same feeling as last week—resolve.

I'm going to do this.

With a bit of pep in my step, I begin my daily duties. I wrap extra silverware and put place settings out at each chair while I wait for my tables to fill up with customers. When some of my regulars begin to trickle in, I greet them with ease, already predicting what they'll order. I've worked here for over a month now, and I finally feel like I'm getting the hang of this.

When the clock in the kitchen shows it's almost six, I sneak the flower from the glass behind the plates and place it on my tray. I think Sarah might notice, but she doesn't say anything, only gives me an encouraging smile as she passes me on her way back into the kitchen.

"Order up!" Shawn yells.

I quickly place the plates on my tray and make my way back into the main part of the café. *Ania* could very well be sitting at her table the next time I turn around, so if I want to give her the flower without drawing too much attention to myself, I've got to do it now. Carefully, I set the tray of food down on the edge of her table and gently place the blue iris just so, right in front of where she always sits, the seat facing the door and closest to the window. After nudging it around, trying to make it perfect, I finally walk away, hoping it has the right effect.

What if she hates flowers?

What if she thinks it belongs to someone else?

Or what if she doesn't realize it's from me?

The panic starts to rise, but I tamp it down, concentrating on slow, even breaths and the possibility of seeing her smile. If that's the only thing I receive from this gesture, it'll be enough.

After I deliver the plates to my other table, I turn around and see she still hasn't arrived, but the iris is sitting where the sun coming through the window hits it perfectly.

It's beautiful, just like her.

I think my dad would be proud.

I'm in the kitchen when I hear the bell on the front door chime. Quickly but quietly, I crack open the swinging door to take a peek, my heart racing, and I'm not surprised when I see her walk through the door. It's like my soul knows when she's near. I grip the door tightly, bracing for whatever comes next—gratitude, surprise, happiness, rejection.

She has her head bent down as she walks toward the table, almost as if she's on autopilot, stepping to the side to avoid a chair until she abruptly stops. Her head snaps up, and she looks at the table for what feels like minutes and then turns to look around the café, waiting for someone to take ownership of the object that's intruding her personal space. I close the door a little more, only leaving a slight crack because I'm not ready for her to know it's me, not yet.

I pry my hands off the door, allowing it to close and step back. As I turn around, I allow myself a few minutes of deep breathing, and I try to center myself.

I did it.

Of course, I've yet to talk to her and let her verbally know how I feel, but I took a step, and right now, that step feels huge.

Steadying myself, I make my way back into the café to check on my tables and try to decide how to handle the flower situation.

I don't have to think on it for long, because *Ania* takes care of it for me by turning around in her seat and blinding me with a smile. It's real and genuine. It almost reaches her eyes, and I can't help but smile back at her. The blush that creeps up on her cheeks makes mine heat up just the same. I feel like a chameleon when I'm around her—what she feels, I feel. The pull she's had on me since day one is even stronger as she makes direct, intentional eye contact. I swear, the smile she's still wearing says more than a thousand words. I wish I could take a picture or commission a painting so that I could remember this moment for the rest of my life.

Fortunately, or perhaps, unfortunately, my section stays extremely busy, and to my surprise, I manage it without spilling or breaking anything.

The boost of confidence I feel from seeing Ania smile makes my feet feel more dependable and my hands steadier. The bad part is, I only get to catch passing glimpses of her, but her entire demeanor seems lighter too. Even though I can't see her face most of the night, I notice her shoulders aren't quite so hunched over. The few times I do get the privilege of seeing her face, it looks pleasant, not a full-on smile, but not nearly as sad as it usually is. It makes me feel good because I feel like I had a part in making her happier, which makes me happier.

When she stands to leave, I hold my ground at the table I'm bussing. Normally, I'd hightail it to the kitchen to take refuge and keep from embarrassing myself. But tonight, I can't. I can't miss any opportunity to see her. I need it like I need the air I'm breathing.

Oh, shit.

Breathe.

She shoulders her backpack and picks up the flower from the table, leaving a folded piece of paper in its place. On her way out, she pauses for a moment and gives me another smile, bringing the flower up to her nose and inhaling. When she nears the door, she dips her head and glances back over her shoulder, giving me one last look before disappearing out of sight.

I don't know how long I stand there, but my feet feel glued to the floor, either unable to move or refusing to. My first thought when she's out of sight is: I want her to come back so we can do that all over again.

When I remember the small piece of paper she left on her table, it brings me out of my trance, and I nearly trip over my own two feet trying to get to it as quickly as possible. My hands are shaking as I unfold it, making sure not to tear the pale pink paper. It's familiar, and I realize it's probably a piece from her journal.

Even if there were no words, I'd still feel like she gave me a piece of her, but there are.

Five little words: *When words escape, flowers speak.*

In this moment, I feel like she understands me, and it's the best thing I've felt in a long, long time.

⚜

DURING THE NEXT SIX DAYS, I cling to the small piece of pink paper. If it's not in my pocket, it's on my nightstand, and if it's not on my nightstand, it's under my pillow. It's become my lucky charm of sorts— the physical representation that I took the first step, and *Ania* met me halfway.

I've had the best week since I can remember. My mind has been clearer, I've felt stronger, and emotionally, I've been in control. I'm trying not to put too much emphasis on seeing *Ania* again today, but the truth of the matter is, I feel like I owe a lot of my good week to her. She's given me something to look forward to, and I want to be able to tell her how I feel. Granted, I probably shouldn't do that tonight. I should probably start with something less scary like, *"Hi, my name is Tripp."*

The first three hours of my shift are the hardest, but I use the time to mentally prepare myself to talk to her. If nothing else, I decide I'm going to go up to her and ask if I can get her anything. It's a start. And hopefully, since it's part of my job, it won't feel too awkward.

I can do this.

I'm going to do this.

Filling an empty glass here, serving an order there, and watching the clock in between—that's how I spend the minutes leading up to *Ania's* arrival. I get caught up fixing an order that was wrong, and when I notice six o'clock has come and gone, my heart begins to beat faster.

She'll be here.

Wyatt asks me to help Julie with a large group that's come in for a birthday celebration. The added responsibilities keep me busier than usual, and when I get a chance to look at the clock in the kitchen again, it's a quarter past six.

She's never late.

I nearly run out of the kitchen with the tray of glasses to see if she's somehow slipped into her booth without my noticing, but she's not there. It's empty.

I help Julie take everyone's order, and when we're headed back to the kitchen to turn them in, I notice that someone else is sitting in her booth.

I want to yell at them and tell them to get out, but I can't. I look around the café, searching for her. Maybe she decided to sit somewhere else today?

She'll be here, right? She has to be. She's always here.

But what if she doesn't come? What then?

How will I ever get the chance to talk to her?

What if the flower spooked her?

Maybe she thinks I'm a stalker or something?

Oh, shit.

What have I done?

I take one more look around, and there's no sign of her. No long dark hair. No crumpled leather backpack. No brown journal with pale pink pages. No sad eyes.

She's not here.

I finish my shift, but the heaviness that replaces the levity from earlier is overwhelming. I feel like I can hardly put one foot in front of the other as I make my way out the back door, blindly acknowledging someone telling me bye as I leave.

I'm not sure where to go or what to do, but I don't want to go home.

Once I'm out in the night air, I breathe deeply, trying to calm the growing anxiety and wild thoughts I've been bombarded with ever since *Ania* didn't show, but I can't. It feels as though my breath is stuck in my throat. I try to think of who to call or where to go, and only one place feels right. Kicking the stand on my bike, I take off until I'm standing in front of the large iron gates.

I haven't been here for a while, but it doesn't take me long to find what I'm looking for. As I approach the wooden bench, I sit down and pull out the note from *Ania*, reading the words for the hundredth time.

When words escape, flowers speak.

Last week, I had been so sure we were at the precipice of something. I didn't know what, but I knew the smile she gave me was enough to give me the courage I needed to talk to her.

"I was going to talk to her," I whisper out into the open air. "I felt like I was making you proud for the first time in a long time . . . following your advice . . . but she didn't show tonight. What if I've messed this up, or even worse, what if something happened to her?"

I stand up and lean into the dark gray piece of stone, my fingers gliding over the engraved words. These words don't even come close to saying what's important. How can you put a person's life into such few words?

"I miss you, Dad. If you were here, you'd know what to do."

"Dad," I sob, letting my tears fall on the headstone, "I know you were sick these last two years, but I still wasn't prepared for this . . . I wasn't ready to let you go."

My chest hurts so bad it feels like it's going to crack open as I let out the anguish I feel inside.

"Thank you for being my biggest supporter . . . and thank you for holding on until the twins were born. I can't believe they're going to miss out on you . . . on your jokes . . . and your good advice. What am I going to do without you here? I already feel like I'm drowning, and it's only been 28 days."

I breathe hard. I'm not sure what a panic attack feels like, but I might be having one.

"What am I supposed to do?"

I wait, but I'm just met with silence. Occasionally, the wind picks up and whistles through the trees, but there's no one to talk back to me. My words are lost in the breeze.

"I just needed to talk to someone, and I didn't know where else to go. I don't think I can do it anymore—football, school—nothing feels right anymore."

I hear my voice crack and then crumble as vivid memories of my dad infiltrate my mind, but I keep going.

"I remember th-the talk we had that one time, and you told me my grades were more important than tossing a ball down the field. I thought you were crazy, but it's like you knew . . . like always, you knew something I didn't." *The anger I sometimes feel when I realize he's gone for good comes erupting from deep within.* "Everything feels so overwhelming right now. I feel like I could just snap at any moment, but I can't. Mom needs me."

The light mist that had started when I got here picks up, and drops of rain bounce off of the thick cold stone.

"I want to make you proud. I want to be able to take care of Mom instead of her taking care of me. I need to be there for her. That's what you would want more than anything. Liza has Ben and the babies, but Mom needs me."

I pound my fist into the stone because I'm so pissed. I'm mad at everything and everyone—my dad for leaving me, the universe for taking him away, my coach for being on my ass, and myself for not being able to handle it all.

"Tell me what to do, Dad. Give me some kind of sign. Please!"

My body feels like it's weighed down, and I can't fight it anymore, so I lie down on the grass in front of his grave, allowing my tears to mix into the damp ground beneath me.

Somewhere in the midst of being asleep and awake, the wind begins to blow, swirling the dead leaves on the ground up and around. I roll over onto my back and look up at the gray sky above, still searching for answers, when the thick clouds part and a small ray of sunshine fights its way through. The brief break in the clouds warms my face, and I close my eyes, soaking it in.

I don't know how, but I feel it—I feel him—and I know what I need to do. I'm so sure of it. It's almost as if he's standing beside me, telling me in person.

I scramble to my feet, unable to move fast enough. The urgency of what I now know I need to do propels me. I jump in the Impala and peel out on the gravel path leading to the main road out of the cemetery.

Twenty minutes later, I pull into the field house parking lot and run into the building.

Knocking once, I let myself into Coach's office and plop down in the chair across from the desk. He looks at me over the top of his glasses, a little startled, but like he might've been expecting me.

"I quit."

nine

KNOCK. KNOCK. KNOCK.
My eyes slowly open and scan my bedroom, trying to find what's making the offending sound.

Knock. Knock. Knock. "Tripp, are you awake?"

Shit.

"Tripp, it's two in the afternoon. Can I come in?"

Did I sleep until two?

I grab my phone off the nightstand and push the 'home' button, groaning when I realize it's Sunday. She's gonna kill me for missing church.

"Yeah, Mom," I yell toward the door as I jump out of bed. "I'm coming. Hold on a sec."

Grabbing a T-shirt off the floor, I throw it on and run to the bathroom to quickly brush my teeth. When I finally open the front door, I see my mom standing in front of me with her hands on her hips and her right toe tapping.

Yep, I'm dead.

"Mom, I—" I start to explain why I wasn't at church and why I've basically been a recluse for the past two days, but the air is practically knocked out of me as she pulls me into one of her bone-crushing hugs.

"I was so worried about you," she mutters over my shoulder. It's then that I notice her voice trembling, and I feel her desperation in the grip she has on the back of my shirt.

"I'm so sorry," I tell her, before I break down. I'm not sure what I'm apologizing for exactly; there are so many things I wish I could fix. My mom is the only person who has this effect on me. She loves me unconditionally; I feel no shame crying on her shoulder.

Claire Alexander may be a small woman, but her hugs are enormous. They block out the rest of the world, allowing me to just . . . be.

After a few minutes, I get control of my emotions and wipe my face on the sleeve of my shirt.

"How'd you know to check on me?" I ask.

"Tripp, a mother knows when something is wrong with her child," she says, her sass back in full force.

"Besides," she continues. "Liza said she hadn't seen or spoken to you since Thursday. I tried to give you space, but when you didn't show up for church or lunch afterward, I knew it was time to beat your door down." She gives me a small smile as she pats my cheek. "Are you going to tell me what's wrong?"

I walk over to the couch and sit down and she follows. Even though I've done nothing but mope and sleep for the last two days, I still feel exhausted.

"I went and talked to Dad," I tell her, figuring that's a good place to start.

"Oh?" she asks, her tone even. "It must've been really important. You haven't been to the cemetery in a while."

"How do you do it, Mom?" I ask, pushing the hair out of my face and looking over at her. "How do you . . . move on?"

"Let me make something very clear. I have *not* moved on, nor am I *over* your father not being here."

"I didn't mean to imply—"

"I know what you meant, but let me finish. I'll never get over losing your daddy. I'll miss him every day of my life, but I can't put my life on hold either. I have to live. We *all* have to keep living. Your dad would be some kind of pissed if he knew we were wasting precious moments here curled up in a ball, feelin' sorry for ourselves."

I know she's right.

It hurts to hear, but she's right.

Dad hated when people focused on the negative side of things. He was always a glass half full kind of guy.

"I also know that all of this doesn't have to do with missing your dad. So, what else has you so worked up?"

"There's a girl," I admit, ready to get it off my chest.

"I thought there might be," she replies, and I can't help but give her a small smile. I'm surprised she hasn't called me on this before now. Claire should be short for *clairvoyant*.

I tell her everything that's happened between *Ania* and me since the day of my job interview, and she listens intently. When I'm finished spilling my guts, we sit in silence for a few moments and I eye her cautiously as she thinks about what to say.

"So, you were worried when this girl didn't show up on Thursday, and that's why you went and talked to your dad?" she asks, still trying to fit all the pieces together.

"I needed someone to talk to and I wanted it to be him so bad. So, I decided that was where I needed to go."

"Then it was," she assures me. "Did it make you feel better?"

"Kinda," I say, shrugging, but obviously I'm sitting here and still don't feel like I have any more answers than I did on Friday and when I think about Ania not coming back to the café, it still hurts. "I think it made me miss him more than I was already. I wish he was here to tell me what to do. What do *you* think he'd tell me?"

"Honestly?" she asks.

I nod my head and swallow the lump in my throat, not knowing what she's going to say, because I know whatever she tells me, I'll do it. I haven't been successful on my own, so I have no choice but to take her advice.

She clears her throat and then levels me with a stare. "I think he'd tell you to piss or get off the pot, and frankly, I agree."

Ahhh, there's the Mom-brow I accused Liza of inheriting a couple of weeks ago. My sister's is good, but it still can't compare to the original.

AFTER GRABBING A QUICK SHOWER, my mom thinks I need to get out of the house and get some fresh air. So, we take a streetcar that drops us off close to the French Quarter.

As we walk to Jackson's Brewery to do some shopping, my eyes scan the people we pass. I can't stop myself from looking for *Ania*, just like I can't stop worrying about her. I mean, New Orleans isn't *that* big of a place, it wouldn't be completely crazy to see her on the street.

However, I don't know what I'd do if I ever *did* see her outside of the café, but I'd endure whatever humiliation I'd bring on myself just to know she was okay.

Two hours later and my ass is dragging big time. When my mom heads into what she says will be "the last store, I promise," I find a nearby bench to rest on while I wait for her.

"Tripp, is that you?"

A mild sense of trepidation creeps up as I turn to search for the person speaking, because I'd know that voice anywhere.

"Hey, Evan," I say, looking up into his familiar face, nerves warring against my desire to appear normal. "How are you?"

"I'm good, man. Whatcha been up to?"

"Just the usual. School, work . . . you know," I utter with a shrug.

"Well, you look good." He says this like he's surprised like he was expecting me to be disfigured or something. Instinctively, I make sure my hair is covering as much of my scar as possible.

"Uh, thanks," I reply, my eyes falling to the ground.

"My mom said she saw your mom with the twins the other day at the French Market. Sounds like everyone is doin' good . . . I'm glad." I look back up when I realize he's not going to dwell on my appearance. He smiles at me, but it's for all for show, because behind the smile is a heaviness that never used to be there.

"Yeah, we're doing as well as we can be. You know, good days and bad," I reply honestly.

"That's great, man. Listen, I'm glad I ran into you. Let's hang out sometime, alright?" he says, already backing away.

"Sure, that sounds good," I agree, even though we both know it'll never happen.

When Evan walks away, I'm hit with nostalgia, remembering when it wasn't so awkward between us.

"Dude!"

"Evan! Man, when did you get back in town?"

Laughing, he slaps my back. "My plane landed a couple of hours ago. You know I wouldn't miss tonight. Watching the sorority pledges being introduced on Greek Row? Hell, yeah! I can't wait to add more numbers to my little black book. I mean, as a junior, it's my collegiate duty to welcome and help any and all fresh-meat, I mean freshman, to Tulane University." Evan places his right hand over his heart as if he's saying The Pledge of Allegiance, and I can't help but laugh at him.

My best friend is a fucking douche, but I know, deep down, he's a good guy.

"You see any potential yet?" he asks, nodding his head toward the large group of girls across the street.

"Nah, I'm just hanging out because I was bored at home."

"Sure you are. If you're here, that means you and Whitney are broken up . . . again. Unless you're looking to reconcile with her . . . again."

Not long after my dad died and I quit the football team, I broke up with Whitney. I was still dealing with all the shit in my life while she was starting to pressure me about proposing.

When high school sweethearts are together for as long as we were, especially here in the south, it's natural for them to get engaged while still in college, or so Whitney told me. She said it made perfect sense to get engaged during our sophomore year so that we'd have two years to plan our wedding, which would occur the summer after we graduate, naturally.

I wasn't ready for that kind of commitment or organization in my life, so I kept blowing her off until one day I simply couldn't take any more. Looking back, I probably could've waited another week to dump her. I don't recommend breaking up with your girlfriend during Homecoming week; I'm just sayin'. We had a huge fight during the annual bonfire, which led to both of us getting shit-faced drunk and hooking up with strangers. I was so hungover and miserable the next day; I missed the parade and the game. Again, not a great weekend for Tripp Alexander.

Since then, Whitney and I have had a convenient on-again, off-again type of relationship, getting together when the need arises, then cooling back off after a few weeks. I still worry about leading her on, but she says she understands that I'm still working through things and that I don't want to be tied down right now.

"You know you two are gonna make it for real," Evan continues. "I mean, you have to. You're perfect for each other."

Whitney and I did get back together, and for a while, I thought it was going to work.

Unfortunately, fate had other plans, which led Whitney to show her true colors, and I've never been happier to be rid of her.

⚜

FOR THE PAST MONTH OR so, I've had some kind of plan for how to interact with *Ania*. Things may not have happened the way I'd hoped, but at least *something* had happened.

This Thursday, I'm at a loss because I don't have a plan. Nothing. Zero. Zip. Zilch. I don't know what to expect because I don't even know if she will be here tonight.

Maybe I scared her off or tried too hard?

It's very possible I embarrassed her or disturbed her solitude so much she decided to find a different place to sit every Thursday evening.

Maybe I'll never know?

It's with a heavy and apprehensive heart that I clock in and grab my apron, ready to start my shift. The first few hours go by as they normally do. Nothing too major happens, with the exception of Julie dumping an entire tray of sweet tea on a table of four. Wyatt, ever the professional, offered to pay for the group's dry cleaning while also not charging them for the food they ordered, including dessert.

"Hey, Tripp! Can you help?" Sarah yells at me when I walk into the kitchen to dump some dirty dishes into the sink.

"Sure. What's up?"

"I have a party of eight, and they've all ordered bread pudding for dessert. Can you help me fix their plates?"

Knowing my current two tables will be fine if I neglect them for a few minutes, I hurry to the dessert counter, ready to help. Sarah has already started scooping the bread pudding into bowls, so I proceed to pour the rum sauce on top before setting them aside. The task doesn't take long, and soon I'm carrying four of the bowls to her table. While Sarah removes the desserts from my tray, my eyes roam the café, looking to see if my customers need me.

I see they're still fine, and as I start to return my tray back to the kitchen, I catch a flash of auburn in my peripheral vision. The familiar gravitational pull is instant.

She's here.

Ania *is here.*

Relief washes over me, but there's something else too.

Anger?

I don't know. I'm not sure if I even have the right, but it's there.

Without telling them to, my feet take me directly to her table. Surprised eyes fly up to meet mine and only get wider when I speak.

"You were gone," I blurt out.

Her large round eyes then narrow at me, glaring, and I know I need to back the hell up.

"I—I'm sorry," I begin, my cheeks burning as I begin to trip over my words and I stop for a second and take a deep breath before continuing. "You come here every Thursday, and then last week, you were gone, and I was worried. Now you're here, and I'm glad, and now I'm rambling because I'm nervous, so I'm gonna leave you alone now."

Turning to leave, I'm stopped by the sweetest sound I've ever heard.

Ania's *voice.*

"Tripp, wait."

She said my name.

How does she know my name?

I've never been overly fond of my name, but the way it falls from her lips makes it shiny and new. I make my way back to her table and pause because I don't know what to do next.

"How do you know my name?" My voice sounds foreign,

questioning. I'm not sure why I'm so bothered by her knowing my name.

Maybe it's because I still don't know hers?

Maybe Wyatt told her?

Did she ask about me?

"It's on your name tag."

I glance down at the tag attached to my apron.

Of course.

"Oh, yeah, right . . . I forgot." My face heats up again, and I can feel the embarrassment clear down to my toes.

Why am I such a moron?

"I did see you last Thursday," she admits, her long hair falling in front of her face as she looks down at the table. I slide into the booth across from her, and her head snaps up—her eyes going wide again—and I'm afraid she's going to ask me to leave, but she doesn't. She sits there, her gaze fixed on me as if she's waiting for me to make the next move on an imaginary chessboard. Her eyes are dark and deep, and I know they hold secrets and stories I'd love to hear, but more than anything, I want her to keep talking to me. She could repeat the alphabet for all I care. So I tell her more in hopes she'll return the favor.

"But I waited, and you never came."

The blush that creeps up on her cheeks is something I've seen before. I assumed it was due to illness. Perhaps it has something to do with me. I don't want to get my hopes up, but I would love to think she's affected by me in the same way I'm affected by her.

"I—I didn't come here. It was later that evening. I saw you going into the cemetery. You were riding your bike. I'd been at the chapel."

Just as I'm getting ready to respond, Wyatt's presence catches my attention, and I notice he's looking our way. His eyebrows pull together, and I can't tell if it's anger or confusion crossing his face, but either way, I know I need to get back to work.

"Could I—uh, meet you somewhere? Like on the bench in front of the café? I get off at eight o'clock." The boldness is a façade. Inside, my heart is racing, and my palms are so sweaty that I have to dry them on the front of my jeans as I wait for her response. Ten seconds feels like ten minutes as her sad brown eyes stare across the table at me, and I can tell she's thinking it over . . . whether or not she can meet me . . . or wants to.

"Okay." She nods her head slightly, her teeth trapping her bottom lip as she hides a small smile.

That simple response has me on cloud nine.

As I walk back toward the kitchen, Wyatt passes me with a tray of food and if I'm not mistaken, he smiles and nods . . . like an approval. Maybe? I don't know, but whatever the look was, it didn't look like he's mad. But, honestly, I don't really care. All I care about is that I talked to Ania . . . and she agreed to meet me after work.

For the rest of my shift, I work fast. In my head, it seems like if I deliver food faster and bus tables faster, the time will pass faster. And the sooner I can finish my shift, the sooner I can meet *Ania* at the bench in front of the café.

Will she be there?

Will she change her mind?

Does she want to talk to me?

As I perform my tasks, those are the questions plaguing me. The subtle smile she gives me every time we make eye contact is the answer. I physically have to hold myself back from walking over to her table. Now that the verbal barrier is broken, I'm not sure if I can continue to orbit around her every Thursday without talking to her. I'm not sure how she feels about that, but the fact that she agreed to meet me after work tells me there's something there.

The look she was giving me across the table earlier was comforting. Something in her eyes was familiar, like I was looking in a mirror. It was an unspoken understanding. I still don't know any more about her, but I decided weeks ago that if all I can be is her friend, then that'll have to be good enough. It'll be hard because I already feel my palms itch when I'm around her, wanting to reach out and touch her long brown hair, stroke her soft cheek. Friends don't do those things.

I let out a deep breath when I have my last table cleared off and see that *Ania* is still there. She glances up at me and then back down at her watch. It's five minutes until eight, and she starts putting her book away in her backpack.

I take that as my cue to put my apron away and clock out. Saying my goodbyes to the kitchen crew and Dixie, I slip out the back door like always.

As I walk around the side of the building, I hold my breath until *Ania* comes into view. Her body is turned away from me, but I can tell she's watching, waiting for me. She glances at the front door a couple of times before standing and gripping the straps of her backpack, as if she's getting antsy or about to change her mind. When she turns around and sees me, the most amazing smile breaks across her face. The corners of her eyes wrinkle, and even though she looks down at her feet as I approach, I don't miss how the smile reaches her eyes and my heart stutters.

"Hey."

"Hey."

My heart is in my throat, and all we've said to each other is a casual greeting. I don't know how I'm going to survive this. She's going to get one good look at me—the real me—and *she's* going to be the one to run.

"I, uh—"

"So—"

We both begin talking at the same time and break off into awkward laughs, recognizing that we have no clue what we're doing. Her insecurity helps put me at ease.

"Could I walk you home?" Somewhere deep within, I conjure up enough courage to spit out those words without tripping over them.

"Uh, well, I drove here," she says, pointing to a red Volkswagen Beetle in the parking lot adjacent to the café.

"Oh, right. Well, I guess I can walk you to your, uh, car." I give her a half smile and run my hands through my hair out of nervous habit.

"Okay."

We walk to the corner and push the button for the crosswalk. I'm fidgeting with the edge of my shirt, trying to think of something to say when she pulls me out of my thoughts.

"Tripp?"

"What?"

"Walk," she says from a few steps ahead of me.

I'm already screwing this up. I don't even know why I thought I could do this in the first place. Mentally berating myself, I follow behind her until we're across the street on the sidewalk.

"So, what were you doing at the cemetery?" Her boldness surprises me, and I almost stumble over an imaginary rock.

"You okay?" she asks, reaching a hand out to grip my shoulder. Her touch feels like an electric shock, and it goes straight to my insides.

"Yeah, I—uh, I'm fine. Sorry. I, well . . . I went to see my dad," I admit, feeling awkward the minute the words leave my mouth. I don't talk about him with anyone except my mom and Liza, and not very often.

"I'm sorry," she says with sincerity.

I nod, unsure of what to say to that. People always say they're sorry, but they're not the ones who took him from me. Thanks to Dr. Abernathy, I know it's just people's way of expressing their sympathy and that the polite thing to say is "thank you."

"Thanks," I mutter.

The late summer sun has almost completely set in the sky, casting pinks and oranges over our heads and making *Ania's* skin take on a warm glow. She's beautiful. It's not that I haven't noticed before, but being this close to her allows me to see so much more. There's a patch of freckles along the bridge of her nose, and her lips almost look like a bow when she's thinking. Her eyes are more than just brown. They have flecks of gold and green in them as well. I could stand here and stare at her forever, but I notice the longer I do, the more the blush on her cheeks grows.

She nervously tucks one side of her hair behind her ear and clears her throat.

Trying to think of something to say to keep her here, I awkwardly blurt out, "So, why were *you* at the cemetery?" My voice squeaks, and I screw my eyes shut, wishing I had thought of something more eloquent. I'm afraid if I don't keep talking, however painful it is, she'll retreat to her car, and I'll be forced to wait an entire week to see her again. That thought alone feels like pure torture, especially after finally getting a chance to talk to her.

"Well, I go there sometimes. It's peaceful. And there's a chapel there. That's where I had been last Thursday—at the chapel."

I want to ask more.

Why?

Did you lose someone too?

Should I apologize for something I had no control over?

Are you engaged?

That last thought has my heart racing. I forced myself not to think about the engagement ring. But now that I'm standing here, talking to her, and feeling things I shouldn't if she belongs to someone else, that's probably something I need to know.

"Are you engaged?" I ask, the thought tumbling out of my brain and into the space between us. I didn't mean to just ask it, without any build up. Looking at the shocked expression on her face, I wish I could take it back.

I see her swallow hard, a bit of pain crossing her face as she looks away from me. But then she answers, "No." It's barely above a whisper and I watch as her arms wrap protectively around her, and I wish I could reach out and hug her. It's a strange thought and I don't know where it came from, but like always, I want to take her sadness away.

I know I've overstepped my boundaries—went somewhere I shouldn't have gone. The look in her eyes tells me she's shutting down—shutting me out.

"I've gotta go," she says, her voice firmer as she turns and walks toward her car.

Desperately, I search for something else to say—something that will fix whatever I just broke.

"I'm sorry," I call after her, letting my voice reach out like my hands want to.

Her steps halt, and she slowly turns back around toward me.

"I just saw you wearing an, uh, engagement ring one time . . . and I didn't want to, uh . . ."

She graciously saves me by interrupting my rambling. "I'm not engaged. I've never been engaged. I don't even have a boyfriend." A small smile replaces the sad expression she had only moments ago, and I return it to her, feeling relieved but still confused about the ring.

"Can I see you sometime? I mean, besides here?" I ask, pointing across the street to the café. "I mean if you'd . . . never mind . . ."

"On Friday nights, I go to the Original City Diner and do homework, sometimes with friends but usually alone. If you want to stop by . . ."

As her words drift off, I nod my head in agreement, unable to find my voice. She gives me one last smile before she opens the door to her car and slips inside.

I stand on the curb and watch as she pulls out onto the road, and I continue to watch until her taillights fade into the distance.

Did she just invite me to dinner?

A study session?

Oh, shit.

I'm going to see Ania tomorrow.

I'm so excited; I doubt I'll sleep tonight. But that's okay, because tonight, instead of nightmares or anxiety, it'll be because of a beautiful girl and an invitation to meet her for homework.

ten

"THIS SMELLS AMAZING."

My mom came over earlier to watch the twins, and being her, she couldn't sit still while they were napping, so she started a pot of gumbo. The aroma has been filling the house for the last five hours, and now that it's finally in front of me, it can't cool fast enough. My stomach and tongue are having an argument over the appropriate temperature for food. Right now, my stomach is winning.

"You two act like you haven't eaten in days," Liza admonishes. I glance over at Ben and see he's mimicking my approach: blow, blow, sip.

Not only am I in a hurry to eat this deliciousness in front of me, but I'm also in a hurry because I'm going to see *Ania* tonight. She said she usually gets to the diner around eight o'clock, and I don't plan on being late. Even though it's just now a little before seven, I want to give myself plenty of time.

"You've been watching the clock all afternoon. What gives?" My mom is eyeballing me suspiciously from across the table.

"I was wondering the same thing," Liza chimes in.

Ben snickers behind his spoon, leaving me to the wolves.

"I, uh, have plans." I leave it short and simple, hoping they'll afford me the luxury of not going into great detail about where I'm going.

"Oh?" Liza and my mom share the same pleasantly surprised expression.

I nod and continue cautiously devouring my gumbo, until two

throats clearing from the other side of the table force me to look back up.

"What?" I ask, trying to play dumb. I glance over at Ben, but he offers no help, just shaking his head and smirking into his steaming bowl. I silently plead with him to help me out on this one, but he stuffs his mouth with flaky bread and grins. Apparently, I'm on my own.

"Uh, I'm meeting An—." *Oh, shit.* The realization that I don't know her real name is disturbing to me. A barrage of negative thoughts enters my mind, mostly emphasizing the fact that I have no idea what I'm doing.

"You're meeting who, sweetheart?" my mom asks, pulling me from my thoughts.

"Uh, a friend I met at the café." I've yet to tell my mom or Liza about this. I confided in Ben earlier today, seeking advice and just to have someone to share it with, because regardless of my nervousness and feelings of insecurity, I'm excited.

No. It's more than that. It's like the best thing that's happened since *Ania* smiled at me. But telling my mom and Liza sets me up for a huge let down if things don't go well . . . and more disappointment. They'll force me to talk about my feelings and try to assure me there will be other girls. The truth is that I don't want another girl. I want *Ania*.

Damn it. I will find out her real name. Tonight.

"This friend wouldn't happen to also be your favorite customer, would they?"

My silence is all the answer Liza needs. There's no getting out of this.

"Tripp," she gushes. "I'm so proud of you! You have no idea!" While my sister offers her praise, I look over to see my mom's eyes glisten in the warm light from the candles that are lit on the table.

This.

This is what I was trying to avoid—them getting their hopes up and me crushing them, once again.

"Stop. Both of you," I plead, trying to sound firm, but I can't. "Please. Just don't act like it's a big deal because it's not. She told me that she studies at The Original on Friday nights around eight o'clock, so I'm meeting her there. That's it. It's not a date or anything. It's two people being in the same place at the same time."

"On purpose," Ben adds. So now he decides to speak.

I glare over at him.

"What? It's the truth! You can try to play this down all you want, but *you* asked her if you could see her outside of the café. *You* did that." He slaps my shoulder with all the proudness he can muster like I've just announced I won the Nobel Peace Prize. As much as this scenario feels so familiar, it doesn't escape me how so much has changed.

"It's been awhile since we've done this," Liza says as her eyes glance around the table.

"It has, and I'm glad we're all here." The tiredness that my mom has seemed to carry for the last nine months finally seems to be lifting. The dark circles under her eyes are lighter than they've ever been, and her smile finally reaches her eyes again.

In comfortable silence, we all begin passing bowls, allowing the familiar aromas to help heal us. This is something we used to do at least once a week before my dad passed away, but all of that went away with him. None of us could bring ourselves to do anything we had done with him. It felt wrong. It's like it doesn't work since he's not here. But for the first time in a long time, this feels like it works. Moments like this make me think that we might make it. Maybe one day the empty seat at the head of the table won't be a stark reminder of the pain we've been through this last year, but a sweet memory.

I'm glad I have some good news to bring to the table. I haven't done a very good job of pulling my weight around here. I've allowed myself to wallow and drown my grief in everything under the sun, and my bad decisions have caught up with me.

I've been fooling myself into thinking I can do whatever I want, whenever I want, and not face consequences for them. Everyone makes excuses for you when you're grieving.

The letter I intercepted in the mail a few weeks ago from Tulane was the wake-up call I needed. It was the slap in the face that helped me realize someone is holding me accountable.

My dad would be so ashamed if he saw where I was a few weeks ago . . . on a three-day bender, skipping class for days, weeks on end, ignoring calls from my family . . . slowly shitting my life away.

But not anymore. All I have left of my dad are memories . . . and I'm going to honor those. I'm going to make him proud of me. It's the least I can do.

After a heart-to-heart with my advisor, I now have a plan to retake the necessary classes to bring up my GPA. He also helped me petition some of my professors to see what I can do about bringing up my grades in my current classes.

"I've declared a major." Everyone simultaneously puts down their forks and looks up at me with a genuine smile on their face.

"Baby, that's great news." My mom knows the struggles I've been facing. I never let her see the letter from a few weeks ago, but she's no dummy. Even though we don't talk about it, I know she knows that I've pretty much been wasting my life away for the last nine months.

"I'm going into the Criminal Justice program. I know it's not Pre-Law, and that's what dad would've wanted, but I feel like it's what I'm supposed to be doing. And it's something I can get into with my current GPA. Hopefully, I can work hard and bring that up . . . and maybe one day I can pursue Law." The feelings running through me are all over the place. I feel relieved, nervous, and a little scared. I know that even though I'm not going Pre-Law, I still have a lot of work ahead of me. It's going to take a lot to get out of the hole I've dug myself into. I also feel disappointed that I shit away an opportunity to follow in my dad's footsteps, but I can't change that.

"I'm proud of you, Tripp." Ben's large hand cups my shoulder, and he pulls me into a manly side-hug. My sister sits across the table and beams at me. It feels good to make them all so proud.

At a half-past seven, I'm making my way down St. Charles, even though I know it'll only take me fifteen minutes to get there. I can't be late. I wouldn't want her to think I'm not coming. A brief flash of last Thursday crosses my mind. There is a slight possibility that I'll be the one who gets stood up . . . I mean, if this were a date, which it's not.

"It's two people being in the same place at the same time," I quietly repeat to myself, because it makes me feel better.

When I reach the garden level of the Lavin-Bernick Center, I begin looking for her long dark hair. I'm trying to imagine what it will be like to see her outside of the café. It feels surreal that I'm meeting her here tonight. It's been a while since I've been here. When I attended Tulane, this wasn't really my scene.

If I didn't know better, I'd think a marching band has taken up residence in my chest. I take deep breaths with each step, willing myself to not run.

I want this so bad.

I can do this.

As I make my way inside the diner, I look more for *Ania* but don't find her anywhere. There're a few girls at a table in the corner and some guy sitting by himself, but no *Ania*. I sit at the table closest to the door but then change my mind, because it seems too out in the open. So I stand back up and scan the room for the perfect spot. I wish I had waited a little longer before leaving the house. If I had let her arrive first, she would have picked our table. *Our* table. I wonder if this could become our thing—meeting here on Friday nights.

I'm getting ready to go back outside and hide around the corner to wait for her, but then I feel her, and a second later, I hear her call my name.

Turning around, I immediately see her. She's giving me a half-wave and smile to match, and she's gorgeous. She motions for me to follow her, so I do, almost certain that I'd follow her anywhere.

"You came," she says as a smile spreads across her face.

I take it that it's a good thing I'm here, so I return her smile.

"There's no place I'd rather be," I admit.

My boldness catches us both off guard. I feel the tips of my ears burning, and her cheeks are a lovely shade of pink.

She clears her throat before asking, "So, where do you normally spend Friday nights?"

"Uh, well, I—"

"What can I get y'all?" The waitress interrupts our awkward exchange, thankfully, giving me a chance to just look at Ania and get a grip on myself.

She orders first, and I'm surprised by the fact that she's eating. She never eats at the café. Not only does she order, but she does it up right, asking for a strawberry milkshake and a pancake with strawberries on top. I guess she likes strawberries.

"And for you, darlin'?" the waitress, asks. Her name is Sally, according to her name tag, and I decide that fits her. She's an older lady with a bun on the top of her head and a friendly smile.

"Uh, coffee?" My order comes out like a question, but she just writes it down and says she'll be back shortly.

"You're not hungry?" *Ania* asks, after Sally leaves. "They have the best pancakes."

"Do you always eat pancakes for dinner?"

"Do you always answer a question with a question?" Her quick retort makes me smile.

Once again, I feel the need to pinch myself. *Am I sitting across the table from her, having this conversation?* If this is a dream, I don't want to wake up.

"I already ate . . . earlier . . . with my family."

"Do you do that a lot?" Her expression is soft but hard to read.

"Well, we usually eat together on Friday nights and Sundays after church."

"That must be nice."

"It is. They're great." I inwardly want to slap myself for being such a dork. *They're great? Who says that?*

A few minutes of awkward silence and I'm getting ready to bolt, looking behind me toward the door, resigned to the fact that I'll never be able to talk to girls like I used to. Not just any girl, Ania. She's the only girl I want to talk to, and I can't. Just before I make a run for it, Sally saves the day, coming back with our order.

"One strawberry milkshake and one coffee," she says placing the drinks on the table and giving me a wink. "Need cream and sugar, Sugar?"

"Uh, no . . . Thank you."

After she walks away, *Ania* throws her head back and laughs. It's the best sound I've ever heard. It's better than the jazz band I love to listen to down at Marketplace. It's better than the lullaby my mom used to sing to me when I was little. It's better than thousands of fans chanting my name at a football game. It's like a bowl of Lucky Charms . . . marshmallows only. I'm not sure what made her laugh, but I want to hear it every day for the rest of my life.

"She was *so* flirting with you." Her eyes are sparkling as she looks across the table at me.

"Who? Sally?"

"Oh, are y'all on a first name basis? Did she secretly slip you her phone number when I wasn't looking?"

"What? I, um . . . no. She wasn't flirting with me." That's ridiculous. She was just being nice. She's a waitress. Waitresses are nice. Generally.

"*Yes*, she was." A small smile stays on her lips as she begins taking books out of the brown leather bag I've seen a dozen times.

"Here ya go, Loren," Sally says, setting down a plate that's holding a pancake the size of my head . . . No. I take that back. It's the size of Ben's head—huge!

Wait. Did she say "Loren"? Is that her name?

"You sure I can't get you anything else, darlin'?"

"No, thank you." I can't quit staring at the girl across the table from me. She wastes no time digging into the pancake. The first bite that touches her lips makes her moan in appreciation, and I shift in my seat, adjusting myself. *What the hell is wrong with me?*

"So, your name is *Loren*?" I ask from a half-dazed state.

"Oh, shit! Um, yeah. I'm Loren. Have we not done this yet?" she asks, shaking her head and wiping the syrup off her lips with a napkin. "I feel like we're doing everything backward," she says, her voice practically a whisper, like she's in awe of the situation. My feelings are mutual. I feel like I know her, but I don't. She's an anomaly—someone who has been the object of my attention and affection for so many weeks, yet I didn't even know her name until just a moment ago.

I nod, and she seems to know I'm feeling the same way.

Loren. Loren. Loren.

That's suddenly the most beautiful name in the English language.

Someone once told me you have to do something seventeen times before it becomes a habit. So mentally, I begin repeating her name over and over in my mind, hoping I don't mess up and call her the wrong name.

Loren. Loren. Loren . . .

Her eyes gaze out the window before slowly turning back to me, and as she begins to speak, her tone is almost as sad as her eyes. "Before you started working at the café, I would go and sit, and sometimes I wouldn't even notice that the time had passed until the lights would get turned off, and I'd have to take that as my cue to leave. No one talked to me, and I didn't talk to anyone. I mean, occasionally, I'd talk to Wyatt, but that's it. Until you."

"Well, we never really talked," I say, rubbing the back of my neck. I have so many things I want to say and ask, but I don't know how or where to start.

"Yeah, but you noticed me."

Those words. I noticed her. Of course, I did. How could I not have? I want to tell her that I know the second she walks into the room, not because I see her, but because I feel her. But I can't say that. That sounds like the words of a crazy person in lo–.

Stop.

"Of course, I noticed you."

She stares at me for the longest time before continuing. "I noticed you, too."

"How could you not have?" I laugh, turning my thoughts on myself. I mean, seriously. I can't believe she's sitting here in front of me because the only thing she's seen from me is an awkward guy who almost spills things on her and breaks plates and says stupid stuff.

"Exactly," she says, but she's not laughing. It looks as though she's breathing harder, and her cheeks flush once again. The way she fiddles with her napkin reminds me of myself. I do stuff like that when I'm nervous or anxious, and I don't want her to feel either of those things. So I try to think of some way to distract her.

"How do you know Wyatt?" I finally ask.

The question does pull her out of her thoughts, but it doesn't relieve the tension etched on her face. She draws her brows closer together and bites her cheek as if she's deciding how to answer. "Well, I've known him for a while, just from going into the café. It's kinda hard not to know someone when you see them once a week for three years."

I nod, trying to think of something else to say. The direction this conversation is going seems to be the wrong one. From the way she's staring out the window, I would guess that she's shutting down; putting up any wall she had dropped, retreating inside herself.

"I like your car," I blurt out.

She turns from the window, and her eyes light up a little.

"It's a classic," she says, with a hint of pride in her voice. By the way her mouth turns back up at the corners, I know I'm on to something the two of us can talk about without things getting uncomfortable . . . well, for now, at least. It's not a subject I've broached for a long time, but if it makes her face light up like that, I'm willing to go there . . . for her.

"I love classic cars," I say, swallowing the lump that's trying to force its way up my throat—the same one that's always there when classic cars are mentioned. I can't think about classic cars without thinking about *my* classic car, and I can't think about my classic car without thinking about . . . *oh, shit.*

Deep breaths.

In.

Out.

In.

Out.

I don't want to do this.

Not here.

Not now.

Dr. Abernathy's voice pops into my head. *"Focus on where you are and who you're with. Don't allow yourself to get swept away. Stay grounded."*

Stay grounded.

"Tripp?" Loren's soft hand touches mine, pulling me out of my head. Her sweet voice sounds concerned, and it helps me focus on something besides the anxiety.

After a few more deep breaths, I finally feel the tightness in my throat loosen, and my breathing starts to return to normal.

"I—I'm sorry," I mutter when I'm able to find my voice.

"It's okay. Are . . . are you okay?"

Normally, I'd feel embarrassed. I'd run, try to get away from whatever situation sent me into the attack in the first place. But when I look across the table, she's there, and it keeps me in place. I've wanted this for so long. I can't run now.

"Yeah. Yeah, I'm fine," I say, convincing her and me at the same time. "What were you saying?"

"What's your favorite?" she asks, but I can tell she's unsure.

"The '60s and '70s. Great solid bodies and timeless designs," I reply.

"Me too," she says, and the twinkle in her eye is back.

"I love the mechanics—taking them apart and putting them back together, knowing everything about them from the hood to the tires," I tell her because this is a safe topic. I can handle this.

She nods in agreement with a day-dreamy look on her face.

From there, our conversation falls into an easy cadence. She asks questions, and I answer, and then we switch.

"Favorite band?" she asks, taking a drink of her milkshake.

"Does Otis Redding count?" I ask, answering her question with a question again.

"Otis always counts," she says seriously.

"What about you? Who's your favorite?"

"Ray LaMontagne," she says. "Hands down."

"I've never heard of him," I tell her.

"What?" she asks in surprise. "Well, I'll have to educate you."

And I like the sound of that.

We both skirt around issues or topics we can tell upset the other. For instance, even though classic cars are a passion for both of us, she doesn't like talking about it that much. There's something there that causes her pain. And I understand, because it happens to me too. I wonder if her reason is anything like mine, but I try not to dwell on it too much because I don't want to ruin this perfect night.

One of my favorite things about talking to Loren, other than the fact that I get to stare at her without feeling like a creeper, is that she makes it easy. She could've bailed when I had my almost-panic attack earlier, but she was calm and didn't even look at me different after it was over. She's patient and allows me time to think about what I want to say without pressing for more information. The same feeling from last night floods my mind, and again, it's as if I'm staring in a mirror, seeing my reflection.

For an hour or so, we sit in comfortable silence, each of us lost in our school work until she looks at her watch and sees that it's almost eleven o'clock.

"I've got an early study group at the library in the morning," she says, but I can hear the hesitancy in her voice as she closes her notebook and snaps the lid on her purple highlighter.

"Yeah, I guess it is getting late." I *know* it's getting late. I can feel my body tiring, but the adrenaline that's been running through me since last night, coupled with the few cups of coffee I've had here, are keeping me artificially fueled.

As we walk out of the diner, I see Sally smile our way. The way her eyes are assessing me, it makes me wonder if Loren is right. Not wanting to be rude, I give her a small wave and smile, but my cheeks heat up under her scrutiny.

"Told you," Loren says, teasing me.

I smile and shake my head as I hold the door open for her.

She pauses on her way out, looking up at me. "Thank you." The smile she gives me as she passes by shoots straight to my insides, causing things to stir inside me that have been dormant for so long.

"Thank *you*," I reply, walking closely beside her. I have no desire to leave her company, but I know I have to.

"What are you thanking me for?" she asks, a smile in her tone.

"For allowing me to join you tonight," I tell her.

"It was great. I, uh . . . I'm glad you came."

"Me too."

The campus is relatively quiet, and the coolness of fall is upon us. I look around, wondering how she got here or if she lives close enough to walk.

When will I see her again?

"I live this way," she says, pointing over her shoulder. "On campus. I walked here."

"Could I . . . Can I walk you home?" If she tells me no again, I'll be forced to follow her, because I won't be able to rest not knowing whether or not she made it safely. And I don't think she's ready to give me her phone number, although I'd like to have it.

"Okay," she says, smiling, but the nervous fidget she had earlier is back, so I keep an arm's length distance between the two of us and follow her lead toward her dorm.

"Do you live close?" she asks as we make our way across the open lawn. The dew is already sticking to the blades of grass and my exposed feet.

"Yeah, just fifteen minutes away. Not bad."

"Do you always walk everywhere you go?"

"Yeah, or ride my bike," I say, watching my feet.

She nods her head, and I can sense more questions in her silence, but she doesn't ask them. I mean, it's not normal for a guy my age to not drive a car. But I'm glad she doesn't ask because I'm not ready to go there. Maybe on our second date, but not tonight.

We pass a group of guys walking in the opposite direction. Loren seems oblivious to their attention, but I notice them notice her, and sense of relief comes over me. I'm glad I took the chance and asked to walk her home. I wish I could walk her home every night.

She slows as we approach her dormitory, adjusting the straps of her backpack and looking everywhere but at me.

"Can I see you again sometime? I mean, outside of the café?" I ask.

"I'd like that," she says quietly.

"Okay," I reply, and it doesn't escape me that I normally don't want to make eye contact with anyone, but when it comes to Loren, I can't take my eyes off her.

"Okay," she says as she swallows and then draws her eyebrows together. "But I'm busy for the next week or so. I have mid-terms to get ready for . . . and . . ."

I can tell she's struggling, with what I'm not sure, but I want to help her.

"It's okay. I have mid-terms too," I tell her because it's the truth and I don't want her to feel bad about whatever took the smile off her face.

"Will I at least see you at the café?"

"Yeah, I'll be there," she says with a weak smile.

"I'll see you then," I tell her, wanting to draw out these last few seconds with her.

"Good night."

"Good night," I say, my eyes locked on her lips as I wonder what it would feel like to kiss them.

When she finally leaves, my chest aches at the loss, and I stand glued in place as I watch her disappear inside the building. She turns around once and gives a small wave when she sees me still standing here.

I can't make my feet move until she's completely out of sight.

On my way home, I replay every moment of our time together . . . and begin counting down the seconds until I'll see her again.

eleven

WEIGHTLESSNESS.

This time, I'm not standing on the shore or watching from an omniscient position. I'm in the water—submerged but breathing. The dark water surrounding me begins to lighten, and I see *her* floating beside me—*Ania*. Her eyes open, and she looks over at me. There's no sadness or fear, but her eyes blink several times as if she's waking from a deep sleep. I reach an arm out to her, and she takes my hand.

Just as I'm pulling her to me, an obnoxious beeping wakes me from the semi-peaceful dream. I lie still for a moment, trying to pull every bit and piece I can from my foggy memory. It's so similar to dreams I've had lately—same elements but different scenario. Regardless, I'll take my murky black and white dreams over the startling nightmares I used to have any day. Even though some mornings I wake up with a pain in my chest from not being able to get to her before my dream is over. This time, I was with her . . . She took my hand.

I reach over and grab the journal from my nightstand, doing my best to scribble down a description of the dream, along with how it made me feel. At my last appointment with Dr. Abernathy, she suggested I start keeping a journal of my dreams, as a way to clear my mind. It seems to be working, somewhat.

As I go through my morning routine, my focus is still on Loren. There's no journaling that can clear her out of my mind. I can't help wondering what we'll talk about tonight. Will she be back to her shy, withdrawn self, or will she be the semi-outgoing and quick-witted girl I saw at the diner Friday night? The contrast between the girl from the café and the girl from the diner doesn't escape me. It's not like she was a completely different person or anything, just better, happier—the color-version of herself. I'm not sure if that had more to do with me or the location, but whatever it was, I'd love to see *that* girl again.

Loren.

Loren.

Loren.

Days later, and I'm still repeating her name to myself, partly because I'm making sure I don't slip up and call her Ania, and partly because I just like the way it sounds in my head.

The afternoon is filled with homework, some Jack and Emmie playtime, and running a couple of errands for my mom. Before I know it, it's time to head to the café for my shift. Wyatt put me on the schedule for a full eight hours today, with talk of adding a weekend shift on in another week or two, depending on how I do this week. The accomplishment I feel from working at The Crescent Moon is huge. I know it's just waiting tables, but I've had to overcome a lot of obstacles to get here, so I'm not going to belittle that.

"Hey, Tripp," Shawn calls from the prep station in the middle of the large kitchen as I walk through the back door.

"Hey," I reply, giving him a nod.

"Tripp, you're just in time. Would you mind helping me move a few tables together to get ready for a large group that's coming in for a late lunch meeting?" Sarah asks, smiling her thanks over her shoulder as she loads down a tray with drinks and heads out into the café.

Tying on my apron, I look around, and a sudden rush of realization hits me—I fit in here. For the first time in a long time, I belong somewhere. I'm part of the team.

With an added boost of confidence, I head out to help Sarah—pushing tables together, rearranging chairs, putting down place settings. One task flows into the next, and I tackle them all with very few mistakes. The mistakes I do make are probably only noticeable to me. I *almost* served the lady at table three a side of shrimp and grits instead of crawfish étouffée, but I caught it just before I loaded up my tray. There was also a near hit with a water glass and an elderly man at table five, but I avoided it. Julie and I collided with stacks of dirty dishes, but somehow we both kept all of our plates in one piece.

I don't think this is the first day that I've been competent at my job, but it's the first day where I've had a clear enough mind to notice—to take inventory—which is surprising, because along with my job requirements, I've also been thinking of Loren. Usually, these days, if my mind is on more than one thing, I screw everything up.

Looking up from the table I've been wiping down, I see her long hair hanging halfway down across her face. She meets my gaze, and a smile breaks. It's not forced. There's no sadness behind it. She holds eye contact with me for longer than necessary, and I know . . . that smile is for me. Just for me. And I smile back. My throat tightens a little, but I laugh, because that's what you do when you're happy.

I'm happy. Loren makes me happy.

I don't know what to do next, but I know when I get a chance, I'm going to go over to table six, and I'm going to talk to the beautiful girl sitting there. Because I can.

I watch her as she takes out her journal and opens it up. She doesn't begin writing right away. For a few minutes, she stares out the window, but when our eyes meet again, there's still mostly happiness where the sadness used to be.

An hour or so later, the dinner crowd has died down, and my last customers are having their after-dinner coffee. There are a few people in Sarah's section, and Julie's taking care of the front two tables, but other than that, the café is quiet.

Walking back into the kitchen, I notice Shawn is in the process of putting away the leftover bread pudding—it was the dessert special today—and inspiration strikes.

"Could I have a slice of that on a plate with the rum sauce?" I ask, nervously wiping my hands down the front of my apron.

"Sure. Did table five change their mind on dessert?"

"Uh, no. It's for . . . uh. Well, I thought I'd . . ."

"Hey, man, no explanation needed," he says, smiling to himself as he puts a piece of it on a plate and pours the warm sauce over the top. After he garnishes the plate and wipes the edges clean to perfection, he hands it over to me.

"Thanks. I'll pay for it later," I tell him.

"Good luck," He says, giving me a knowing smile.

I give him a half-smile in return. I'm glad he's cool. I don't think I could handle it if he started asking a bunch of questions. It'd make me even more self-conscious than I already am about what I'm getting ready to do.

When I walk back out, I almost lose my nerve and turn right back around, but seeing her sitting there and knowing how good it felt to talk to her last week, I know I can't. I have to do this. I *want* to do this. I *need* to do this.

As I slide the piece of delectable dessert in front of her, she pauses, eyes cast down at the plate in front of her. Slowly, she looks up, a small smile playing on her lips.

"I, uh, thought you might . . . Well, last Friday, you ordered all sweet stuff. So I thought you'd like this."

"It's my favorite."

"It's on the house."

"Thank you."

I don't want to hover while she eats, so I make myself useful and help Sarah clear off a table. Every once in a while, I look up and see her taking a bite of the bread pudding. I wasn't sure if she'd eat it, seeing as though she never orders anything while she's here, but I hoped she would. She looks over at me about the same time her tongue darts out to lick the rum sauce off the fork, and a tightening in my stomach catches me off guard. I'm not stupid. I know what it is, and I know why it's there—attraction, desire—I just haven't felt it in so long that I almost forgot what it's like to *feel* something.

"You just gonna stand there?" Sarah asks, nearly making me drop the bucket of dirty dishes I'm holding.

I clear my throat and hold the bucket lower to cover what I'm sure is an embarrassing outward display of my inward affections.

"Sorry," I mutter, dropping my gaze from Loren and heading for the kitchen.

After I deposit the dirty dishes and preoccupy myself with the mundane task of spraying them off, I feel more in control. So, I step back out into the café to check on my customers. My two coffee drinkers have left, and there's hardly a soul in the place, except for the couple at the front and the beauty at table six.

Tentatively, I begin walking toward her, but before I can get to her, she turns around and smiles at me.

"Hey," she says, her eyes inviting me in.

"Hey," I reply and slide into the booth across from her.

My eyes go down to the book in front of her, but I don't get a chance to see what's written on the pages because she quickly closes it, holding it to her chest. I wasn't trying to pry. My curiosity just got the best of me.

"I'm sorry. I wasn't . . . I mean, I didn't see . . ." I stumble over my apology, hoping she's not mad at me.

"It's okay. I just . . . well, I . . ." she begins, trying to explain.

"Don't worry about it. I get it." I do. I get it. I know that we both have secrets we're not ready to tell, and that's okay with me. The last thing I want to do is push her away, so I'll take whatever she wants to give me. It's already been more than I ever could've dreamed of getting in the first place.

"Um, there's this thing . . . on campus at the Rat on Thursday nights," she begins, her fingers nervously running up and down the uneven pages of the journal. "I was . . . do you like jazz music?" she finally asks and her cheeks instantly turn a lovely shade of pink.

She's nervous.

I know that feeling too.

Instinctively, my hand inches across the table and gently grabs hers.

The entire interaction was completely unplanned, making my eyes grow in surprise. I only wanted to make her forget whatever it is she's worried about—take away her nerves.

As I glance across the table at her, she laughs, shaking her head.

"I love jazz," I tell her. I also want to tell her that I love the way her hand feels in mine, but I don't think it would come out right, and I don't want to ruin this moment.

"Well, I just thought that if you don't have anything to do after work, maybe you'd like to go to Jazz at the Rat with me?"

"I'd love to."

"Really?"

"Of course."

We sit there, exchanging slight smiles that turn into larger ones, until I physically have to pry myself out of the seat and go back to work.

I only have about ten minutes left on my shift, so I help Sarah tidy up the kitchen to pass the time.

When I walk around the side of the building, Loren is waiting patiently on the bench at the corner. I watch her for a second, soaking in the fact that she's here and she asked me to meet her. I can't help the cheesy grin on my face when she looks up at me.

"Did you drive here?" I ask, hoping she didn't, as I scan the parking lot across the street, but the little red Volkswagen is nowhere to be seen.

"No," she replies as she turns her head toward where she had been parked the week before. "I was kinda hoping you'd say yes, and I thought we'd walk there together." Her statement comes out more like a question, and I realize she was unsure of what my response was going to be. It seems so strange that she could think for one minute that I might turn her down.

She has no idea.

Once again, the happiness I'm feeling erupts from deep inside, and I let out what sounds like a nervous laugh, but it's just her . . . It's how she makes me feel, and it's unexplainable.

"Yes." It's all I can manage, but it's enough. I unlock my bike from the rack and release the kickstand so that I can walk beside her. For a few minutes, the only sound filling the air between us is the click of the gears on my bike.

"Soooo . . . have you always lived in New Orleans?" she asks, fidgeting with the straps on her backpack.

"Born and raised here. How 'bout you?"

"I moved here for school. I'm originally from a small town outside of Houston."

"Not too far away from home, then."

"No, but far enough."

The way the words come out makes me want to ask more questions, but the shift in her demeanor tells me that maybe I shouldn't.

"Did you always want to go to Tulane?" I ask, changing the subject a bit.

"Uh, well, it wasn't technically *my* dream . . . but, I guess . . ." Her voice trails off. When I look over at her, she's worrying her bottom lip and her eyebrows pinch together.

"Hey," I say, getting her attention. "Let's talk about something else. Anything. You choose."

She relaxes a little, allowing the smile back on her lips, and asks, "Favorite song on the radio?"

"I don't listen to the radio much, but I like this song called 'Demons', which sounds creepy, but . . . it's, uh, a great song. The lyrics, I mean. They're great." I feel so lame. But it's the only song I can think of. I've overheard it from the garage when Ben's in there. I don't go in, but I sometimes sit on the steps leading up to my apartment and listen, thinking.

"Imagine Dragons," she says, nodding her head. "Yeah, I like them. That is a great song." The way she smiles up at me sets my mind at ease. The oranges and pinks hanging on in the western sky are casting a warm light over her, making her skin glow, just like last week when I walked her to her car. I'm instantly distracted from my insecurities by how shiny her hair is and how soft it looks.

I wish I weren't pushing this damn bike. I might try to hold her hand, which seems crazy, but the way she looks at me gives me confidence I didn't even know I possessed anymore. I thought it was long gone with so many other things.

Instead, I ask her the same question, wanting to know everything about the girl walking beside me—the good, the sad, the bad . . . her deepest, darkest secrets . . . and even her favorite song.

"'Shake It Off'," she says matter-of-factly.

I glance over my other shoulder, trying to figure out what she's talking about and then back at her just in time to see a smile cross her face. And then she laughs. As she tilts her head back and squeezes her eyes closed, I can't help but join in, if for no other reason than not wanting her to stop.

"It's a song. By Taylor Swift," she explains, and I have no idea what she's talking about. I mean, of course, I know who Taylor Swift is, but that's about as far as it goes.

"There's not any deep, philosophical meaning behind it," she continues. "I just like it. On days I'm feeling sad, I can play it, and I don't feel so sad anymore. It's just mindless words and they help me forget whatever the hell I'm dwelling on at the time."

I hate that she's sad, but this "Shake It Off" might be my new favorite song.

Her eyes stay on the concrete beneath our feet until we reach the grass in front of the Student Union. There are quite a few people milling around, and we look to each other, both silently asking where or what we should do next.

"I could walk over to my dorm and grab a blanket so we can sit over here on the grass away from the crowd."

"Whatever you'd like to do." I'd sit on the moon if that's where she wanted to be.

I lock my bike to a rack and escort her over to her dorm.

"I'll be right back," she says, looking back over her shoulder.

"I'll be waiting."

She smiles again and shakes her head as she walks through the glass doors.

Minutes later, we've secured a spot on the lawn, close enough to hear the jazz that's coming from the Rat, but far enough away that we can still have a quiet conversation of our own. We discuss school, and she tells me she's just recently declared her major—Sociology. I can tell from the way she talks about it that she wants to help people. That makes me like her even more than I already did, if that's possible.

We're both leaning back on our arms, legs kicked out in front of us, shoulders almost touching but not quite, and something in my mind starts to stir . . . like a fuzzy television station coming into focus . . .

Valentine's Day.

The official day of love.

The day men are pressured into doing something romantic for the woman in their life.

Don't get me wrong. I have nothing against romance. What I don't like is being pressured to show my feelings for someone, especially when I don't know how I truly feel about them.

Whitney and I have been seeing each other yet again, ever since we hooked up at a New Year's Eve party. It's been less than two months, and she's already starting to put the pressure on me to get serious. Monogamy has never been an issue with me. I'm totally committed when I'm in a relationship, but I'm simply not ready to make any major plans for my future right now.

Regardless, here I am, laying out a picnic for my girlfriend and me to enjoy on this breezy February fourteenth at Audubon Park, while she watches me with lovesick eyes. I like Whitney. I do. I have for years. I just wish she'd stop demanding so much from me. I put enough pressure on myself as it is.

"Tripp, this is so sweet of you," Whitney gushes. "I love it." She gracefully sits down and accepts the plate of fruit, cheese, and crackers I hand her.

"I'm glad you like it. I thought we could visit that new jazz club in The Quarter later too if you'd like."

"Dancing the night away sounds perfect!" She takes my hand and laces our fingers together before leaning toward me, speaking quietly. "Then we can celebrate our news in private." I stare as her tongue sweeps across her full bottom lip for a moment before her words catch my attention.

"What news are we celebrating?"

"Our engagement, of course, silly!"

"We're not engaged,*" I tell her, that last word coming out with a bit of disgust. Extracting my hand from hers, I run my fingers through my hair, willing myself not to flip the fuck out.*

"Well, we will be as soon as you ask me, so go ahead!"

"What the hell are you talking about?"

"Tripp, stop playing around. You said you had a surprise for me here at the park . . . It's Valentine's Day . . . What else could it be?" Her voice starts to squeak, causing the ducks in a nearby pond to fly off.

"The picnic was the surprise, Whitney! We've only been back together a few weeks. What the hell? You thought I was going to propose tonight?"

This girl is unbelievable. I can't even do something nice for her without her thinking it's a damn proposal.

"You make it sound like we've only known each other a short time. We've been together since high school! Why are you so afraid of commitment?" Her eyes fill with tears, but I immediately recognize them for the ploy they are.

"Why are you so ready to get married? Why can't we just enjoy our time together without putting added pressure? We have plenty of time to settle down after we graduate, if that's what we decide to do."

"I don't know, Tripp. I don't think I can wait that long. I was there for you when your dad died, I didn't complain when you gave up football, and I've forgiven you for being with other girls when we were broken up. I think I've earned a damn ring by now!"

A cold sweat covers my body, and I quickly stand up, not stopping until I'm across the lawn. When the panic rises that fast, I always feel like running, like I'm trying to escape whatever is chasing me down. Loren is close behind. I feel her, and when I finally turn to look at her, there is nothing but worry and concern etched on her beautiful face.

"Tripp, are you okay?"

I honestly don't know how to answer her. Technically, I'm fine, but to have that particular memory hit me out of the blue like that has shaken me to my core.

"D-do you mind if we sit on that bench over there," I ask, pointing a few feet away.

"Of course not." For a second, it looks like Loren might grab my hand, but she quickly changes her mind—not that I blame her.

Once we're seated, I close my eyes and breathe deeply. The faint sound of jazz still fills the night air, and it helps me to refocus and calm myself until I feel comfortable enough to speak. Turning to face Loren, I see she's watching me. Self-consciously, and out of habit, I tug on my hair, which only causes her gaze to sharpen, focusing in on my scar.

Her fingertips ghost over my eyebrow, making my skin hum.

Softly, she asks, "What happened?"

I know if I'm going to have any kind of relationship with Loren, I need to be honest and tell her something about myself, something to help explain the crazy. If I don't, she'll never begin to understand and I doubt she'll waste her time. Even if I do tell her, she still might not want to waste her time.

And that scares me.

I know we've only been talking for a few days, but they've been the best days I've had in a long time. I'll be crushed if she wants to stop seeing me, although I'll understand why.

"Tripp?" she asks, a hint of alarm in her voice and I know I have to say something, give some explanation to my behavior.

"I'm not . . . normal," I finally begin, struggling to find the right words to say. "I'm sure that's obvious, but I feel like I should give you fair warning. That way, you'll be able to make an educated decision on whether or not you still want to talk to me." I breathe out deeply, eyes trained toward the ground, willing myself to continue even though the fear and anxiety are crippling. "I'm not ready to tell you everything, but I can at least explain what happened just now."

This might be for me as much as it's for her, because the memory of my date with Whitney is still making me dizzy, and talking about it might actually help.

"I'll listen to whatever you want to say, Tripp, but I wish you wouldn't be so hard on yourself. None of us are *truly* normal," she says in a soft, comforting tone.

This time, she's the one to grab my hand, and her touch empowers me.

"This is going to sound crazy, so I'll apologize ahead of time," I say, wincing at the thought of what I'm getting ready to admit. "I had a girlfriend. Her name was Whitney, and we were together for a long time—since high school. She was putting a lot of pressure on me to propose, and I just wasn't ready, you know?" Loren nods her head, encouraging me to continue.

"Anyway, for the last year or so we were together, we kept breaking up and getting back together. It wasn't pretty and nothing I'm proud of. Toward the end, something *bad* happened," I say, choosing my words carefully because I'm not ready to go there. "I don't remember much of the end of our relationship, because of what happened. My memories are sparse, but just now, when we were sitting on the blanket, this memory just hit me out of the blue . . ." I pause, breathing deeply as I recall the way my heart was pounding out of my chest. Memories like that catch me off guard and for some reason, scare the shit out of me. "It was something I'd never remembered until tonight."

Feeling her thumb rub circles over my knuckles causes me to look into her eyes. I'm expecting any number of things: pity, disgust, alarm, but there's no sign of discomfort on Loren's face. I can't find a hint of judgment within her features either, only acceptance. Maybe even understanding. I've experienced this with my family, of course, but to receive this gift from her, my *Ania*, it makes me feel warm all over.

For the first time in a long time, I feel like the dark cloud that's been hovering over me for so long is lifting. For once, something is going right in my life. Loren makes me feel like there's a chance for normal. But she's so far from normal. She's anything but. She's extraordinary—a beautiful girl, with sad eyes, and hidden secrets—but she sees me, the real me, and she doesn't run. She stays.

twelve

"WELL, I WAS DRUNK . . . THE day my mom . . . got outta prison
And I went . . . to pick'er up . . . in the rain!
But, before I could get to the station in my pickuuuup truck
She got runned over by a damned ol' train!"

"Fucking hell, Tripp. I thought you were going out with Whitney tonight. Why on Earth are you here at the frat house hammered out of your mind? Oh, wait. Let me take a wild guess. Y'all broke up again, huh?"

"Shut up, Evan. You're messin' with my favorite drinkin' song." Damn, I really am messed up. Even I can tell my slur is strong.

Evan turns down the old-school country music that's a staple here at the Kappa Sig house before tossing me a bottle of water. I take a swig to appease him, then promptly pop open a can of beer.

My best friend just rolls his eyes at me. "Come on, man. Tell me what happened."

"Fuckin' Whitney, man. I set up a really nice picnic . . . you know, tryin' to be all romantic and shit . . . and she tells me she was expectin' me to propose! I mean, what the fuck, man!"

"Damn, that girl will never give up trying to get a ring from you. What did you say?"

"I told her I wasn't proposin', that we'd only been back together for a few weeks!"

"Well, my friend, looks like we need to hit Bourbon, STAT."

I guzzle the rest of my beer and let out a roaring belch before agreeing. "Let's do this."

I sit on my bed and breathe deeply, trying to focus on the here and now. These recent flashes of memories have been shaking me up. First, the flashback of Whitney and me on Valentine's Day. And now, this.

It feels almost like an out-of-body experience—like the memories are mine but not. It's like playing with a jigsaw puzzle, taking what my mom and Liza and Ben have told me and piecing it together with what's coming back to me. Part of me wishes I could keep all of that locked away for good. The bit I do remember already gives me nightmares. I don't think I want to remember any more than I have to. It feels easier to deal with if I have no first-hand accounts.

Regardless, I'm not going to let this deter me from what I'm planning on doing today. First, I have class, and then I'm planning on waiting for Loren outside her dorm so I can ask her on a date.

⚜

AS I PACE IN FRONT of her dorm, I feel like a damn stalker, but it's the only way I know to contact her. We still haven't exchanged phone numbers, and I don't want to wait until tomorrow. I need to see her. At our coffee date earlier this week, she had mentioned having class until three o'clock on Wednesdays, so I'm hoping I've timed it right. I rode my bike as fast as I could to make it from Loyola to here before three, so I wouldn't miss her. Looking at my phone, I see it's now a quarter after three. For all I know, she could have other plans, but it's worth a shot. She's worth it. The more I know about her, the more I want to know about her. I'm hoping that with time, she'll feel comfortable enough to tell me about her past as well.

After another ten minutes of walking up and down the sidewalk outside her dorm, I decide to have a seat on the bench. I'm tired after being in class all day. Normally, on days I have classes, I go home afterward and take a nap. I probably need to text Liza and tell her I won't be home. She'll be worried if I don't show up to help with dinner.

I quickly shoot a text off to Liza and get a fast response telling me to "be careful and have fun," with a winky emoticon added to the end. I roll my eyes at my sister's assumptions but smile to myself, because I always have fun when I'm with Loren. Whether we're at the café or studying at the diner or drinking coffee at the espresso bar down the street, I can't get enough of being with her.

With every passing day and every encounter, I find myself wanting more . . . more than I feel I deserve . . . more than I feel I'm worthy of . . . and it scares me. For the last few months, all I've thought about is talking to Loren, but I never really thought about what would happen once I did. I guess all along I thought she would reject me, and I would never have to cross the proverbial bridge. I feel like I've given her a fair warning. She's seen me practically lose my mind over a conversation about cars, and she didn't run. I told her I'm not normal, and she still didn't run. But I can tell she's had a lot of sadness in her life, and what if I just bring her more sadness? What if there's too much sadness between the two of us? She deserves someone who will make her happy, and I'm worried that's not me . . . And I'm worried that it's too late to turn back now. She'll have to be the one to walk away, because I can't—I won't.

So, my new fear is Loren realizing all of this and wanting nothing more to do with me.

I have to believe it's all worth it and that I'd survive if she walked away. Nevertheless, it's a risk I'm willing to take.

"Tripp?"

I'm a little startled by her proximity. Normally, I know when she's near, but I must have been too deep in thought.

"Sorry. I didn't mean to scare you," she says, her voice light with a hint of laughter. "I thought you might be sleeping. What are you doing here?"

I can tell she's just curious and wasn't expecting me, because the smile is still on her face. I glance over to see a girl with curly blonde hair standing next to her, and I feel myself shutting down and closing in. *I wasn't expecting her to have company.*

"I, uh. Well, I was just . . . stopping by. This is a bad time. I'll just wait and see you tomorrow at the café." I keep my eyes focused on the ground beneath me and walk swiftly past the two of them.

"Tripp?" Loren's concerned voice makes me stop in the middle of the sidewalk. "Grace, I'll see you in the room," she says, dismissing the girl. I turn back around just in time to see her friend walk through the glass doors, giving me an odd look as she goes.

I don't know if it's being caught off guard or the path my thoughts were taking before she walked up, but I've lost all the confidence I had when I got here. I suddenly can't remember what I had worked out in my head—the words are lost on my tongue.

"Did you need something? Did you want to talk?" she asks, slowly walking toward me as if I'm a caged animal. The analogy isn't far off. My insides feel twisted and unsettled.

"I'm sure you think I'm weird for camping outside your dorm, waiting for you." I think I'm weird, so why shouldn't she? In my defense, I wouldn't have had to do this if I had her number. "I don't have your phone number," I blurt out, immediately wishing I hadn't.

She purses her lips and walks closer to me, grabbing my hand and taking a pen out of her pocket. The ink feels weird on my palm, but the warmth from her touch is something I would pay good money for. "There. Now you have my number."

She puts the pen back in her pocket and shields her eyes from the sun as she looks up at me. "So, what did you want to talk about?"

What did I want to talk to her about?

Sometimes the way she looks at me makes me feel more stupid than usual.

A date. That's right. A date. A *real* date.

"I was wondering if you'd like to go on a, uh, d–date . . . on Saturday?" I ask—questioning her, myself . . . the whole fucking universe.

She looks out across the lawn at nothing in particular, but I can see the side of her mouth turned up in a smile, so I take that as a good sign and continue.

"I thought we could go down to The Quarter, maybe get a bite to eat, listen to some music." I push my hands deep down into my front pockets to keep from fidgeting.

"That sounds like fun." She squints an eye when she looks back up at me, and she's so cute. Her nose is scrunched, and the few freckles across her cheekbones are on display. Her hair wisps around her face as the breeze blows. And at that moment, she's everything good in life.

And I'd love to kiss her.

I can't help but stare at her lips. The tension between us is suddenly thick, and we both clear our throats at the same time, simultaneously trying to clear the sudden heaviness in the air.

"So, Saturday night?" I ask, making sure she's really on board.

"Sounds good. We can talk about the details tomorrow night."

"I guess I could've waited until then to ask you."

"I'm glad you didn't."

"I'll see you tomorrow, then."

"See you tomorrow."

⚜

WHEN I WALK INTO THE house, Liza is cooking away in the kitchen, and my mom has the two rugrats practically tied down at the kitchen table. She has a measuring tape draped around her neck and a few straight pins pinched between her lips. That looks dangerous.

"Uncle Tripp!" Both kids start whooping and hollering and trying to get away from my mom, but she has a pretty tight hold on them. She's no stranger to wrangling kids. I can only imagine what Liza and I were like when we were that little, but at least there's a nearly five-year age difference between us. These two are hell on wheels. What one doesn't think of, the other does.

"Oh, look. It's Chicken Nugget and Big Mac," I say with a smile, causing Emmie to giggle, but Jack gives me his signature glare.

"I'm not a hamboorger," he says with a humph.

"Well, you look good enough to eat," I tell him as I get closer, leaning down and pretending to munch on his neck.

"Tripp, you're not helping," my mom admonishes. "Why don't you make yourself useful and hold one of these?" She hands me a giggling Emmie. Her lime-green fairy wings slap me in the face as she climbs on my lap.

"So, who's ready for Halloween?" I ask.

"Me! Me!" They both scream.

Another look from my mom tells me that I'm *still* not helping. I think they're already hyped up on sugar.

"You ready to scare people with your mummy costume?" I ask Jack with a serious look.

"Yes! Rawwwwwwr!" He growls loudly, both hands out in front of him. My mom does her best to continue tacking pieces of material on to his costume without sticking the little dude.

"I don't fink mummies roar," Emmie says from her perch on my lap. Her legs are crossed, and her hands are daintily placed on her knees. "They're dead."

"No, they're not!" Jack yells.

"Yes, they are!" Emmie fires back.

And the fight is on.

⚜

"JACK AND EMMIE, FRONT AND center," Ben barks, the orders sounding like they're from a drill sergeant. Both kids play the part of the dutiful soldiers, standing at attention in front of him. "There will be no running. No crossing streets. You must be holding a grown-up's hand at all times."

"Is Uncle Tripp a grown-up?" Emmie asks, interrupting his tirade.

I can't help but laugh. It's a legitimate question.

"Well, that depends on who you ask," Ben answers. I punch him on his beefy arm, and then we're both laughing.

"Did you guys see that mosquito that just bit me?" Ben asks, teasing me as he brushes off his arm, but it flies right over the kids' heads. No pun intended.

"I didn't see no mosquito," Jack says, swatting the air.

"Okay, so who's ready for trunk-or-treat?"

Everyone cheers as we step out onto the sidewalk and make our way toward Audubon Park. Some of the fraternities, sororities, and other social organizations from Tulane and Loyola join forces and put on a trunk-or-treat for the kids, large and small.

I really would rather be sitting at home, catching up on my school work for the week so that I'll be free to take Loren out on our date on Saturday, but my mom and Liza insisted that I come and participate in the festivities.

One thing we know how to do well in New Orleans is be festive.

Let the good times roll.

While we're walking down the sidewalk, Emmie sidles up beside me and takes my hand. "Uncle Tripp, why didn't you dress up?"

"I did." I glance down to see her looking me up and down. Her little nose scrunches up, and her eyebrows pinch together, just like my mom and sister. "I don't fink so, Uncle Tripp. Dis looks like your regular clothes." She drops my hand and pulls at my flannel shirt. I quickly grab her hand back up before I pull a Saints ball cap out of my back pocket and place it on my head.

"There."

The frown is still on her face, so I unbutton my shirt and show her the Saints T-shirt underneath.

"See? I'm a Saints fan."

Her giggles erupt, and the frown leaves her adorable face. "But you're always a Saints fan! You supposed to be somefin' different!"

I tickle her as I pick her up and carefully place her on my hip, avoiding the green fairy wings. "Well, you're always a princess, but look at you," I say, gesturing to her tiara.

"Yeah, but tonight, I'm a fairy!" She reaches into her little purse and throws glitter into the air.

"Sparingly!" my sister yells from behind us.

"I told you that was a bad idea," Ben grumbles, licking the inside of his shirt to get the glitter off his tongue.

We're all laughing as we approach the mass of people who have gathered at the park. I hold Emmie a little tighter. She helps me feel grounded and gives me something to focus on besides the crowd of people and the loud noises.

As we make our way up and down the rows of cars, Emmie and Jack flutter between the three of us adults. Sometimes, they're brave enough to let go of our hands and walk up and get candy on their own, but other times, they're too shy or scared and need someone to go with them. When we come upon a large tent with flashing black lights, Jack leaps back and grabs my hand. Emmie holds the other. They're both mesmerized by the college-aged girls hovering around in neon garb with their faces made up like skeletons, but neither of them budges.

"You know those are just people with painted up faces, right?" I ask, bending down to their level. They both nod their heads but don't take their eyes off of the skeletons. A few other kids come up. Some run right into the tent and come out with candy, but some are hovering around the entrance like Jack and Emmie.

"Wanna skip this one?" I ask, not wanting them to be scared. They both shake their heads but still make no effort to enter the tent.

"Want me to go with you?"

Nods, again, are all I get.

I stand up straight and walk toward the opening, both of their hands gripping mine tightly. The spooky music gets louder, and the flashes of light get brighter. And I get pissed off at myself, because with each step, I feel my palms sweat and my head throb.

Not now.

Not here.

"Ben," I call over my shoulder, needing him to take over for me.

"Tripp?" a familiar voice asks from deep within the tent. Even with the makeup and odd-looking clothes, I'd know that beautiful dark hair anywhere.

"Loren?" Somehow I manage to keep myself together, holding tightly to Jack and Emmie's hands.

"Tripp?" Ben asks as he steps inside the tent. "Everything okay?"

"I, uh . . ." Truthfully no, but I don't want Loren to know that.

"You need to go back outside?" he asks quietly, taking Jack and Emmie's hands from me.

I look between Ben and Loren a few times, warring with what's going on inside my head and what I want. That's when the knowing look falls across Ben's face. "Loren?" he asks. We both nod. "I'm Ben," he says, helping the kids get some candy and freeing up a hand to reach out to her. "Tripp's brother-in-law."

"It's nice to meet you," she says, shaking his hand.

"It's nice to meet you, too," he tells her. "Tripp, I'm going to give you a few minutes, yeah?" he looks back at me with a worried expression but like it's a risk he's willing to take.

"Yeah."

"Uncle Tripp!" Emmie yells as they're walking back out of the tent. "We can't just leave him!"

Ben assures her that I'm fine, but I don't feel fine. I reach up to rub my temples and take some deep breaths, trying to regain some balance and keep a migraine from hitting me full force. I feel a hand gently touch my shoulder, and when I draw in a cleansing breath, it's her I smell—sweet, light, and comfort.

"You wanna step outside?" Loren asks, her voice like a soothing balm to an open wound.

I turn on my heels and walk outside the tent. She follows close behind until we're standing between two cars, and the noise and light fades into the background.

"Are you okay?"

I look up to see her stunning eyes shining through the paint covering her face.

"With all the strobe lights and music, I felt like I was getting a migraine, but I'm better now." Something about her being near calms me, and I feel the throb in my head begin to subside.

"Good," she says, brushing her hand down my arm.

I allow myself to get a good look at her. She's wearing a tight black mini-skirt with tall black boots and a cut-off black tank top. There are white stripes on her that resemble the body of a skeleton, but it leaves little to the imagination. In all the times I've ever seen her, she's always been fully clothed. This is a new kind of overwhelming feeling. The throb in my head has moved further down my body, and it's taken my voice with it. I can't think of any intelligent or polite words.

Fuck me.

"So, what are you supposed to be?" she asks, a sly smile on her face as she continues to stand incredibly close to me, her hand still resting on my arm.

I laugh, remembering the lame response I gave Emmie. "Just myself, I guess. Although I told my niece I was a Saints fan so that she'd be happy."

"I like yourself," she says, looking down at our feet and then back up. "But the Saints fan works, too." She reaches up and grabs the bill of my baseball cap. The motion pulls her shirt up even higher, and her bare stomach is on display. There's a weird pull in the pit of my stomach. Part of me wants to see what else is under there, and part of me wants to rip my shirt off and cover her up with it.

"And you are?" I ask, knowing but wanting our conversation to continue.

"A skeleton." Her real teeth flash as she smiles. "It was required," she says, gesturing to the banner that's hanging on the side of the tent.

"So you're in a sorority?" I ask.

"Phi Mu," she says, nodding. "How about you? Are you in a fraternity?"

"Not anymore," I tell her as I rub the back of my neck, partly out of nervous habit, but also to help the tension subside.

I can tell by the way she squints her eyes and bites down on her lip that she wants to ask more, but just like every other time we hit one of these walls, she doesn't. We don't push. We just let the other have their secrets or past or whatever.

"It was really good seeing you tonight," she finally says.

"You too. I should probably go . . . and, uh . . ."

"Yeah, your family is probably wondering where you are. Was that your niece and nephew?"

"Yeah, Emmie and Jack," I tell her, smiling at the thought of the two of them.

"They're adorable."

"Thanks."

"So, tomorrow night?" she asks, never taking her eyes off my face. Normally, that would make me nervous and self-conscious, and I do feel nervous, but not for the normal reasons. I feel it because she notices me and I like it. And because I want to touch her, maybe kiss her lips, even though they are covered in black.

"Yes, I'll meet you at the streetcar stop by the coffee shop, if that's still okay?" I tell her, shoving my hands down in my pockets to keep from reaching out and grabbing onto her. We made plans last night at the café. I wish I didn't have to wait until tomorrow to be alone with her, but I've waited this long, so what's one more day.

"It's perfect. I'll see you then," she says, smiling as she walks backward toward the tent.

I tug on my baseball cap to hide the ridiculous smile on my face and then reluctantly walk away to find my family.

Tomorrow can't get here fast enough.

thirteen

I'M NERVOUS. I SHOULDN'T HAVE left the house so early. I know exactly how long it takes to walk to this streetcar stop, yet I left thirty minutes early anyway, and now I have all of this time on my hands to stand here and overthink everything.

This is a bad idea.

I know this isn't our first date . . . or maybe it is? I guess that would depend on who you ask. According to my mom and sister, this is the first *real* date because I asked her out, and we're going somewhere we don't normally go. Ben could tell that their fawning and flailing was making me nervous, so he pulled me aside and assured me there was nothing to be nervous about and that we've already been on dates, regardless of who asked who.

Loren and I know each other.

We've done this.

We can do this.

There's nothing to worry about, and no matter what, Ben assured me he'd only be a phone call away, should any emergencies arise. I've mapped out the entire evening in my mind, thinking of how we'll take the streetcar down to Canal Street and then walk down Decatur to The Quarter. I'm planning on taking Loren to a small restaurant that sits adjacent to Jackson Square. It's a family favorite. We used to go there all the time when my dad was alive. We haven't been there much in the last few years, but it's somewhere I feel comfortable. Plus, it's in a great location. There's so much to do around there—people to watch, music on every corner.

I'm distracted by the familiar pull. When I look up, Loren is approaching with her hands pushed down into the pockets of her jacket. Her long hair is pulled loosely to the side, and her eyes are darker, lips pinker . . . cheeks a bit flushed. She's gorgeous.

"Have you been waiting long?"

"No," I lie, because it's my damn fault I've been here for half an hour. She doesn't need to know that. "The next streetcar should be here any minute. Are you cold?" I ask hesitantly.

"No. I'm great. I love the fall weather."

"Me too."

"It was good seeing you last night," she says, smiling up at me. The sun has already set, and the only light is coming from the street lamp on the corner.

"Yeah, that was a nice surprise."

"So, where are we headed?" she asks as the streetcar pulls up to the curb. I walk up to the steps, but move aside, allowing her to walk in front of me. Fortunately, there aren't many people using the service this late in the evening, so it's easy to get a seat, and the windows are closed, so it's not too cold.

"Stanley," I say when we're seated. "Have you been there?"

"No, I mainly just stick to campus and St. Charles," she says as she pulls her hair over the side of her shoulder and smooths it down. It looks so soft, like always. Sitting this close, I can smell her sweet scent. It's also soft and girly, and I love it.

"And Bourbon?" I ask, knowing that all college students head to Bourbon occasionally.

"Maybe twice," she says with a grin.

"Really?"

"Yes," she laughs. "I know it's shocking, but I'm not a lush."

"I didn't . . . I mean, I wasn't trying to insinuate . . ."

"It's okay, Tripp." Her hand rests casually on my arm, just like last night. "I'm teasing."

She may be teasing, but her touch is searing—electrifying.

"It's not that I don't like Bourbon Street. I just haven't been much."

"Yeah, it's not my scene either. But I've had some good times down there." I smirk, thinking back on the days before I even had a legal ID. Evan and I had some fun there. I shake my head, refusing to go down that road right now.

"So, where's Stanley?" she asks.

When the question is out of her mouth, she laughs. It's that really good laugh, like the night we were walking to the Rat.

"Sounds like a person . . . or like we're looking for Waldo," she continues, still laughing.

The way she tilts her head back and her eyes glisten, I feel like this is *her*—the real her. When she lets go of the sadness and allows herself just to *be*. I've seen it a time or two, and I'm so glad she feels comfortable enough around me to let down her guard . . . or wall . . . or whatever she's built up around her.

I'm sure I pause for too long, watching her. She stops laughing, but the soft smile stays.

"Tripp? That's funny, right?"

I smile back at her, but all I can think to say is, "You're beautiful."

The blush on her cheeks is instant, and she immediately looks the other way, out the window of the streetcar, and I'm worried I shouldn't have said that. But when I feel her fingers playing with the sleeve of my shirt, I know I didn't mess up too bad.

"Thank you," she finally says and turns back to look at me. The spark in her eyes intensifies. "I'm not sure anyone has ever told me that."

My brows furrow, and I find it hard to keep a scowl off of my face because she should've been told that . . . every day . . . at least once.

"Well, you are." I decide to play it safe and keep most of my inner dialogue to myself. "And Stanley is on Decatur. It'll be a few blocks walk after we get off the streetcar. Are you okay with that?"

"Yes, it sounds great! I love walking down to The Quarter."

When we get off the streetcar and begin making our way down the street, I feel Loren's hand brush mine. Somewhere deep inside, instinct takes over, and I reach down and link our fingers together. She pauses for a moment but doesn't miss a step.

"Is this okay?"

"It's perfect."

Dinner at Stanley is just as good as I remember it being. The atmosphere is casual and laid back. They used to only be open for lunch, but thankfully they expanded their hours awhile back. For a brief moment, I allow myself to miss my dad and think about how much he would've enjoyed the oyster Po-boy with cole slaw and remoulade sauce that I ordered.

"What's wrong?" Loren asks from across the table, lightly wiping her mouth with her napkin.

I'm not sure if this is the time or the place, but I feel like being open and honest with her. My mom gave me some good advice earlier about being myself. She said if I care about Loren, I should trust her enough to tell her about my past. I definitely care about the girl sitting across from me—my *Ania*.

"I was just thinking about my dad and how much he would love this," I say, holding up the last bite of my sandwich.

"That's who you were visiting that day at the cemetery, right?"

"Yes."

"Do you mind me asking what happened?"

No. I can honestly say for the first time in a long time that I want to tell someone about my dad. I want her to know how wonderful he was.

"He died a few years ago of lung cancer."

"That sucks," she says with honesty and sincerity, and I smile across the table at her, because she's right. It sucks.

"It does, and I miss him. This was one of his favorite restaurants."

"Thank you for bringing me here."

"Thank you for coming. Do you want to get out of here, maybe walk around the square?"

She nods and reaches for the check, but I stop her. "This is my treat."

"You don't have to pay for mine."

"Yes, I do. I asked you to come here, and I wouldn't feel right not paying . . . and it's not because I want anything in return. It's because I enjoy being with you, and if my dad were here, he'd kick my ass if I didn't."

"Thank you." She smiles and puts her arms through the sleeves of her sweater.

"So," I begin as we walk back out into the cool of the evening, "do you mind if I ask what you were doing at the cemetery that day?"

She lets out a deep breath. "No." She hugs her arms across her body, pulling her sweater closed. "I was there at the chapel. I go there sometimes when I need to collect my thoughts, pray, feel some peace . . . I don't know."

"You weren't visiting someone?" I ask, not wanting to dig but knowing that there's more there that she's not saying.

"That someone isn't here. He's back home."

He's, meaning what? A boyfriend? A friend? Right when I'm trying to think of the right way to ask the question, a man in a mime costume walks up in front of us.

He proceeds to act out a scene of a girl and a boy . . . and what appears to be a proposal. The whole situation begins to feel uncomfortable. I've always hated those stupid mimes. The way they move and never speak freaks me out. I notice Loren stiffen and move closer, so I pull her to me and walk around him. Neither of us comments; we just keep walking, both lost in our thoughts.

"Gelato?" I ask as we pass one of my favorite dessert shops.

"I love gelato."

And just like that, the smile is back, and the awkward atmosphere around us lifts.

Loren likes strawberry everything. She orders a double scoop of strawberry gelato, and we find a small table in the corner. My two scoops of limoncello hit the spot, and we sit in comfortable silence for a few minutes, watching people pass outside the window.

The interior of the shop is decorated in vintage signs, mostly related to cars and old gas station memorabilia. I see Loren looking around the shop before she spots a big "VW" sign on the opposite wall.

"Tell me about your car."

"Well, when I first bought it, it was a piece of shit," she says, shaking her head and smiling at the memory. "I just needed some wheels, and I only had a few hundred dollars. PJ . . ." Her voice drops, as well as her eyes. She plays with her spoon for a second, drifting off, as if she's not even here.

"Who's PJ?"

"My . . . the uh . . ." She struggles with how to say whatever it is she's trying to tell me.

And I suddenly get it. *He* is who she goes to the cemetery to visit, the one who's back home . . . whoever she's lost . . . PJ.

I just nod my understanding, encouraging her to continue if she wants to.

"He convinced me we could make something out of nothing." She smiles sadly, looking out the window as she continues. "I didn't know anything about cars, but over the course of our senior year, we somehow managed to take the beast apart and put her back together. The summer before we came here, I saved up enough money to buy a new paint job and have a little body work done on her. She's run like a champ ever since. And that's how I learned to love the classics." She looks back at me, a proud smile on her face. I'm not sure if it's just pride in what she accomplished with the car or pride in sharing that bit of herself. Regardless, I return the smile, silently thanking her for telling me.

"What about you? Do you have a classic?"

I swallow hard, trying to think of the best way to answer that question without having a full-blown panic attack. I owe her something.

"I have a '67 Chevy Impala." I guess that's a good place to start. No need to go into too many details.

She nods, looking at me with a face full of questions, but she responds with, "Nice." Her appreciation of the car is evident in her tone. "Did you rebuild it yourself, or was it already in mint condition?"

"It wasn't as bad off as your Volkswagen, but it needed a lot of work under the hood."

"Did you do the work yourself?"

"No, no," I answer, shaking my head but smiling at all of the good memories that flood my mind of working on the car. Those were good days and ones I don't mind talking about. "My dad did a lot of the initial work, but when I was about fifteen, I got interested in cars . . . well, *that* car, in particular. I swore I'd have it finished by the time I took my driver's test."

"And did you?" she asks, leaning over the table.

"No." I laugh at the disappointment I felt. "My sister, Liza, had to work that day, so I couldn't use her car, and my dad was in court. It left my mom to take me, and the only available vehicle was her Subaru." I shake my head, remembering her telling me that it wouldn't be the end of the world. "I could've waited, but I *had* to get my license the day I turned sixteen. There just wasn't another option."

She looks down at the table, allowing her hair to fall over her shoulder. "I didn't get mine until I was seventeen. Didn't really have a use for it until then," she says, shrugging her shoulders and smiling back up at me. "So, when did you finish the Impala?"

"Just before my seventeenth birthday. Thankfully, Ben came along and married my sister. He and I would work on the car every day after school when he didn't have to work; sometimes even when he did, he'd come over in the evenings."

"He seems like a cool guy."

"The coolest."

"Why don't you drive the Impala anymore?" she asks. Hesitation is thick in her tone, and she fidgets with the wadded up napkin in her hand.

"It needs some work." I feel the familiar trepidation deep down in my gut, but it doesn't grow like normal. It stays down, allowing me to think through my answer, to give her something without freaking the hell out.

"Did something happen to it?"

"Could we go?" I ask abruptly. "I need some fresh air."

She quickly gets up and throws our trash away, offering her hand to me as we walk out the door. No words. Just her hand in mine as we walk down Decatur, passing by Jackson Square. Soon, it's only our footsteps on the concrete blended with the faint sounds of jazz coming from the House of Blues as we approach the corner at Canal Street.

"I didn't mean to push," she says softly, squeezing my hand.

"It's fine." And it is. Even though I wasn't able to tell her everything, I did tell her some of it, and the most important part is that I got through it without having a panic attack.

"I had a great time tonight." Her body leans into mine, and it feels so good.

"I did too."

The streetcar pulls up, and I put my hand on the small of her back as she climbs aboard. She turns around and looks back at me, her eyes holding a level of intensity I haven't seen yet. When we slide into the bench, she remains close, her hand in mine and her head on my shoulder.

The ride back to St. Charles passes too quickly. Before I know it, we're stepping off and standing awkwardly at the corner where we met just a few short hours ago.

"Can I walk you back to your dorm?"

"Please."

We make small talk on the way to her dorm. She tells me about a report she has to work on tomorrow at the library, and I tell her about the test I have to study for. When we're standing in front of the dorms, she stops and turns toward me.

"Who's going to walk you home?"

"I'll be fine." I laugh at her mock concern.

"Would you text me, so I know you made it safely?"

"Yes." My throat tightens, and the familiar feeling is back—a marching band in my chest—as I realize she's concerned about me.

And she wants me to text her.

I'd like to do more than text her.

I want to kiss her.

She starts to pull away, but I have a surge of confidence flood my body, and I pull her to me. Our bodies flush, I reach up to brush a loose strand of hair off her face, cupping her jaw. Before I know it, my lips are on hers, and the coiling in my stomach is now a blazing fire. I feel hot from my head to my toes. Her lips remain closed, but she doesn't pull away. I feel her grip the front of my shirt, pulling me closer, but then it's like a switch flips—her arms stiffen, her lips pull back, and she averts her gaze to anywhere but me.

"I should go," she says abruptly. "Thank you so much for tonight." She stands on her tiptoes and wraps her arms around my neck. It takes a second for my brain to catch up, but when it does, I fold in around her. We stay in the warm embrace until she ends it, taking a couple of steps back. I watch her as she goes into the building, even walking closer so I can see her enter the elevator at the end of the hall. When she's long gone, I finally turn around and head home.

My heart and my head are battling as I walk. One is elated that I kissed her, but the other is worried I shouldn't have. She seemed to want it at first, but then it was like she regretted it . . . and then she hugged me. I'm so confused . . . but happy.

A few guys walk past me, reeking of alcohol—all of them wearing Kappa Sig shirts—causing a flood of memories to hit me like a brick wall.

"Come on, bro. Just make your shot, and put me out of my misery," Evan begs.

Leaning over the table, poised to strike, I wait a few more seconds before sinking the eight ball in the corner pocket right where Evan is standing.

"Next round's on you, asshole!"

I laugh as he tosses his pool stick down on the table and heads toward the bar, grumbling the entire time.

Evan is nearly as drunk as I am, which makes him a real shitty pool player. I, on the other hand, get better as I drink, which only adds to his humiliation. Maybe his crappy playing is what makes me look good, but I don't care. I'm winning, and he's buying, so it's all good.

After leaving the frat house, we found a parking spot on a side street in The Quarter before making our way to Bourbon Street. Seeing that I was too drunk to drive, Evan was more than happy to take the keys to my Impala and drive for us. Bourbon is party central any time of day, but after walking the strip a couple of times, we were bored and decided playing pool was the way we should spend our evening. After turning a few corners, we found ourselves at Mollie's Pool Hall.

Even at five o'clock on Valentine's Day, Mollie's has a nice crowd, but it's not crazy packed, so we can enjoy our game in peace.

As I rack the balls for another game, I feel a small hand slide up my arm and grip my bicep.

"What's a guy like you doing all alone on Valentine's Day?"

I turn my head and see an attractive girl with very glassy eyes looking up at me. As politely as I can, I remove her hand from my arm and grab the blue chalk, applying it to my pool stick.

"I'm not alone. I'm hanging with my buddy tonight."

"I should've figured a pretty boy like you isn't into girls. My mistake."

"Oh, I'm not gay. My girlfriend and I had a fight, so now I'm having a guy's night instead of a romantic one," *I explain. I mean, I guess Whitney's still my girlfriend. We didn't officially break up. We just had a huge fight, resulting in me leaving her ass at the park to clean up the picnic I'd made for us, while I drowned my frustrations at the Kappa Sig house.*

Fucking Whitney.

Fucking Valentine's Day.

The girl's eyes light up, and she licks her lips before telling me to find her by the jukebox if I decide I want some female company before walking off.

Yeah, no thanks.

Evan finally shows up with our pitcher of beer and pours us both a glass.

"What took you so long?"

"I was just seeing if you were going to hook up with that chick that was after you," *he laughs.*

"Fuck you," *I tell him before breaking the balls and sending two stripes and one solid into their respective pockets.*

Evan groans before saying, "This is the last game, fucker. I can't take this anymore."

"Fine, pussy, but you're still driving, so lay off the beer."

fourteen

LOREN

I WATCH WITH EXCITEMENT AS Wyatt sets a warm bowl of bread pudding in front of me.

"Here's your usual, darlin'."

"Thanks. I've been looking forward to this all week." The first bite melts in my mouth, and I don't even try to quiet the moan that escapes. "So damn good. Wyatt, you must share the recipe with me."

"If it were up to me, I would, but you know my Livie . . . She's very protective of her creations, especially when they make her a lot of money. I bet she'd make an exception for you, though."

Wyatt gives me a wink before walking back to the kitchen, whistling a happy tune.

"I don't know how you can eat all those sweets, Loren. I guess that's why you're so sweet, huh?" PJ smiles at me and grabs my empty hand because he knows better than to grab my spoon-hand. "How was your day?"

I finish my dessert before answering, trying to hold on to my sugar-induced joy for a moment longer.

"It was fine. School was good, as usual, but my hours at work were cut back again for next week, which means another week of struggling to make ends meet. Maybe I should take a break from school. You know, work a year, save some money, then finish my degree. Doing both at the same time is getting hard."

"You can't do that, Lo. You're so close to graduating; you only have a few semesters left. Soon, you'll be out of school and making your own money, but until then, let me take care of you."

PJ's dark eyes are so earnest and full of love, and it kills me I can't look at him in the same way. I've tried for so long, but I'm beginning to think it'll never happen.

"You do take care of me, PJ. You have for a long time. Sometimes I worry that I'm taking advantage of you."

"That's crazy. You're my girlfriend, and one of these days, you'll be my wife. Why wait until then to live together? Move in with me now, and that's one bill you won't have to worry about paying. As an added bonus, we'll start celebrating "Naked Sundays" like we always dream about. What do you say?"

I quickly grab my glass of water and take a drink, avoiding all eye contact with PJ. It'd break his heart if he saw the panic in my eyes. I've obviously allowed this to go too far if he's thinking about marriage. I can't marry PJ, but I don't want to hurt him either.

I have to tell him we can only be friends, but not tonight.

Tonight, I want to enjoy his warmth, his smile, and his positivity, because I doubt he'll want anything to do with me after I break up with him. So, I'm going to be selfish this one last time.

"Loren?"

I look up to see Tripp standing over me, eyes full of sadness and concern.

He's so beautiful. I know he doesn't realize it. I can tell by the way he hides behind his long bangs. But he so is—so beautiful it hurts. His green eyes are like marbles; they're mesmerizing. I have a hard time looking at him and remembering to speak.

Angrily, I wipe away the tears that have fallen. I'm not sure if I'm mad at the memory or the feelings I can't shake, but I'd give anything to be free of the guilt and grief that have consumed me for the past nine months. Well, technically, the guilt has been lingering longer.

"You wanna talk about it?" he asks.

I nod my head in response because I don't trust my voice not to break, and because I *want* to tell him. He's slowly claiming my heart. He should know how it got in the condition it's in now. He may not want me after he hears what I have to say, but he deserves to know. I feel like he's opened up to me so much—telling me about his dad and his ex-girlfriend. But I feel like there's more for him to share. Maybe he's waiting for me, or maybe I've been waiting for him. Regardless, it's time, because the secrets are holding us back.

My therapist tells me the truth will set you free.

I hope he's right.

As Tripp and I begin walking down the sidewalk, he tangles his fingers with mine. This has become my favorite thing about walking with Tripp. He has no idea how just being close to him makes me feel. I've never felt this way about anyone . . . and here comes the flood of guilt again, so powerful, it almost knocks me over.

When we cross the street, I realize he's leading me to the park.

It's probably only seven o'clock, but the sun has set. The park is dark except for the light posts, which is probably a good thing because I'm not sure I can make it through what I need to say without falling apart and I'm not a pretty crier.

This will be the first time I've told anyone about this, except for my therapist and Grace, and that realization is making it hard for me to breathe. Internally, I want to retreat—forget all of this—and go back to whatever this is we've been doing for the last few months.

A pseudo-relationship with Tripp is better than no relationship at all.

His cool fingers brush along the side of my face, and the familiar tingle I get every time he touches me comes along with it.

"Tell me what's wrong," he pleads. The tone in Tripp's voice is pained as if he can feel what's inside me. "I hate seeing you sad, and I've been worried about you ever since I kissed you the other night . . . I shouldn't have done that . . . or I shouldn't have done it without asking first. I'm sorry, An-"

He stops himself, and his hands leave me and go straight to his hair. His expression shifts, and I wonder what he was about to say. It wasn't my name.

"Don't be sorry." I'm still confused about what he was getting ready to say, but the last thing I want is for him to feel guilty about Saturday because that night was beautiful. Everything about our date was perfect and made me fall for him even more than I already had. "You didn't do anything wrong. The date, the kiss—it was . . . Well, it was one of the best nights I've had in a long time, if not ever." I pull my jacket tighter, trying to keep the chill out, while holding myself together. Leaning over on my knees, bracing myself, I begin.

"I don't even know where or how to start, so it's probably going to come out a jumbled mess. But," I pause, hesitating. "Please, just promise you'll hear me out."

"I'm not going anywhere, Loren."

"You haven't heard what I have to say yet."

"You could tell me anything, and I'll still be sitting right here when you're finished."

I give him a weak smile, hoping he's right. Clearing my throat, I start from the beginning.

"My dad is a fireman in the small town I'm from. He put a roof over my head, but that's about it. My mom never wanted kids, which is why she left when I was eight. Funny thing is I didn't even miss her after she was gone. She wasn't ever the 'bake cookies, curl up and read a book with you' kind of mom. She only ever cared about herself . . . *still* only cares about herself. My dad was raised by his dad, who was a widower, so he didn't have a nurturing bone in his body. In his defense, he did as well as he could, but he was a shitty parent . . . still *is* a shitty parent. From the age of eight, I made my own meals, got myself up and dressed in the morning, and put myself to bed at night. When I was fourteen, I got a job at the local diner. I worked there all through junior high and high school. I bought my own clothes, anything school related, and then eventually a $200 car."

Taking a deep breath, I collect my thoughts and release a long exhale. Tripp's patience and gentle strokes on my hand are what help me continue.

"The diner I worked at is also where I met PJ. He was my best friend. He stood up for me when kids at school would bully me for not wearing the right clothes or when they would make fun of my family, or lack thereof. *He* was my family. I spent every holiday and summer vacation at his house. When he decided to apply to Tulane, I applied to Tulane. I knew he was my only ticket out of the small town we're from, and truthfully, when I thought about living there without him, I wanted to kill myself. There was no way I was staying behind. So when we both got accepted and I was able to secure a little financial aid, I took the biggest leap of my life, loaded down my car, and left Texas for good. I used up all of my savings by my sophomore year. I didn't realize how tough it would be to make it without financial support from home. PJ had his dad, and even though they weren't well off, they had enough. Plus, he had a college savings fund to dig into when he needed it. Occasionally, he would spot me cash, but I tried to always pay him back. The beginning of my junior year was when things got hard. I was close to dropping out of college and saving up some money, but PJ talked me out of it. He encouraged me, gave me options, just like he always did."

I pause, swallowing the enormous lump in my throat. "I always knew that he liked me as more than just a friend, and we tried to have a relationship. I honestly don't think I've ever tried *so* hard at one thing in my entire life. I wanted it so bad." I turn to look Tripp in the face, begging him to understand, and I'm met with nothing but soft eyes and comfort. "I wanted to fall in love with him, and I felt like there was something wrong with me when I didn't. The guilt I felt almost pulled me under sometimes, and I was finally ready to tell him that it just wasn't working . . . I loved him, but I wasn't *in love* with him. I needed him to know that . . . to clear my conscience. He'd always been such an amazing friend to me. I felt like I was lying to him and holding him back from finding someone who could love him the way he deserved to be loved."

Fresh tears are pouring down my cheeks. When I think about PJ, I miss him. I miss my confidant and protector. But most of all, I miss my friend. I might not have been in love with him, but he was the best thing that ever happened to me up to that point. I felt like I had been walking around with a black cloud hanging over my head until he walked in—very similar to how I feel about the guy sitting beside me. But, unlike PJ, I can see myself loving Tripp . . . being *in love* with Tripp. That epiphany hit me a couple of weeks ago, and I haven't been able to stop thinking about it. I've watched dozens of sappy love stories and read about them in countless books, and everyone says that you'll know when you know . . . and I know."

"Did you tell him?" Tripp asks.

"No," I say, with overwhelming sadness, and it's hard to get the next few words out because they carry with them so much guilt and regret. "I never got the chance."

"What happened?"

This is the horrible part—the part I don't even know if I can talk about without breaking down and becoming an incoherent mess. But here goes nothing.

"I was supposed to meet him for dinner."

"At The Crescent Moon?"

"Yes," I tell him, recalling the day in my mind with such clarity. Sometimes, it feels like it was only a month or so ago, but other times it feels like years.

"What happened?" he asks, prompting me to continue.

"He never showed. I waited and waited . . . for almost two hours I sat in the booth at the café, just waiting, but he never came. About the time I was giving up, figuring he'd gotten tied up somewhere and forgot to call, my phone rang."

"Was it him?" Tripp asks.

"No, it was the New Orleans Police Department asking me to come down to the station. At first, I thought he'd been in a fight or maybe gotten drunk on Bourbon Street . . . something . . . anything except for what they told me when I got there. *Not that. Not PJ . . . that's* what I kept saying over and over and over . . . *Not PJ . . . Not PJ,*" I repeat, much the same way I did that night.

"What happened?"

"He was going through a stop light when a car ran a red light coming from the opposite direction. He was hit on the driver's side. He died at the scene."

"Oh, God. Loren . . ." Tripp says, anguish in his voice.

"One of the police officers finally took my phone and called my friend Grace. She came and got me, but I barely remember anything after finding out the news. I stayed in bed for three days, until she forced me out and drove me home for the funeral. That entire day is hazy. I couldn't look at anybody . . . or talk to anybody. My dad didn't even try to console me. It was the worst day of my life and all he could offer me was a side hug," I tell him, my body reacting to the memories and starting to shake.

Tripp rubs my arms, warming me from the outside, but it's not enough to stop the tremors I feel on the inside.

But I continue, "PJ's dad, Jess, walked up to me and dropped a golden ring in my palm. That's when I hit rock bottom. I thought it was the night at the police station when the officer told me he was dead, but I was wrong. It was that moment. The moment I realized PJ was actually going to propose—that he'd bought a ring and everything. It killed me. I passed out. The last thing I remember was Jess placing the ring in my hand. I vaguely remember Grace driving me home, but the next real thing I remember is waking up in my room and three days had passed."

"I don't even know what to say. I'm so sorry," Tripp says, his voice is tortured, breaking. And I hate that I'm burdening him with my past, but I don't know what else to do, except keep going until I've told him everything.

"He was going to propose to me . . . and I was planning on breaking up with him. He didn't even know."

"That's why you go to the cafe every Thursday?" he asks.

"I honestly don't know why I go to the café. I guess I go to force myself to remember him. Guilt?" I say, shrugging, because as crazy as it sounds, I know that's a big part of it. "Sometimes, it still feels like he could walk through the door."

"So, you're punishing yourself?"

"Wouldn't you?" I ask, my voice rising an octave. The precarious grip I have on my emotions is slipping. "I was going to break up with him, Tripp. And then he died! He died thinking I was in love with him, and I don't know if I'm supposed to be happy about that or hate myself for it! It's a horrible feeling. The worst part is that everyone who knew us as an *us* thought we were in love . . . They all think I've been mourning my lost love for the last nine months. But I haven't been. I've been mourning the loss of my best friend and the lost opportunities to make things right. I didn't even get to say goodbye."

Sobs wrack my body, and Tripp's strong arms wrap around me tightly. He pulls me onto his lap, holding me, allowing me to cry until I can't anymore—until my throat feels strained from the onslaught of emotions.

When I begin to shake from the chill in the air, Tripp slips his arms out of his jacket and drapes it over my shoulders. He lightly kisses my cheek, inhaling deeply as his lips touch my skin before I settle my head back on his chest. Being this close, I can hear and feel his heart beating wildly.

"It's not your fault, Loren," he says, nearly choking on his words. "You didn't do anything wrong." Now he's shaking, and I don't know if it's because he's cold from giving up his jacket or something else. "Sometimes, the universe steps in and makes decisions for us, and we don't get a say. It . . . it sucks, and it's not fair. I'm . . . I'm sorry. I'm so sorry you lost your friend . . . and I'm sorry you've carried this guilt all on your own, but it's not your fault."

The words coming out of his mouth are similar to words other people have told me—my friend Grace, my therapist—but they sound different coming from him.

I *want* to believe him.

After we sit in silence for awhile, me trying to convince myself that what Tripp said is true and him probably trying to process all the shit I dumped in his lap, he quietly asks, "Why don't we get you home?"

I nod and slowly stand up, unwrapping his jacket from my shoulders.

"No, you keep it. I'm fine," he says, helping me slide my arms into the sleeves.

As we begin to walk toward campus, Tripp's hand slips into mine. With my free hand, I pull the jacket tighter around me and inhale. It smells like him—clean, spicy . . . manly. It soothes my frayed edges and calms my soul.

Tripp seems to be deep in thought as we walk, but he never lets go of my hand, sometimes squeezing tighter or rubbing circles with his thumb.

When we arrive outside of my dorm, I don't want to let him go. I wish I lived somewhere I could invite him in, ask him to stay the night. Falling asleep in his arms would surely keep the bad dreams away.

"So, if you don't mind me asking . . ." Tripp starts.

I shake my head, encouraging him to continue. I'd rather get everything out in the open tonight so that we can move forward from here.

"When was the accident?"

"Valentine's night," I tell him, realizing just how horrible the date alone makes it.

"This year?"

"Yes," I reply, but I can hardly focus on my answer because Tripp is now squeezing my hand, and it looks as though the color has drained from his face. "Are you okay?"

"Yeah . . . yeah, I'm fine." He drops my hand and leans in to place a kiss on my cheek. "I just . . . I've gotta go."

"Text me when you get home?"

"Sure. Goodnight, Loren."

"Goodnight, Tripp."

This is the first time I've seen him walk away. Typically, when I step into the elevator, I can still see him watching me from outside the building. But not tonight. He walks hastily, and I'm now the one waiting until I can't see him any longer . . . until he eventually fades into the black of the night. A weird feeling in the pit of my stomach begins to grow, but I wrap myself up in the jacket Tripp left behind and try to ignore it.

I hope he's not too cold on the way home.

I hope he texts me when he gets there.

I hope I didn't ruin everything.

fifteen

TRIPP

"SLOW DOWN, FUCKER. YOU CRASH my car; I'm gonna beat your ass." *The slur of my words is softening the blow, but I mean every one of them. If Evan puts even a tiny scratch on the Impala, it's on like Donkey Kong.*

"What are you laughing at, Tripp?"

"Donkey Kong," *I tell him as if it should make perfect sense.*

"Oh, man. That game is the best!"

See, that's why Evan is my friend. He gets me.

I hold up my palm, but when he moves to return my high-five, the entire car swerves, causing him to grab on to the steering wheel with both hands while I hold on to the "oh-shit" handle for dear life.

"Dammit, Evan," *I yell as passing cars honk at us.*

"Sorry, man. I didn't think I was this fucked up. I'm good now, though." *He slows down at a red light and lets out a deep breath.* "Nothing like nearly slamming into a parked car to sober you up, right?"

The sound of tires screeching and metal crunching catches my attention, and I look over Evan's shoulder just in time to see another car coming straight for us. There's no bracing for impact, no time to prepare. The words "Oh, God" *barely leave my mouth before the collision. Glass explodes around me as my head slams into the windshield. The loud horn blaring keeps me alert long enough to register that something bad has happened, but too soon, the bright flashing lights overwhelm, and my brain does what it can to protect itself: it shuts down.*

My screams pull me from my restless sleep, while my body is tangled in my sheets and covered in sweat.

No.
No.
It can't be.
It can't be the same.
It's not possible.

I close my eyes and try to remember more, but my brain is at war with itself. One part is struggling to remember, to free the last of my memories, while the other part is pushing back just as hard to keep me ignorant and protected. To be honest, I don't know which part I want to win. For a while, I've wanted to remember and get the pain over and done with, but it's obviously not going to be that easy. And *no one* could've expected this—for mine and Loren's lives to be connected, entwined, like this.

I immediately recognize the sight, sounds, and smells of the hospital, and for a moment, I assume I'm here to visit my dad, but no. This time, I'm the patient. In between my mother's and sister's cries, I hear words like "trauma," "brain injury," and "wait and see."

This time, my stomach wakes me, and I hurry to my bathroom to empty its contents. After cleaning myself up, I slip on my shoes and head to Liza and Ben's house. It's barely six o'clock in the morning, but I need answers. *Now.*

I let myself in through the back door and walk into the kitchen. If I'm going to wake my family up this early, the least I can do is make them coffee. Soon, I hear the sound of shuffling feet, and when I see the sleepy faces of my sister and brother-in-law, I feel guilty for doing this to them. But I'm too impatient for answers to turn back now.

When Liza sees me, her steps quicken until she's right in front of me, completely alert.

"What's wrong? What's happened?" She's demanding but still gentle, with her hands gripping my arms.

"I'm ready to talk about the accident."

Liza turns to Ben and points to the stove. "You start the bacon, and I'll call Mom."

Considering we have a lot to talk about, the four of us are quiet as we eat our breakfast. It's as if we're carb-loading, preparing for battle. To be honest, I don't know what to expect. I have so many questions, but I also have to deal with the answers I get. I don't know what I'm dreading more.

The dirty dishes are left in the sink as we each refill our coffee cups and walk to the living room. I watch as the people I love most in this world—my family—sit on the couch in front of me, patiently waiting for me to begin. I know I owe them so much. I'm about to learn exactly *how* much, though.

"Tripp, son, what's brought this on all of a sudden?" my mom asks.

"I've been having flashbacks—memories—leading up to the accident. They started shortly after I started spending time with Loren."

"Who's Loren?"

"She's my new . . . friend. We met at the café."

My mom's eyes flash over to my sister, and they share a subdued smile, but I can see the excitement all over their faces. I want to share in their happiness, but I'm not sure if it's possible right now.

"Anyway, these flashbacks have been about things I'd never remembered before . . . things about Evan and . . . Whitney."

At the sound of my ex's name, Liza starts grumbling under her breath.

"Last night I remembered what happened . . . the wreck . . . but only parts of being in the hospital afterward. Can y'all help fill in the blanks? I *need* to know what happened that night."

My mother immediately starts wringing her hands and taking deep breaths, making me realize this is still traumatic for her too.

"Mom, if it's too hard, we can wait—"

"No," she stresses. "If you're ready, then so am I. I'll be fine." She steadies her breathing and continues. "You and Evan were in a car accident. You'd both been drinking a lot, but that's not what caused the wreck. In fact, strangely enough, it's probably what saved your life."

My eyebrows draw together at her odd statement while Ben explains.

"You know how statistics show most drunk drivers survive when they're involved in a crash because their bodies are so loosened up by the alcohol? Well, you and your buddy supported those numbers. You were both inebriated, and you didn't have time to tense up or react before you were hit. Fortunately for you, but unfortunately for another guy, the driver that hit you crashed into another car first. It slowed his car a bit, but he still had enough speed to slam into the Impala, throwing you into the windshield because you two idiots weren't wearing seatbelts."

My stomach flips at the mention of *another guy*.

PJ. Loren's boyfriend. I know it's him, but I need them to confirm it for me.

A cold sweat trickles down my back, and I close my eyes tightly, willing the nausea away. Slowly, I lower myself to the floor, and when I feel able to hold my shit together, I look back up at my family.

"Was I in a coma?" I ask. I know it sounds crazy, but I haven't wanted to know anything about the accident, until now. Now, I need to know. I have to know.

This time, Liza speaks. "Yeah, for about a week. You had a mild brain injury, but other than that, you were fine. It's a miracle, actually," she says brightly.

I rub the scar on my forehead and laugh, but there's no humor there.

"Sure. A miracle." I might not know the details of how my brain got this way, but I know all about the condition, and I don't feel like it's a miracle. It's why I can't remember things, why I have to set alarms just to make it to class or remember I have a test . . . why I have migraines and panic attacks. It's the reason I get confused and irrational. "I know all about the brain injury. I live with it every day," I spit out.

"But you're getting better every day. I see positive changes, good changes, every day," she says, leaning forward, pleading with me to believe her words. "Like Loren."

I stand up and begin to pace, feeling the anger building inside me. Stupid fate and destiny and all the fucking stars that align.

"Yeah, well, when she finds out the truth, she'll probably never want to see me again." The second the thought is in my mind and the words are out of my mouth, I feel sick. I want to make it all go away. I want to go back to me and Loren just being me and Loren. I don't want all the rest of the shit that goes with it.

"Why do you say that?" my mom asks.

"The first guy that was hit," I continue, needing to know every detail. "Did . . . did he die?" I'm still hoping that somehow my calculations are off—that somehow it's some other guy.

Liza nods. "He was killed instantly."

"What was his name?" I ask, dread thick in my throat as the words come. I close my eyes, waiting for the response I know will come.

"Peter Jacoby," my mama says reverently. "I'll never forget his name or the sacrifice he unknowingly made that saved your life." When I hear her voice quiver, I'm done.

I can't do this.

I stumble out the back door and run straight to the garage.

I don't know why I instinctively come here, but I do. I need to see my car. I need to remember. I want it all—every regret, every fear, every failure, every what if.

My hands are shaking as I touch the dust cloth that's been covering the car.

I haven't looked at it since the night of the wreck. I couldn't. Too many memories and the thought of seeing it banged up has kept me away these last nine months. But now I have to see it.

In one hard pull, the cloth is on the ground.

I know it looks better now than it did after the wreck, but it's still not perfect. Ben has done his best to fix it up even though his time has been limited and he's had no one to help him. It has a new windshield, and it's cleaned up, but the bumper is still hanging on by a piece of wire, and the side mirror is missing. The passenger side door and fender have been replaced but still need to be painted. It pains me to see it this way, and not just because of how it got like this. It's more than that.

This was my baby. It was a piece of my dad and a piece of me . . . and even a piece of Ben. It means the world to me. I know Ben thought that by mending it, it would help me . . . mend me—make things better or normal—but for some reason, it pisses me off. It's another reminder of how I've failed.

Hurt, anger, and guilt course through me, and if I don't let it out, I'll explode.

I frantically search the garage for what I want, finally finding my old baseball bat.

I don't think.

I don't question.

I don't even feel.

I just let go.

Deep down, there's a small voice telling me to stop . . . telling me that I'll regret this later, but I tell it to shut the hell up, and I keep going.

I can't stop.

I don't want to.

I need this.

Every swing, hit, scratch and dent are like drops of holy water on my forehead, absolving me of my sins.

My arms are sweaty and straining from exertion, but I still don't stop. I keep hitting the car for myself, my family, and my past . . . for Evan, Loren, and PJ. I hit it and let every emotion drain from my pores.

Eventually, strong arms wrap around me from behind, causing me to stop and the bat to slip from my fingers.

Ben pulls me to the floor and lets me cry, encouraging me to "get it all out." His heavy hand on my shoulder makes me stay put, but truthfully, I don't have the energy to go anywhere or do anything more. I can't fight him.

When I finally feel ready to move, I lift my head and assess the damage.

"Holy shit, Ben. I'm so fucking sorry," I whisper, covering my mouth with a shaky hand.

"Don't. Don't you dare apologize to me. Cars can be fixed, Tripp.

I'm more concerned about you than the Impala."

"I don't know if I can be fixed," I admit, hanging my head between my knees.

Looking back up at the car, I'm hit with a new wave of nausea. I don't know if it's the result of the adrenaline that was pushing through my veins or the reality of what I now know.

"Fuck that, bro. You don't need fixing. You need to cut yourself some slack. I've never seen anyone work as hard as you have since the wreck. You learned some major shit today, and you dealt with it. Now, what are you going to do to move forward?"

"I wish it was all over, but there's more."

He watches me expectantly, waiting for me to explain.

"The guy that was killed . . . his nickname was PJ. He was Loren's boyfriend."

Ben exhales sharply before cussing under his breath.

"How can I tell her the truth?" I ask. The question is for me as much as it's for Ben. At this moment, I wish I was someone else—someone who deserves Loren and could make her happy. "She'll never want to see me again."

"Why do you think that?"

"He was going to propose that night, but she was planning on breaking up with him. She feels incredible guilt over that. The reason she sits at the café every damn Thursday is to punish herself." I let out another sob and wipe my snot on my sleeve because it's just Ben, and he's seen me at my worst. "Sh-she has no one in her life now, other than her roommate, and when she finally allows herself to open up to someone new, he just happens to have been involved in the same wreck that took her best friend? How could anyone overcome that?" I look up at him, begging for him to tell me that she can . . . that she will. Something to give me hope that it's not all over.

"You have to tell her, and she'll have to decide for herself how she wants to handle it. But don't blame yourself for things out of your control. And don't take that decision away from her." He pauses, giving me a second to catch my breath.

"You might be alive because of him, but he's not dead because of you," he says forcefully, trying to make me believe his words.

I nod, knowing he's right. Of course, I have to tell her, but when and how, I have no idea.

"Right now, I'm too worn out to do anything." I slowly stand up and dust myself off, looking over at the Impala and feeling a lot like it looks—broken, shattered, and beat to hell. "Thanks, Ben. For everything. I don't know what I would've done without you."

He gives me a mock punch in my shoulder before saying, "Don't mention it, man. You'd do the same for me."

I nod my agreement and leave the garage. I hear Ben behind me, kicking some shit out of the way, and the guilt settles heavy in my gut. I feel bad for losing it and for leaving Liza and my mom the way I did. I know they're hurting too. I'm not the only one who was hurt, but I know they'll understand.

In my room, I fall back into bed, hoping for dreamless sleep.

My eyelids are scratchy, my throat is sore, and I can't quit thinking that I must have done something really bad in a former life. I never believed in any of that shit, but it's the only explanation for why everything in my life seems to get fucked up.

First, my dad dies. The person I confided in, depended on, and trusted most in this world left me.

Then, when I couldn't deal with that, I was forced to give up football—the thing I loved, what I was good at.

And, as if that weren't enough, on a drunken Valentine's night, after breaking it to my girlfriend that I was, in fact, *not* proposing, Evan and I were in an accident. Fortunately, it wasn't our fault, but it left me with scars, physical and mental, that I'll have for the rest of my life.

And just when I thought I was coming to terms with all of that and had finally found my place in the world again—found Loren—it just so happens that the wreck I was in killed her best friend.

How am I ever going to tell her that?
She'll hate me.
I'm here, and he's not.
I can't tell her.
I can't do that to her.

I can't hurt her like that.

I can't open up that fresh wound and pour salt on it.

The best thing I can do for her is disappear. It might hurt her a little at first, but in the long run, it'll be better. She'll forget. And she'll escape without having her heart broken again.

I reach up and rub at the spot over my own heart, wincing at the pain I feel when I think about never seeing her again.

The wreck didn't kill me, but this might.

Eventually, my mind slows down enough for me to fall asleep, but it's not peaceful. The dreams are filled with sounds of scraping metal and smells of gasoline and burnt rubber. There are bright lights and screams . . . those might have come from me.

When I wake, my pulse is racing, and I feel sick again. After splashing my face with water, I take a look at myself in the mirror. I wish I had dreamed all of that shit up, but the fresh cut above my eye proves it was all real—the truth, the car, PJ, Loren—all of it. I pop two sleeping pills and wash them down with water from the faucet.

At some point, my mom uses her key to come in and check on me. I hear her tiptoeing in, and then I feel her cool hand on my forehead, but I don't let her know I'm awake. I don't want to face her. Not yet.

Sometime later, Ben stops by and even though he doesn't feel my forehead, his actions are similar to my mama's—checking me over, pacing for a while, then leaving.

When I'm awake, I think of Loren, and the tears come. And I let them because the pain I feel from losing her is worse than any pain I've felt in a long time, and the only way I can relieve the ache is to let it out.

It's worse than a migraine or any panic attack.

If I had to compare it to something, I'd compare it to how I felt after my dad died. Not as painful, but close. It's a loss, but it's not permanent like my dad. It helps knowing that, eventually, Loren will go on with her life.

She'll find someone who can make her truly happy.

That thought leaves a hole in my heart, a vacant spot where she was . . . is.

But I can't let her stay.

Letting her stay means telling her the truth and I can't do that.

⚜

I LOOK AT THE CLOCK; it's after twelve, but I'm assuming it's twelve midnight because I can't see even a sliver of light from the window. I'm pretty sure I slept through Friday and Saturday. I vaguely remember my sister bringing me some soup, but I don't know if that was yesterday or today.

I reach over to my nightstand and pick up my phone. It's almost dead, but there are several missed calls from Loren, a text also from her asking if I made it home safely, and then another one saying she's worried about me. I almost reply back and tell her I'm fine, but that's a lie, and I can't lie to her. So, I toss the phone down on the floor and roll over in my bed.

I continue to lie in the dark for countless hours, playing over in my mind the different scenarios that could happen if I tell Loren about the wreck, but all of them end with her never wanting to see me again, not wanting to be constantly reminded about what she lost. Nowhere in my brain can I find a reason why she'd want to continue her relationship with me. I know Ben said that I should give her a choice—tell her and let her make her decision—but it feels like this is a situation where not knowing is the best option.

She might hate me for disappearing, but I'd rather her hate me than see her hurt more than she already is.

sixteen

LOREN

I KNEW IT WAS A bad idea to tell Tripp about PJ. I don't know why, but deep down, I just felt like it was going to change things between us. I had no idea it would hurt like this, though. Tripp has been in my life for a few months and has only been absent for a few days, but I miss him more than I can express . . . more than PJ even, which is weird to admit.

It's different.

When I think about him, my whole body aches, like I have the flu or something, but the only thing I'm suffering from right now is missing Tripp.

I call him, but he doesn't answer.

I text him, but he doesn't reply.

I tried waiting around the Loyola campus for him, hoping to catch a glimpse of the mess of dark hair and the flannel shirts I've come to love and find comfort in, but nothing. He's nowhere. It's like I dreamed him up. The only evidence that he does exist is the jacket he left behind when I saw him last . . . the jacket I've wrapped myself in at night when I try to sleep. The one I'm wearing right now.

Last week, when Thursday rolled around, I felt like the weight had been lifted from my shoulders, because I just *knew* he'd be here at the café when I arrived, but he wasn't. I could tell he wasn't here the moment I walked in the door.

Even so, I did something I haven't done in a long time. I stopped the girl with the dark hair—Jamie? Jenny? I can't remember, but I stopped her and asked her if Tripp was here, thinking that maybe he was just in the back or he'd left early.

Maybe he was waiting for me on our bench . . . *our* bench?

Listen to me. Just because we've met there a few times, it suddenly becomes *ours*?

What the hell is wrong with me?

How could I let myself fall like this? Trust like this? Let someone in?

I roughly wipe away the few tears that have trickled down my cheeks. I'm so pissed at myself . . . at Tripp . . . at PJ.

With PJ, everything was so final. He was gone. There was nothing that could bring him back. As much as I hated every second of it, I had to accept that. It took months of therapy for me to get that, even though I still think I'm in the denial phase sometimes. Then Tripp came along, and he made everything right again. He filled all of the cracks in my broken heart, and then he just left. And it's worse because I know he's out there somewhere.

When the bell on the door chimes, I can't help but look to see who's walking in. Just in case. But it's not him. It's two of Tripp's regulars—an older couple who're usually here around the same time I am every week.

They sit down at the table behind me, and I hear the lady ask where the *handsome waiter* is. I lean farther back in the booth so I can hear better; when the girl with the dark hair tells her he's out sick—the same excuse she told me—my shoulders slump.

I thought maybe she'd say something different. Somehow, I know it's a lie.

I wonder if he'll quit.

Maybe he already has?

I wish there were something I could do, but I'm at a loss. Besides, if he wanted to see me or talk to me, he would've answered one of the dozen phone calls or text messages.

He would be here.

I don't know why I thought he'd still want me after everything I told him. I don't blame him, but I had hoped he would understand. I know he has secrets too and I thought I saw something in him that my heart identified with.

I guess I was wrong.

"Excuse me," a voice says, pulling me out of my thoughts.

I look up to see a woman standing pensively by the table. Her hands are gripping her shoulder bag, and she looks around the restaurant before looking back down at me. I stare at her, waiting for her to speak again.

"Are you Loren?"

I nod, and when we make eye contact, she's familiar to me.

"Do I know you?" I can't place her name or how I know her, but . . .

"I-I'm, uh . . . My name is Liza," she says, sticking out her hand for me to shake. My hand grips hers, and I know. "I'm Tripp's sister."

"I know."

She smiles and begins to slide into the booth across from me. "Do you mind if I sit here?" she asks.

"No. Please." I wave my hand in the direction of the booth.

Something inside me shifts.

I feel something in the pit of my stomach.

Hope?

I don't know if that's it, but I quickly shut it down. Just because Tripp's sister is sitting across the table from me, it doesn't mean anything. She could be here to tell me off or to ask me to leave Tripp alone.

"I know this is weird," she starts. "And I swear, I'm not stalking you. It's just that Tripp told me you come here every Thursday, so I thought I'd take my chances that you'd be here."

"It's fine," I smile back at her because something about her puts me at ease. Maybe it's her striking resemblance to Tripp? I don't know, but I like her.

"Listen," she starts but is quickly interrupted by Wyatt bouncing up to the table.

"Well, look who the cat dragged in," he says, beaming at Liza. His purple bow tie and yellow suspenders add to his cheerful disposition.

No matter what, Wyatt always has a smile and a kind word. Even after the accident, when I was at my lowest, I knew when I got here and saw him, I'd feel better. I'm not sure he ever knew exactly what happened because he never asked me. He just offered his sympathy without pushing or prodding. Every once in a while, he'll sit down and ask me how I'm doing, but that's about it.

"Wyatt!" Liza jumps up out of the seat and hugs him.

"You here for dinner?" he asks. His eyes shift over to me, and he looks a little perplexed, probably wondering what the two of us are doing sitting together. I shrug my shoulders, and he looks back at Liza.

"Uh, no. I'm just here to talk to Loren. I hope you don't mind that I'm taking up space."

"No, no. That's fine." He looks back over at me with a questioning glance, but whatever he sees on my face must convince him that everything's cool. "Y'all take all the time you need. Could I get you a tea?"

"That'd be great," she says. "Loren?"

"I'm fine, thanks."

"You know Wyatt?" I ask, pointing over my shoulder as he walks back toward the kitchen.

"We go *way* back." She chuckles and leans back in her seat. Her eyes are locked on mine, and a soft smile settles on her face. "We've known each other since college. It's been a while, but you know how that goes . . . when you see an old friend, and it's like no time in the world has passed."

My face falls a little, because I don't know what that's like, but I wish I did.

Wyatt comes back and sets a glass down in front of Liza, and she smiles, telling him thanks. They exchange a few words while I stare out the window.

When Wyatt leaves, I feel Liza's eyes on me. I turn to look at her, and she has a sad smile on her face. There may even be tears there. I'm not sure. I guess at this point, it's a stand-off to see who mentions Tripp first. Normally, I'm a competitive person, but this is a competition I don't mind forfeiting. I need to know he's okay.

"How's Tripp?" I ask. The second the words are out of my mouth,

I can't help the flood of emotions. My throat tightens, and I feel my face crinkle, but I refuse to ugly-cry in front of someone I've only known five minutes. "He won't return any of my calls or texts."

Liza blows out a deep breath, looking out the window for a second. "He's okay," she starts, turning back to look at me. "I mean, he's safe and at home." She shrugs her shoulders. "I'm normally not one to meddle in other people's lives, but Tripp is my brother, and I love him . . . He's . . . Well, he's . . ."

I sit and watch as she struggles to explain how Tripp is, but I already know. He's special. He's genuine. He's sincere. He wears his feelings on his sleeve. He has secrets. He's a fighter and a lover. I could tell her all of those things, but instead, I say, "I know."

She smiles at me, and I return it. We have a silent exchange of understanding.

"He needs you," she says softly as a tear slips out of the corner of her eye. "I haven't seen him hurting like this since . . . well, in a long time."

I hate knowing Tripp is hurting, and I hate thinking I caused that pain. Wiping my face with the sleeves of Tripp's jacket, I look back up at her. "Tell me what I can do. I . . . I don't know what I did . . . or, or . . . what to do," I stutter out.

"It's not your fault, Loren," Liza soothes, her hand reaching across the table to hold mine. "I wish I could put your mind at ease, but it's not my place. I want to help you both. I thought if maybe you went to Tripp, he'd be forced to tell you what he needs to tell you. It can only come from him."

"Take me to him," I whisper. I feel like my feet can't move fast enough as I climb out of the booth and grab my bag.

Liza doesn't hesitate. She puts a few dollars on the table and follows me out the door.

I'm scared. Liza refuses to say anything more about what Tripp needs to tell me. Her demeanor is sad, resigned maybe, but not angry. I feel like, if she were taking me to him just for him to tell me he doesn't want to see me anymore, she'd give me some warning. She wouldn't let me walk in there with my guard down. She's nicer than that. I've only personally known her for twenty, maybe thirty minutes, but I know that much. I read people well. I can smell an asshole from a mile away. Liza is definitely not an asshole. She's kind and sincere. Occasionally, she leans over and pulls me into her, giving me a side hug.

"Any chance you can give me a clue as to what I'm walking into?" I ask as she shows me the back steps leading up to Tripp's apartment.

"Tripp," she begins but hesitates as she looks up the stairs. "He's been through a lot, and it's changed him. But the one thing I know for sure is that he cares about you and this thing he's doing . . . this distance he's put between the two of you, it's out of fear and his need to protect your heart. But if I were you, I'd want to know the truth so I could make the decision on my own."

"Okay," I say, with resolve, looking up the stairs and then back at her. For a few seconds, I can't make my feet work. It's the fear of not knowing that's paralyzing me, but the thought of seeing Tripp finally pulls me forward.

I miss him.

As bad as the feeling in my gut is at the moment, I want to see him that much more. Whatever he has to say can't make me feel any worse than I did an hour ago sitting in the café, wondering how or if I was ever going to see him again.

When I make it to his door, I turn back around and see Liza is gone, and suddenly I'm even more nervous. I knock twice on the door and wait . . . and wait . . . and wait.

Maybe he's not here?

I decide to give it one more try and knock again. "Tripp? It's . . . it's me, uh, Loren . . ."

I press my ear to the door and hear movement inside.

I *feel* him.

I know he's in there, so I knock again.

"Tripp. I know you're there. Please . . ." I don't know what I'm asking for, but I have to see him one more time. Even if he doesn't want to see me anymore or pursue whatever this is, I at least want to say goodbye and have some closure.

"Tripp—"

The breath is sucked out of me when he abruptly opens the door. The dim light from his apartment mixed with the yellow glow from the street below are all I have to see him by, but I can see the scruff on his jaw and cheeks, something Tripp never has, and his red-rimmed eyes are gray underneath.

Instinctively, I reach out to brush his hair away. There's a fresh cut above his left eye, the one without the scar. Tripp is quick to move my hand away. His head ducks, making his hair fall back over the wound.

"What are you doing here?" he asks. His voice is thick and rough.

"I, uh . . ." I don't know what to say. I haven't thought this through enough. I've pretty much been on autopilot since Liza sat down across from me in the café.

"How did you know where to find me?"

"Your sister," I say with a shaky voice. "She came to the café."

The look on his face is pained, and his features begin to crack and break, but he's still so beautiful. "Loren." My name falls from his lips, and there are so many emotions packed into that one word. I can tell he's hurting, and I reach out again to comfort him—to find a way to help him.

"Please. Just leave."

"No." I shake my head, emphasizing my reply. "I just want . . . Why didn't you text me?" I ask. The anger I've felt off and on the last couple of weeks is coming back. "I called you, and you didn't answer. I was worried about you!"

He slowly picks his head up, and his eyes meet mine. There are unshed tears, and I take a step toward him, wanting to know . . . wanting to hold him and fix whatever is broken.

"I don't want to hurt you."

"Then don't. Let me in . . . Tell me what's wrong," I plead.

"That's the thing," he says, shaking his head. "If I tell you, then I *will* hurt you. He reaches out and plays with a piece of my hair. "And I can't do that. It's the last thing in the world I would ever want to do."

"I don't know what to do," I admit. I feel like we're at an impasse, because if he doesn't tell me what's wrong, I can't help him. But I also can't leave, not without a reason.

"You're going to hate me," he says, but it's barely audible.

"No." I shake my head emphatically. "There's no way I could ever hate you."

He quickly bridges the gap between us and pulls me into a bone-crushing hug, and it feels so good. One of his hands grips my shoulder, while the other grips my hip . . . so, so tightly, like he's drowning and I'm his life raft. I squeeze him back as hard as I can, never wanting to let go.

"Please tell me." I breathe deeply, taking in as much of him as I can.

"I can't."

"How can I help you if you won't tell me what's wrong?"

"You can't."

"I *want* to." I feel like punching him or slapping him or kissing him. I *need* him to tell me. I refuse to take no for an answer. This time, I get to choose.

"Just promise me . . . Promise you won't leave." His voice stutters and his body shakes, and I'm worried he's having some sort of breakdown. I wonder if I should get Liza, but the second I pull away, he pulls me back in even tighter.

"I'm not going anywhere." I press my lips to his exposed neck, trying to comfort and calm him any way I can.

Tripp pulls me into his apartment and leads me over to a big oversized chair. He practically falls into it and takes me with him, gathering me up and holding me close. We sit like this until his breathing evens out.

"Tripp," I whisper, not wanting to startle him or wake him if he's asleep. I'd gladly sit here in his warm embrace and let him rest.

"I just need a few more minutes," he replies. His breath is warm on my skin as he inhales and exhales. He places soft kisses on my hair until he finally begins. "Y—you know how, uh . . . how I told you something bad happened that made me lose my memory about some stuff?" he asks.

"Yes."

"And, uh, you know how you told me about what happened to PJ?"

"Yes," I reply, swallowing hard, forcing my emotions away. Tripp mentioning the accident puts me immediately on edge. And fear creeps in as he continues to fumble over his words.

"Well, uh . . ." He pauses again, and I know he's nervous by the way he fidgets, and I can tell he's scared by the way he won't look me in the eye, but he finally starts talking again. "I . . . I don't even know where to start."

I wish he'd just spit it out. I don't know where he's going with this.

"At the beginning, Tripp. Just take your time, and start at the beginning," I say trying to sound calm, even though my insides feel like a raging storm. I have no idea what he's trying to tell me, but I just need him to say it. The anticipation is killing me.

His breathing picks back up, and it worries me. I don't want him to have another panic attack.

"Tripp?" I say, forcing him to look me in the eye, and that's when I see he's crying. I can't hold it together any longer, and I begin to cry too, but I don't know why, other than the fact that I can't stand to see him so sad. And if he's this sad, whatever he's trying to tell me must be really bad.

"Please don't cry," he says, brushing his thumbs under my eyes.

"Then tell me what's wrong. You're scaring me."

He takes a deep, cleansing breath and roughly wipes his face on the sleeve of his shirt. I see the resolve on his face as he begins again.

"The thing . . . that made me lose my memory?" he asks, and I nod, encouraging him to continue. "It was a car wreck . . . on Valentine's Day. Well, that evening."

My body stiffens at the mention of the day, and my mind reels with scenarios—the worst kind. My breathing quickens as he continues.

"I'd had a really bad day because of a fight with Whitney, and I ended up drinking way too much." He stops and sucks in a deep breath of air before continuing. "My best friend, Evan, picked me up from the Sig house, and we went down to a bar to shoot pool. We drank some more. Evan was more sober than me, so he drove us back to campus . . . except we didn't make it."

The blood starts to gush through my ears, and Tripp now sounds like he's in a tunnel. I grip his shirt, hoping he's not getting ready to say what I think he's going to say.

Please, God.

No.

Not this.

"We were sitting at an intersection . . . and a guy . . . He, uh, well, he ran through a red light and hit the car in front of us and then . . . then he hit my car. I—I wasn't driving, but we were, uh, in my car . . . my Impala. The impact threw me into the windshield. It knocked me out. I was in a coma for about a week after the wreck. I had a nasty cut on my head, mild traumatic brain injury . . . and retrograde amnesia, which is why I couldn't remember anything about that day . . . and, uh . . ."

I begin to sob uncontrollably—every emotion flooding my body is coming out in an anguished cry. More than anything, I'm relieved Tripp *wasn't* responsible for PJ's death. If that had been the case . . . if he had been responsible, I don't know what I would do. I'm not sure how I could get past it. I also don't know how I could live without Tripp. My insides, along with my mind and my emotions, are so twisted right now; all I can do is cry.

"Is PJ's real name Peter?" Tripp asks.

I can't answer him. I only nod.

"Loren. Say something. Please."

"Hold me." And he does, without hesitation. He pulls me back, and I melt into him, wishing the whole messed up world would go away.

He cries.

I cry.

At some point, the emotional and mental exhaustion take over, and I drift off to sleep.

When I wake up, I'm no longer curled up in a ball on Tripp's lap. I'm stretched out on cool sheets with warm arms wrapped around me. My eyes feel swollen, as does my throat, and I can feel my heartbeat throbbing in my head. I groan at the realization that everything wasn't a bad dream. Tripp's arms tighten around me, and he kisses the back of my head.

"Tripp?" I ask, testing my voice. It's scratchy and raspy, but at least I can speak.

"Are you awake?" he asks softly.

I nod.

"Wanna talk?" he asks as his arms loosen from around me.

I slowly sit up, leaning back against the headboard of his bed. I've often wondered what it would be like to share a bed with Tripp, but I didn't think it would be like this—under this circumstance. The thought of Tripp's revelation hits me again, and the lump is back in my throat. I don't even know what to feel.

Happy, because Tripp is here, and he didn't die.

Guilty, because I'm *happy* that Tripp is here. But that doesn't mean I'm happy PJ isn't here.

Angry, because I hate this.

I didn't ask for any of this.

Tripp didn't ask for any of this.

PJ didn't ask for it.

My mind goes to something I was thinking about right before I fell asleep, as I was trying to make sense of everything. I remember one day a few weeks after the accident; I wanted to find out more about what happened. I knew the basics, but I went searching for more. As I was going through the newspaper articles in the library at school, I remember seeing the names of other people involved in the accident. It didn't mean that much to me back then, so I must have pushed it to the back of my mind. But when Tripp started telling me how his accident and PJ's accident were one in the same, the name Alexander came back to me. But it wasn't 'Tripp Alexander'.

Maybe Tripp is confused?

Maybe the two accidents aren't related?

"Uh, I'm confused about something," I begin, and I feel Tripp tense up beside me. "I read an article after the accident . . . and I vaguely remember the names mentioned. But I know for sure there wasn't a Tripp in the wreck. I would've remembered that. It was something different—Sal? Sid—?"

"Sidney?" he asks, his voice low and gravelly.

"That's it. Sidney, *he* was the other one." I almost feel happy, because Sidney is not Tripp. And if Tripp was in some other accident on

Valentine's Day, then this is just some crazy coincidence. And I can still be sad that PJ died, and be happy that Tripp survived, without feeling guilty about the two contradicting emotions.

It wasn't Tripp.

I want it not to be him.

"Sidney Alexander," he says solemnly, pointing to himself. "That's me. There were three of us—my grandfather, my dad, and me—I *am* the other one. It was me in the other car." He hangs his head, and my heart falls again into the pit of my stomach.

seventeen

TRIPP

"I'M SORRY," I WHISPER BECAUSE I don't know what else to say. I'm so sorry. I'm sorry that PJ died. I'm sorry that I was in the same accident. I'm sorry that everything seems so complicated now. I feel guilty for being here . . . and for being able to hold Loren, yet I'm happy at the same time. The fact that she's here feels like a miracle . . . one that I don't deserve.

Everything inside my head is so jumbled up and confusing, even more than usual.

"It's not your fault," she whispers back. And for that, I'm so thankful. How could I live with myself if Loren blamed me? I'm having a hard enough time as it is. I can't even begin to imagine how I would feel had Evan or I been responsible for PJ's death.

"This is so fucked up."

Loren nods her head against my chest in agreement.

"What are we going to do?"

"I don't know. Just . . . just when I felt like I was finding my way again . . ." she says, her voice drifting off so low I can't hear her, but I feel her. I know what she means. I feel the same way.

I kiss the top of her head and tell her I know.

"Thank you for not leaving." I know there's no guarantee she'll still want a relationship with me, but the fact that she's still here gives me hope.

"I told you I couldn't leave you."

"I don't know why that is, but thank you." I don't know what I'd do without her right now. Her presence alone kept me from having a full-blown panic attack last night . . . or tonight . . . whatever. It's three o'clock in the morning. Loren fell asleep in my lap last night, and I sat and held her for hours, but when my legs started falling asleep, I carefully moved her from my lap to my bed, which felt so surreal. Since Loren and I have been seeing each other, I've thought a lot about having her in my bed, but never like this.

I couldn't have predicted this.

"Are you mad at me?" I ask. I need to know where we stand. I have to know how she feels.

"No," she answers quietly, sadly.

"Do . . . do you wish PJ was here . . . instead of me?"

"No," Loren replies, followed by a loud sob, and she wraps her arms around me, squeezing me so hard. "Th—that's what's so messed up." Her words come out as wails, and her whole body shakes. I wrap myself around her, trying to hold her together—trying to keep her, trying to fix what's broken.

I wish I could make it all better.

"Tell me what to do," I plead, crying with her. "Tell me how to make it better. May—maybe if . . . if I'd told you sooner . . . I'm sorry . . . I should've told you sooner. Wh . . . while you could still walk away. You deserve someone who makes you happy." I sob into her hair while rocking us back and forth on the bed.

Loren cries louder, telling me that I'm wrong, but I know I'm right. If I had been upfront with her about all of this—about the wreck, my past—she could've left before she got hurt . . . again.

"I'm always going to be a reminder that PJ is gone."

Loren shifts in my arms and turns her body until she's straddling my legs, my face firmly between her palms. "Stop," she orders, tears streaking her face. Her hair is stuck to her cheek, and I reach up to pull it away. "It wasn't your fault," she says again, punctuating each word. "Neither one of us asked for this. We're all innocent bystanders." She breathes deeply and shakes her head. "Do you believe in fate . . . destiny?"

I nod my head yes. Of course, I do.

"Maybe," she says, wiping her face and taking a deep cleansing breath to calm herself. "Maybe we were supposed to find each other."

Without thinking, my lips crash into hers. When I tighten my fist in her hair, she moans into my mouth and grabs on to my shirt, pulling me closer to her. Our teeth clash as the kiss quickens, urgency taking over.

Just as I think that this might be a bad idea, and I begin to worry that Loren might pull away again, she bites my bottom lip, sucking it between her teeth.

I lay her back into my bed, but soon the frantic kisses are replaced with gentle brushes of lips. Neither of us has the energy to take this any further, and I'm okay with that. I'm just glad she didn't push me away this time. Loren wedges herself under my chin, her head on my arm, and eventually, we fall asleep.

The light coming through my window wakes me, and that's my clue that it's way past time to get up . . . or way past the time I *normally* get up. I've lost track of days, but I think it's Friday, which means I should be going to class, but I don't have it in me. I'm pissed off at myself for slacking off so much. I know I've been dealing with a lot of shit, but it seems like there's always going to be shit to deal with. So I have to suck it up and get through these last few semesters.

Loren is resting so peacefully. I can feel her slow, steady breaths against my arm.

I don't want to wake her, so I slowly pull my arm out from underneath her. She moves slightly but settles on snuggling the pillow instead of my arm. I hope she sleeps for a while longer. I'm not ready for her to leave or to face the day. I don't know what today will bring. Loren may still decide she doesn't want this. She may decide that it's too much for her to deal with.

It would kill me, but I would understand.

"Tripp," she whimpers, and I pause, ready to climb back into bed with her if she needs me. But when I turn around, her eyes are still closed and she snuggles up closer to a pillow. I continue to watch her until her face relaxes. She was restless most of the night. Sometimes, I wondered if she was having nightmares or dreaming about PJ.

When I'm convinced she's going to stay asleep, I quietly walk over to the kitchen area and busy myself with brewing coffee. Occasionally, I glance over at Loren, just to make sure she's still asleep and still here. Not that she'd be able to leave without me knowing, but I feel like she could disappear at any moment.

Thinking back over the last day—fuck, the last two weeks—I wonder how much more shit either of us can take. My brain keeps holding onto what Loren was saying about how maybe it was meant for us to find each other. I feel like that's been my life preserver these last few hours.

I want to believe it.

I want to believe that I'm meant to be here.

I want to believe that Loren and I were meant to find each other.

I want to not feel guilty for living.

But it's hard.

Doubt creeps in from every crevice of my mind. It won't let me forget the fact that I lived, and PJ died. It won't let me forget that every day Loren looks at me, she'll more than likely think of him. I'll always be a reminder of someone she lost. I don't know how a relationship can survive that, but if there's a chance it can, I want to try.

God knows I want to try.

"Good morning," she says, pulling me from my thoughts. Her voice is raspy and her hair is a mess. Some of it is still stuck to her face. But she's gorgeous. The lump stuck in my throat is different from the one that's been permanently lodged there the past week. It's her. And the fact that after everything, she's still here. She hasn't run away. And that makes me want her more.

"The coffee smells good." A small smile graces her face and I can't help mirroring it, because if she's drinking coffee, that means she'll be staying, at least a little while longer.

⚜

"YOU DIDN'T HAVE TO WALK me home," she says, smiling up at me as she blocks her eyes from the early afternoon sun.

"Yes, I did . . . and you didn't have to leave. You could've stayed for lunch." I squeeze her hand tighter, feeling my anxiety build the closer we get to her dorm.

"Is the reason you don't drive because of the wreck?"

The question catches me off guard, and I take a deep breath before answering. "Yeah, Dr. Abernathy . . . my, uh, therapist," I begin but stop when I think about how crazy that probably makes me sound. I'm not used to telling people this stuff. Besides my family and Dr. Abernathy, no one else really knows the extent of my injuries.

"I have one of those, too." She wraps herself around my arm, leaning her head on my shoulder and easing my worries, just like always.

I don't know how she knows what I need or when I need it, but she does. It's like she was made just for me. That thought makes me incredibly happy and scared shitless at the same time.

I don't want to lose her.

I can't.

"Well," I continue, "she said that sometimes people who have been in car accidents . . ." Again, I pause, wishing that none of this was our reality. I feel like saying anything about the wreck is torture for her . . . and me. "Anyway, she said that a lot of times people develop a fear of cars or driving . . . sometimes both. I guess I'll eventually get past it, but it's something I'll have to work through. I can't avoid cars for the rest of my life. I've tried a few times . . . since the wreck, but I haven't got any farther than sitting in the passenger seat. I had a major panic attack the last time."

We walk in silence the rest of the way, without any more questions from Loren. She seems deep in thought as we make our way down the sidewalk that leads to her dorm.

"When am I going to see you again?" I ask.

This morning, it dawned on me that next Thursday is Thanksgiving, so the café will be closed. I can't go two weeks without seeing Loren again. The last two weeks almost killed me.

"I, uh," she starts but hesitates, not making eye contact. And my heart drops. "I feel like I need some time to process everything." She nervously plays with a thread on the sleeve of my jacket. "I don't want you to think I don't want to see you . . . because I do. But the last day has been a rollercoaster, and I just need some time to get my head on straight."

I swallow hard, trying not to jump to conclusions or think the worst. She needs a couple of days. Of course, she does. I can give her that.

"Okay." I nod and pull my jacket closed around her. The wind has picked up, and it's kind of cold out today. I should let her go inside, but I'm finding it hard to take my eyes off her.

I'd give you anything. I'd even let you go, if that's what you needed.

That's what I want to tell her, but I'm afraid.

What if today is the last day I see her? What if this is the last time I get to touch her?

I don't know what to do next.

Do I say goodbye?

Is it okay to kiss her again?

Do I call her? Text her?

She stands on the tips of her toes and grabs the front of my sweatshirt, pulling me to her. "This isn't goodbye. I can see the worry on your face, but that's not what this is. I meant what I said yesterday. I'm not going anywhere."

"Okay," I whisper again, praying she means it. Wrapping my arms around her and holding her close, I press my lips to the top of her head. I breathe her in and hope I don't have to wait too long to see her again.

"I don't know where we go from here, but I want to find out," I tell her, leaning my forehead into hers. "What are you doing for Thanksgiving?"

"I don't have any plans."

"Spend it with me."

"I don't know . . . I don't think . . ."

"Don't think. Just come."

"Are you sure?"

"Yes."

"But Thanksgiving is for families . . . and I . . ."

"Everyone would love for you to be there." I feel confident answering for my family because I already know they'll love Loren. "I promise."

She hesitates for a minute, worrying her lip.

"Please come." I'll get down on my hands and knees and beg if I have to.

"Should I bring something?" she asks, crinkling her nose.

"Just yourself."

⚜

"TRIPP ALEXANDER, IF YOU DON'T stop pacing, you're going to wear grooves into your sister's hardwood floors!"

The sound of my mama scolding me stops me in my tracks. In a funny way, it makes me feel kind of . . . normal again. She's been so gentle with me since the wreck, treating me like I need to be wrapped in bubble wrap or something, that I haven't had many chances to push her boundaries. The old me would've jumped on any opportunity to drive my mama crazy, but this new version of myself . . . I don't know. I've always loved my family, but I'm not sure I always showed my appreciation. And I've been working on changing that.

Besides, I've put them through enough hell. I don't want to ever willingly do that again, and right now, I'm putting my life in danger by potentially damaging Liza's floors, and on a major holiday at that.

I make a show of tip-toeing over to my mom and kiss the top of her head.

"Sorry, Mama. I'm just nervous."

"What is there to be nervous about? So your friend, who just happens to be *female*, is coming over for Thanksgiving to meet your mother for the first time? I don't see the big deal. If you love her, then I'll love her."

"Mom, I never said I loved her. I don't think we're even officially dating yet!"

"You didn't have to say it, son. A mother knows." I scrunch my face up while she pats my cheek a couple of times before walking back into the kitchen.

I'm not sure why I'm nervous either. Liza and Ben have already met Loren and liked her a lot, and there's no reason the same won't happen when my mom meets her. After explaining to Mom about how Loren and I are connected through the wreck, I could tell she was heartbroken for her but yet hopeful we can help each other heal.

That makes two of us.

I think what's bothering me is the fact I haven't seen Loren all week. We've texted and spoken on the phone a few times, but I haven't seen her beautiful face or held her soft hands since I walked her home on Friday.

I miss her.

And there's a small part of my brain that's worried she won't show. I know she said she would, but what if she doesn't? What if she's decided all of this is too much to handle? What then?

"She'll be here." My mother gently pats my shoulder as she passes from the kitchen to the dining room with another plate of food.

Two knocks at the front door send my heart racing.

Why the fuck am I so nervous?

"I'll get it," Emmie yells as she rounds the corner coming from the living room.

"No, you won't," Liza yells back. Ben intercepts Emmie and hauls her with him to answer the front door, but I beat him to it, squeezing between him, Emmie, and the door.

"I got it," I tell him.

He nods and backs away from the door. I take a second to collect myself, breathing in deeply and exhaling, before finally opening the door. Loren is standing there on the front porch looking absolutely beautiful. Her dark brown hair is hanging loosely around her face and the cream-colored sweater she's wearing. It looks soft, like her hair. My fingers itch to reach out and touch it . . . her . . . making sure she's really here, but instead I back away from the door, allowing her space to enter.

"Thanks so much for coming," I whisper as she walks in, handing me a plate wrapped in foil.

"Thanks for having me." She smiles nervously, looking up over at

Ben and Emmie, who are still standing behind me.

"Hi!" Emmie squeals. Ben tickles her sides as he puts her down. "I'm Emmie. You're pretty. Wanna see my animals?" My niece is adorable and never meets a stranger, but it's obvious she already likes Loren because she wants to introduce her to her animals. Not everyone gets to meet the animals.

"Uh," Loren starts, a smile on her face.

"Let's let Loren meet everyone else. Maybe you can show her your animals after we eat?"

Ben gives Loren one of his big cheesy-ass grins. "Good to see you again."

"You too."

I look up to see my mom and Liza standing in the doorway that leads to the dining room. Walking up behind Loren, I place my free hand at the small of her back. "Mom, Liza . . . this is Loren. Loren, this is my mom, Claire, and my sisters, Liza, who I believe you've already met," I say, giving my sister an eyeroll and silently thanking her. "Yes. Nice to see you again, Liza. And it's really nice to meet you, Mrs. Alexander."

"Oh, call me Claire!" My mom swoops over and wraps Loren in a hug.

To my surprise, Loren hugs my mom right back. "Okay," she laughs.

"Well," my mom says, with one arm around Loren's shoulders. "Who's ready to eat some turkey?"

"Me! Me! Me!" Emmie and Jack both yell in unison as they run between us and into the dining room.

"Can Loren sit by me?" Emmie asks, bouncing with excitement.

"Sure she can! If she wants to," my sister replies, looking over at Loren.

"Of course. I've always wanted to sit by a princess."

Emmie beams up at Loren. "I'm not a princess today. Mom says no costumes at the Fanksgiving table." Her smile falls a little, and everyone chuckles at how adorable she is, even when she's unhappy.

"Well, real princesses don't need costumes," Loren tells her.

Emmie's smile is back, and she leans even closer to Loren's chair. The look she gives her is verging on hero worship.

"I'm saying Grace!" Jack yells because he only has two volumes, loud and louder.

"Short and sweet, Jack," my sister reminds him as we all bow our heads. I look to my side to see Loren with her hands folded on the edge of the table and her hair blocking her face from my view, until she tilts her head my way.

"Thank you," she mouths silently, but it's me who's thankful. I'm thankful for her being here . . . for not giving up on me, for giving me a chance, and for hearing me out. I'm thankful for fate and destiny and all that shit, even if it seems messed up. Peeking up, around the table, a lump forms in my throat, because I'm incredibly grateful and thankful for every person . . . all of the people I love the most in the world in one place. I don't know how I got so lucky.

"Lord, thanks for the turkey and for Mom, Dad, Grandma Claire, Uncle Tripp, Emmie, and . . . and," he pauses. "Loren," I hear my sister whisper in his ear. "And for Loren. And thanks a lot for the pie that Grandma said I can eat later, and for all of the starving children in Africa . . . I hope they get some turkey too. And also, thanks for Papa Sid. We hope he has turkey with you."

"Amen," I hear my sister whisper to him, prompting him to end his prayer.

"Amen," he says, and we all join in unison.

I notice Loren wipe under her eye, and I hope she's not sad. I never want to see her cry again. Ever. I only want her happy.

"Are you Uncle Tripp's girlfriend?" Emmie asks as she passes a basket of rolls to Loren.

"Emmie!" Ben warns.

I cringe because I should've thought this through better. I'm about to come to Loren's rescue when she speaks up.

"Yep, I'm his girlfriend. Is that okay?" she asks, scrunching up her nose. Every time she does that, I want to kiss it . . . and her. Emmie excitedly nods her head.

I notice that Mom, Liza, and Ben are all staring at us with ridiculous smiles on their faces.

Wait.

Did she just . . . ?

Her hand reaches under the table and squeezes my leg. I look up and see her questioning me with her eyes. Leaning over, I place my lips to her cheek, letting them linger and whispering, "Thank you."

For everything.

eighteen

TRIPP

THIS WAS THE BEST THANKSGIVING I'd had in ages.

After our meal, there was football on TV, board games in the living room, and then we all helped decorate the outside of Liza and Ben's house with Christmas lights. Loren was by my side the entire time.

It's now dark, and my sister's house is quiet as Loren and I slowly step off the front porch. Ben and the twins crashed early, and Liza and my mom soon followed, knowing they'd be getting up in only a few hours for their Black Friday shopping tradition. Now, it's just the two of us, and we both seem reluctant to end our time together.

"Will you walk me home, Tripp?" Eyes the color of warm chocolate look up at me, filled with hope and . . . desire, maybe? I hope I'm right because I'm feeling the same, and she should know.

"Stay with me."

It's only a whisper, but the intensity of my words leaves us breathless as we continue to gaze at each other, my hands cradling her face while she slides her thumbs through the belt loops of my jeans.

"Nothing has to happen, Loren. I'm just not ready to let you go."

"You're not tired of me yet?" she jokes.

"I want to kiss you so badly."

"What's stopping you?"

"Once I start kissing you, I won't want to stop. Ever."

"Then don't."

My heart is frantically beating in my chest, like a caged animal trying to break free. *This*. This is what falling in love feels like.

I can do this.

But first, I have to ask. "Did you mean what you said during lunch?"

She tilts her head to the side in confusion but soon realizes what I'm asking.

"Do you mean when I said I'm your girlfriend?"

Words fail me, and I can only nod my head 'yes' as I wait for her answer.

"Do you want me to be your girlfriend, Tripp?"

My breathing and the nodding of my head both pick up in speed, so much so, I fear I may pass out. That would be mortifying, so I push out the words, "very much so," before taking a deep breath and calming myself, if only marginally.

Her smile is glorious when she tells me she'd love to be my girlfriend, but it doesn't stay because it's now being covered with my mouth. I kiss her like I've wanted to all day—like I've wanted to for so long.

This kiss is frantic with passion and longing, and when Loren wraps her arms around my neck, I automatically pull her up, causing her legs to hug my waist so I can carry her to my apartment. A few stumbles and bumps as we make our way up the stairs cause us to giggle into our kiss, but we finally make it inside without causing too much damage.

Loren makes no move to leave my arms, so I carry her to my bed, laying us both down. As much as I want Loren, I don't think I can make love to her tonight. Being this close to her is overwhelming enough . . . in the best of ways . . . but I want to savor this, savor her, and not rush things.

She must sense my apprehension because she stops kissing me to look directly into my eyes and forces me to do the same.

"We have all the time in the world, okay? No rush. I just want to be with you," she says as she puts her hand over my heart.

I close my eyes, and before I can stop myself, I whisper, "My Ania."

"What did you call me?" Her tone is sharp, and although she didn't raise her voice, it's enough to pop the lust-bubble we were just in.

Way to go, dumbass.

"I . . . I . . . called you 'Ania'."

"Why? What does that mean?"

My face flushes at having to explain my nickname for her, but it was bound to happen sooner or later. Better to get it out now, I suppose.

"I saw you the day I interviewed with Wyatt at the café. Do you remember? I was walking to the front door, and you glanced up at me. I'd never seen anyone so sad yet so beautiful in all my life."

Loren looks down and starts chewing on her bottom lip. I brush my thumb over her mouth, then her cheek, causing her to look at me again.

"I was immediately drawn to you. I wanted to know you, to know why you were so sad. It hurt my heart to see you in pain. I looked for you every time I went to the café, and I thought about you constantly. Does that make me a creeper?"

My question surprises her, and she laughs out a "kinda", but I see the tears forming in her eyes. I gently kiss both of her eyelids before continuing.

"I needed a name for you, something I could call you when I thought of you—something other than *the sad girl at the café.*"

"You could've just asked me my name."

"No, I couldn't." I laugh without humor. "You remember what I was like back then, what I'm still like sometimes."

"Stop," she demands.

This time, she's the one to reassure me with a kiss, and I let her.

"Now finish your story," she says with a small smile.

"I tried to name you after a saint," I tell her and it makes her toss her head back in a laugh.

"I'm so not a saint."

"Yes, you are. You're with me. If that's not qualifications for sainthood, I don't know what is."

She continues laughing and I take the opportunity to press my lips to her exposed neck, inhaling her sweet scent.

"So, not a saint?" she asks a second later, her voice sounding distracted.

"No, nothing fit," I tell her as I continue. "Then I moved on to mythological names, because I thought they would suit you more."

When she blushes, I smile and kiss her again, simply because I can.

"The Algea are spirits of pain and suffering, and there's one specifically for grief, distress, sorrow, and trouble called Ania. I thought it was perfect, but now, maybe I should change it or not call you anything but 'Loren'."

"Why?"

"Because I don't want to label you with something sad. You're so much more than that."

Warm, soft lips attack mine, distracting me so much, I don't notice that Loren has pushed me onto my back and straddled me until my hands instinctively grab her ass. I give it a few squeezes before I move my hands, not wanting to push any boundaries, but Loren pushes.

"Uh-uh. Put 'em back," she murmurs between kisses.

Who am I to deny her?

Returning my hands, I grasp her cheeks even more firmly than before. Loren doesn't hold back, grinding herself against my crotch, eliciting moans from both of us.

It feels so good to be like this again—to feel something—especially with Loren. But if we don't stop soon, there won't be any going back. And I don't think I'm ready for that. Yet.

Loren's mouth is traveling down my throat, and fuck me, it feels amazing. I don't want to end it, but I also don't want to go too quickly and mess everything up. A hint of anxiety mixed with trepidation creeps up deep inside. "Baby, we need to stop," I whisper, running my hand through her hair.

I'm not going to lie. There's a part of me that hopes she doesn't listen—that she keeps going. Of course, that part of me is hard as a rock, begging for release, but I need to think with my brain and not my dick.

I tell her again that we need to slow things down, and she finally pulls away and looks at me with her swollen lips begging to be sucked back into my mouth. I run my hands over my face a few times to help clear my head.

"I guess I got carried away again. Sorry."

"Don't ever apologize for that. I'm not complaining, I promise. I . . . I guess I'm just nervous."

"I am too, and I know we're not ready for . . . *that*. When we kiss, though, all reason leaves my body, and I just can't get enough of you."

"Shit, Loren, I feel the same, believe me. Is it wrong? I mean, is it too soon to feel like this?" My hands grab on to her hips, anchoring her to me, while she runs her fingers through my hair, briefly touching my scar.

"I don't think so. We've been working our way to this point for months, you know? It's just so intense, and I've never felt this way before. It's scary."

"It wasn't like this with PJ?" I don't want to hurt her by bringing him up, but I need to know.

Loren sighs and touches my scar again. "Never. It was always tame . . . safe. Never this passionate. What about you and Whitney?"

"We had crazy times, for sure, but we'd been together since high school. We were able to trust each other and experiment . . . learn what we liked and didn't like."

"Did you love her?"

"For a while, I did, yeah. She was with me through some major life events. Eventually though, I realized there was no substance between us, only history."

"Did you break up right before the accident?"

"No. My mom didn't know we'd had a fight that day, so after I was admitted to the hospital, she called Whitney. And Whitney was there for a while. At least, that's what they told me. I don't remember anything from the hospital. But after Whitney heard my prognosis, while I was still in a coma, she told my mom she couldn't handle it."

I watch as Loren pushes up just enough to look me in the eyes.

An internal fire blazes across her features—eyes squinting, nostrils flaring—before she calmly speaks. "What a stupid bitch."

Seeing this side of Loren—this slightly jealous, extremely protective side—does nothing to ease my raging hard-on, and I instinctively push myself against her.

Her eyes close, and she hums with pleasure as she rubs her hands over my chest.

"Have you seen her since then?" she asks, attempting to keep up with our conversation, but slowly losing ground and giving over to the pleasure.

"No," I say roughly, loving the way her body feels against mine.

She rocks her hips into me once more before declaring, "Her loss; my gain."

I pull her back down to me and claim her mouth with my own. The intensity from before is back, but there's no urgency, only passion as tongues swirl and fingers touch. Eventually, we have to come up for air and after a few more soft kisses, we give ourselves some distance. I think we both know we want more, but we also know tonight isn't the night.

When Loren mentions going home, I tell her I'll take her home tomorrow. We might not be ready for sex, but I'm also not ready to be apart from her, already dreading being in my bed without her.

"Today was the best day I've had in a very long time," she says softly. "Thank you." Her words are sleepy as she snuggles into my chest, one arm draped across my body while the other plays with my hair.

"It was for me, too," I reply, kissing the top of her head and feeling completely content as we fall asleep.

⚜

THE SOUNDS OF CHILDREN SQUEALING and laughing wake me from the best dream I've had in a long time. When I open my eyes, I see my beautiful girl still curled into me, and nothing—not even the sex dream I was having—can beat this.

Not wanting to disturb Loren with my morning wood or my niece and nephew playing outside, I slip out of bed and get myself ready for the day. Ben waves at me when I step outside, and meets me at the bottom of the stairs.

"Sorry if the kids are bothering you. I had to get them out of the house to burn off some energy. Liza and your mom didn't get back from shopping until 5:30 this morning, so they're both crashed inside."

"It's all good, man."

"So, you have a girlfriend now . . ." Ben never was a subtle guy.

"Yeah, I do," I answer. I don't even try to keep the smile off my face.

"That's great, Tripp. I really am glad you two were able to work through the accident and everything."

"Me too. Can I ask you something without you freaking out?"

"Tripp, I'm hurt. When do I ever freak out?" The seemingly innocent expression he's wearing only makes me laugh, calling him out on his bullshit.

"Whatever, Ben. But seriously, I need some advice. How soon is too soon to take things to the next . . . you know . . . *level?*"

I should probably feel bad for laughing at him as he sputters coffee out of his mouth, but I don't. This is Ben; he deserves it.

"Shit, man. I know this isn't the first time you've been . . . intimate . . . with a girl. Why is it different this time?"

"Because it is, and you fucking know it." I glare at him to emphasize my words, making his hands fly up in front of him in a peaceful gesture.

"Easy, tiger. I was just testing you. I'm glad to see you're serious about this . . . about Loren . . . but I can't tell you when the right time to get physical is. That's for you two to decide together."

"She's asleep upstairs." Ben's raised eyebrows encourage me to continue. "We haven't done anything but kiss, but things are starting to escalate. Quickly. It's just so intense with Loren. Being with someone has never felt like this before. It's getting harder and harder to hold back, no pun intended, and I don't know if I can handle it yet. Emotionally, I mean. We're only beginning, and I don't want to mess it up."

My brother-in-law is quiet for a moment, and I wonder if I've shared too much.

"Tripp, what you just said tells me two important things. One, you're not ready for sex yet, so don't push it. There's plenty of time for that later. Two, you're in love, dude. Congratulations."

I expect the increase in my heart rate. I expect the flush that runs from my neck down to my fingertips. I even expect my breaths to become shallow. What surprises me is how those responses in my body quickly calm, leaving a peaceful hum deep into my bones.

⚜

A COUPLE OF HOURS LATER, Loren and I are sitting at the same coffee shop we've visited a few times.

"Are you worried about finals?" I ask her.

"Not really. I'm just so ready to be done with this semester. One more and I graduate!" A proud smile covers Loren's face before she asks about my finals.

"I'm not too worried either. There's only one class that I need to study for, and thankfully, it's my last final of the week, so I'll have extra time to study."

"I can help you study," she offers. Her smile is now playful and causes me to laugh.

"I'd love that. I'm sure you can come up with an incentive or two to keep me on track."

"I'm sure I can think of something to reward you with," she says with a smile.

When I grab her hand and kiss her fingers, her giggle warms me up more than my coffee.

"Will your work hours change much in December?" she asks, letting me hold onto her hand.

"Wyatt asked if I'd be willing to work a couple of extra days a week leading up to Christmas, and I told him I would. I'll have the time, and the extra money will be nice. Will I still see you on Thursdays?"

Loren gently takes her hand back and silently stirs her coffee for a moment before answering me. "I've been thinking about that."

Crap. She's going to stop coming to the café. I just know it.

I force myself to remain calm and wait for her response instead of immediately overreacting.

It won't be the same without her there on Thursday nights, but I'll handle it. *It just means we'll have to figure out other ways to see each other. We can do that.*

"I don't think I should go to the café on Thursday nights anymore. I don't want to punish myself anymore . . . or whatever it was I was doing. Besides, I'm not so sure I want to substitute one ritual for another. I just don't know if that's healthy for me . . . or us. Does that make sense?"

"Yeah, it does. I have a tendency to do a lot of things in a ritualistic manner since the accident, and sometimes it hurts more than it helps. I'll miss you, but we'll figure something out."

Loren reaches across the table and squeezes my hand tightly, and the apprehension I was feeling melts away.

We'll be okay.

We can do this.

nineteen

TRIPP

THE WEATHER IN SOUTHEAST LOUISIANA can vary greatly this time of year. Even though it's technically almost winter, it can still be humid and muggy in December. Thankfully, a cold front came through last night, keeping today's temperatures in the low fifties. The strong breeze works in my favor, causing Loren to snuggle into my side as we walk throughout The Quarter. Finals are over, and we're celebrating the end of the semester by doing some holiday window shopping.

"Are you sure you're okay with not seeing your dad for Christmas?" I ask, brushing a stray hair off her beautiful face.

"Yeah, we only speak a couple of times a year, so he'll be satisfied with a phone call," she says with a small smile.

"Will *you* be satisfied, though?" I ask. I couldn't care less if Mr. Jensen is okay with their arrangement. My only concern is Loren.

"I'll be fine, Tripp, especially if I'm with you." She smiles up at me, her eyes as bright as the Christmas lights decorating the streets.

"You'll be with me. That's a given. My mama can't wait to spoil you." After kissing her lips, I pull back to see a panicked expression on her beautiful face. "What?"

"What do you mean?" she asks. "Please don't go overboard on my account. My income is very limited, and it'll make me feel uncomfortable if I can't reciprocate."

"No, baby. Don't worry about that. I mean, I can't promise we all won't go overboard with each other. It's kind of an Alexander holiday tradition. But we're excited to include you in our traditions and spend as much time with you as possible. My mama was giddy as a loon this morning, talking about teaching you all her holiday recipes." I chuckle to myself at the memory before looking back at Loren. "We'd never do anything to make you uncomfortable. My family is very close, and we're very affectionate. If that makes you uneasy, we'll tone it down."

"Tripp, I don't want your family to change anything for me. I adore them. I'm just not used to the whole close-knit family thing. I've never had that. So, this is all new to me."

I watch as her fingers wrap around the front of my jacket, pulling me closer. She loves doing that and I love it when she does. It makes me think there's a chance she wants me as much as I want her.

Her eyes stay level with my chest as she says softly, "But I want that with you."

My Ania.

Cupping her face in my hands, I tilt it so that she has no choice but to look at me. "I want that too, Loren. So fucking much." Our mouths meet, and it isn't long before our tongues start exploring, the kiss deepening. A passerby clears their throat, and I reluctantly pull away. Loren whimpers as we part, resting her forehead against my chest.

"Maybe we should go back to my place," I suggest with a smirk.

"I think that's a great idea," she agrees before taking my hand and pulling me down the sidewalk.

I've been using public transportation for almost a year and have never regretted it. It takes longer to get to my destination, but it's comfortable. Not today, though. Today is the first time in my recovery I'm wishing I could drive so Loren and I can get home as soon as possible.

As we sit on the bench watching the city pass us by, Loren's hand travels up and down my thigh at a soothing pace. I love how she knows what I need and when I need it, but this time, her movements are having the opposite effect on me. When I feel myself begin to harden, I place my hand on top of hers and lace our fingers together, forcing her to stop.

"What's wrong?" she asks quietly, her lips so close to my skin I can feel her warm breath.

Facing her, I blurt out the truth. "I was feeling frustrated that I can't drive us home, but then you started rubbing my leg . . . and well, now I'm a different kind of frustrated."

Loren's cheeks redden before she hides her face in my shoulder. I'm worried that I've embarrassed her by being too honest, until I feel her body shake with laughter. I poke her side and make her yelp, causing us both to laugh loudly.

Once we've calmed down, she settles back into to me, lacing our fingers again. "Have you thought about trying to drive again?"

Her question is innocent enough, yet it causes anger to surge through me. "I can't, Loren."

"But—"

"Just drop it," I snap and the sharp tone surprises me. If it surprises her, she doesn't show it. It also doesn't stop her from pressing the topic.

"Tripp, I think we should talk about this."

"I think you should mind your own damn business." I don't know where that came from and I immediately feel guilty for saying it to her.

When the bus stops, I waste no time getting off. I don't even wait for her before I start walking toward my house.

"Tripp Alexander!" she yells from behind me, causing me to stop. I feel like an asshole. I know none of this is her fault and I don't know why I'm taking my frustrations out on her, but I don't turn around to face her. I can't. She doesn't deserve my anger, but I don't know where else to direct it.

I sense her more than hear her when she walks up behind me. "What the hell was that?" she asks with a hint of anger, but more concern than anything. "Tripp, look at me."

I don't move, so she walks around in front of me and tries to block my view of the ground.

"Hey, talk to me." Her tone is soft now—much softer than I deserve. "I'm not letting you shut down on me, so tell me what happened back there on the bus."

I close my eyes tightly and take a deep breath before answering. "I'm such a fucking loser; I can't even drive my girlfriend to the store or on a date or anywhere," I admit. "I want to, but I can't, and I *hate* it. When you started pressuring me, it made me feel even worse. I got pissed, and I lashed out."

I think for a second that she might be gone, because it's dead silent, except for the random passing car.

When I open my eyes, she's still there, and she's glaring at me. "For the record," she says, narrowing her eyes. "I was *not* pressuring you. I simply asked you a question."

Her hands go to her hips and I know this pose. What small amount of self-preservation I have left makes me internally flinch.

"I was only trying to help," she continues. "To be honest, sometimes I think you need to be pushed out of your comfort zone. You'll never know if you can drive again until you try, and if you'll let me, I'd like to help you."

Her eyes are ablaze and her hair is a bit crazy, but she's never looked more beautiful. Even through the anger, I can see how much she cares about me and it makes me want to be better, but what if I can't?

"But what if I fail?" I ask, my voice rising in volume and my hand going instinctively to my hair, pulling as I feel the spiral of irrationality coming over me.

"Then you try again," she says with conviction, making it sound so simple.

Her faith in me is astounding. I don't know if she realizes what she does for me, just by being here, just by being her.

"Why?" I ask as my throat tightens around the question.

"Why what?" Her confusion is apparent, but I'm having a hard time answering her.

A moment passes before I let out all my worries.

"Why everything," I say, laughing, but there's no humor in it—laughing so I don't cry. "Why are you with me? Why do you care if I fail or not? Do you realize I might never drive again? What if I work at the café for the rest of my life . . . and live over my sister's garage? You deserve better than that, Loren, and I'm scared I'm not going to be enough for you."

My words are coming out in short gasps, so I bend over with my hands on my knees, trying to get my breathing back under control.

Loren gives me a few minutes to collect myself before reaching her hand out to me, waiting patiently for me to take it.

When I do, she leads me across the street, around the corner, and up the stairs to my apartment, never saying a word. She's still not speaking to me as she waits for me to unlock the door, and I can only assume she's letting my words sink in and agreeing with them.

Once inside, she pulls me to the couch and sits me down before straddling my lap.

"I understand your fears; I have some of my own." When she pauses, I start to reply, but she places her hand firmly on my chest and shakes her head 'no'. "You, Tripp Alexander, are enough. You're *more* than enough. I don't care if you never drive again, and I couldn't give a rat's ass if you live here and work at The Crescent Moon forever. What I *do* care about is you giving up and not trying. If we're going to be together, I'm not going to sit by and let you wallow in self-loathing. I'm going to push you to succeed, to reach your goals . . . because I believe in you. And I'm with you because I love you."

I'm afraid to move, afraid to blink because I don't want this to be a dream. When Loren whispers, "I love you," this time against my lips, I become alive again, crashing my mouth to hers.

Only when I need to breathe, do I move my lips across her jaw and down her neck, not wanting to break contact with her skin. It finally dawns on me that I never told her how I feel about her, and I can't get the words out fast enough.

"I love you" I tell her in a rush. "Never . . . never did I believe I'd ever find someone like you. Someone who sees me, knows all of my secrets and flaws and loves me anyway."

"You're perfect . . . perfect for me. Never doubt that." Her demanding tone carries over into her kiss, claiming what already belongs to her.

In the month and a half we've been together, Loren and I have only kissed. Nothing else. Now, though, I need more. I want more. Her lips are heaven, but I want to feel her skin on mine. With the way she's grinding on my lap, I'm pretty sure she feels the same way.

Taking the initiative, I stand up, holding her to me, and carry her to my bed. Now that we're here, and this is happening, I want to slow down, savor her.

"Can I see you?" I ask, desperation thick in my voice . . . in my veins. All I can think about is showing her how much I love her, memorizing every inch of her.

"Only if I can see you, too," Loren answers, pushing my jacket off my shoulders.

Such an impatient girl.

I sit up and remove my button-down shirt, followed by my T-shirt. Loren cusses under her breath as she watches, and this time, I'm the one to blush. She takes off her sweater and tank top, leaving her bra for me remove.

It's been so long; I wonder if I remember how to even undo a bra. Thankfully, I notice that Loren's fastens in the front, so I don't have to feel around too much, torturing both of us in the process. With one small click, I'm able to slowly peel away the sheer fabric covering her beautiful breasts.

Just like riding a bicycle, thank heavens.

My fingers trail over her delicate skin, marveling at how it pebbles at my touch.

"Touch me, please," she says softly. It's all the permission I need. Leaning forward, I wrap my lips around one of her peaked nipples, sucking it into my mouth and swirling my tongue around it. Loren's hands go to my back as she searches for purchase, anything to hold onto as her body begins to writhe beneath me.

I used to be an ass-man, but not anymore. Now, I'm all about Loren's amazing boobs. They're fucking perfection.

She pulls my face back up to hers, and kisses the hell out of me. Before I realize what's happening, I'm on my back and her hand's on my zipper. My dick is so hard; I think it might be trying to help her pull the zipper down.

Her soft hand gently strokes me beneath my boxers and it's incredible, so incredible that I need to distract myself; otherwise, it'll be over for me way too soon.

I roll Loren back over and pull her jeans and panties off in one quick motion. She's perfect, so perfect that I forget how to breathe. Looking up at her, I silently ask for permission. The look in her eyes tells me everything I need to know—she wants this, she wants me. Slipping my finger between her folds, I find her swollen and wet. I brush over her clit and then lean down to mimic the action with my tongue on her nipple.

Loren rolls onto her side, and at first I'm worried I've done something wrong, but when I realize it's so she can reach my cock, I'm relieved and turned the fuck on. Angling my body closer to hers, she strokes my cock while I slide one, then two fingers inside her. My senses are on overload, and I struggle with concentrating on everything that's happening. I must be doing okay, though, because the sounds coming out of Loren's mouth are only words of adoration and praise, making my dick impossibly hard. Soon, I feel her walls begin to tighten around my fingers, her whole body tensing as I increase the pace, and then I watch her come.

Hearing her yell *my* name sends me over the edge, and I come harder than I have in years, the result of my orgasm covering Loren's stomach.

After my breathing stabilizes, I start to move, intending to get a warm washcloth for to clean her up, but she stops me.

"Don't leave this bed." Her words don't have much strength behind them since she's practically falling asleep as she says them, but still, I obey, only moving to cover us up with my blanket before succumbing to sleep myself.

Waves are crashing around me as rain falls from the gray sky. A vision of white floats ahead in the water, and I strain to keep my eyes focused on it. At first, I'm not sure what it is I'm watching, but I know deep inside my bones that I need it. My dark clothes are heavy, soaked, and stuck to my frame. It's difficult to move through the ocean, but I command my muscles to push me forward, my only goal being to reach the white object.

It feels like an eternity has passed when I finally arrive at what I now can see is gauzy white material. My body aches, and I'm out of breath, but still my arm is outstretched, reaching for my prize. The cotton slips through my fingers, so I grab again, this time finding something firm yet delicate.

A hand.

I tighten my grasp and pull, not stopping until a female form is cradled in my arms. Rejuvenated by my find, I waste no time walking back to the beach, each step lighter than the one before it. I lay her down and move the thick wet hair away from her face, revealing the most beautiful creature I've ever seen.

Without another thought, I place a kiss on her mouth and whisper, "You're safe now."

My dream is fresh in my mind when I wake up, and I use this quiet time to analyze it further. I've never been one to put much stock into dreams, but this recurring one is different. It's shown a progression between the dream-me and the girl in white that parallels my relationship with Loren. With my previous dreams, I've always felt scared . . . unsure when I awakened, but not today. Today, I feel comforted, as though I'm exactly where I should be . . . where *we* should be.

I gaze down at Loren sleeping beside me, and I know without a doubt she's the one I rescued in my dream. But the truth is, she's the one who's saved me.

Moments later, I have a plan. I feel bad for waking Loren up and making her get dressed, but I'm too keyed up to stop myself. I need to show her how serious I am about her . . . about us . . . and that I want to move forward in my recovery. With her.

"Where are we going?" she asks, slipping her arms into her jacket.

"You'll see."

Once we're both bundled up, I lead Loren downstairs and to the garage. She seems to know what's behind the door, and I hear her suck in a deep breath as it rolls open, exposing the Impala.

It hurts my heart to see my car in this condition, but I only have myself to blame.

"The wreck did all of this?" she asks.

"No, I did most of this the night you told me about PJ . . . the night I realized our wrecks were the same." I turn away from her, shame covering my face. "Ben had worked on it from time to time, trying to fix it for me. I ruined all of his hard work."

The feel of her hand on my back warms me, and I swallow the lump in my throat before turning to face Loren again. "I need you to push me when I need it, but I also need you to catch me when I fall. I'm gonna mess up." Her arms wrap around my waist in reply. "You once said PJ taught you about cars and how to fix them up." I pause, gauging her reaction. "Will you help me fix my car?"

A single tear slips from her eye as she nods emphatically. "Of course, Tripp."

I've made her cry. Shit. Maybe this is too much, too soon. Maybe this will be too painful for her.

"I'm sorry, baby. I wasn't thinking clearly. I should've thought more about how this will affect you and your own healing. We don't have to fix the car now. It can wait until we're both ready, I promise."

I cradle her face, ensuring she sees the sincerity in my eyes, and I pray she believes me. Her hands cover mine, and she's smiling through her tears.

"Thank you for thinking of me, Tripp, but I'm ready. I swear. I think we both need this."

My shoulders sag with relief, and I'm suddenly exhausted, needing more sleep that the few hours we've had. Loren must have a sixth sense, because she simply takes my hand and leads me back upstairs without another word. She undresses me, down to my boxers, and then she does the same. We both crawl under the cool sheets and she wraps her arms around me, holding me. I pull her to me, as close as possible, loving the way her bare skin feels against mine.

And we sleep.

And it's the best sleep I've had in months.

twenty

TRIPP

"Here," Loren says, sitting on the chair across the room from me, staring at her laptop. "This junkyard out in Kenner says they have a lot of parts for cars from the '60s and '70s, specializing in Chevy models. We should call them and see if they have the side mirror or the front fender we still need."

"But that's all the way out in Kenner. It's too far." I roll over in my bed and place the book I've been reading on my nightstand.

"It's not too far if we drive." She continues to stare at the computer, waiting for me to respond. She already knows how I feel about driving . . . or riding for that matter.

"Not an option." I feel bad shutting her down so quickly, but I can't do that. I'm not ready. "I'm sure they'll show up at a junkyard closer to town."

"And we might be waiting a year for that to happen!" She closes the screen to her laptop roughly, shoving it into her bag. "You said you want to get back to driving. This is the first step."

"I don't know," I tell her, because just thinking about getting into a vehicle makes my heart beat faster, my palms start sweating, and my throat feels like it's closing in.

"You can't live your life in fear, Tripp. It's not healthy. No one knows what's going to happen from moment to moment or day to day, but would you really want to?" She pauses, looking over at me with her deep brown eyes. Her hair is in a messy bun on top of her head, and she looks gorgeous. I want her. I want everything with her. "Are you even listening to me?" she asks, her brows furrowing.

"Yes."

"What did I say?"

"I can't live my life in fear . . . and then . . . Well, I'm not sure, because I got distracted by how sexy you look sitting over there with your hair all messy, wearing my sweatshirt."

A pillow makes direct contact with my head, causing me to laugh.

"You're incorrigible," she huffs.

"You're adorable when you're mad."

"I'm not mad."

"Okay, well, whatever you are, it's cute."

She tries so hard not to smile but fails miserably.

"I should go. I promised Grace that I would be around tonight to celebrate Christmas with her before she goes home."

"I wish I could walk you home."

"Well, I drove since I knew it'd be late."

"You could stay the night."

"I'm not going to be one of those girls who ditches her friends when she gets a boyfriend." She smirks over at me as she finishes packing up her books. I hate when she doesn't sleep over. It's strange, though, because I've never shared a bed with anyone before, but it feels like something's missing now when she's not here. Hopefully, after tomorrow, she'll be all mine until Christmas break is over. That's a solid three weeks of good sleep and alone time. I can't wait.

"I'll at least walk you to your car." I grab her overstuffed backpack and toss it over my shoulder.

I close the door behind me on our way out, and I nearly bump into her as she pauses at the top step. For a second, I think she's possibly changed her mind. She turns to me, leaning into my chest and gripping my shirt.

"Think about what I said." She places a soft kiss on my jaw before turning around and making her way down the steps.

She doesn't have to say another word. I know what she means, and I will think about it. For her.

I'd do anything for her.

⚜

I WISH I DIDN'T HAVE to work today. Loren's roommate, Grace, left this morning for Christmas break, which means that Loren is all mine for a few weeks. I would love to be spending the day with her instead of waiting tables.

"Order up!" Shawn calls from the other side of the counter.

As I load up my tray, Julie comes into the kitchen carrying a bucket of dirty dishes. She has a ridiculous Santa hat on her head and a cheesy grin on her face. Apparently, Christmas is her favorite holiday. Who would've guessed that under all that dark hair and dark eyes and back-alley smoking habits, is a Christmas enthusiast?

"Need help with those?" she asks, motioning to my overloaded tray.

"Nah, I'm good." I carefully lift the tray and balance it on my shoulder as I back out of the kitchen. Before the door swings shut, I catch a glimpse of Shawn whacking Julie's hat with a spatula. I'd always wondered if there was something between the two of them. I smirk to myself, knowing that when guys tease girls, it usually means they're into them. Good for them.

While I'm serving the large table, I hear the bell chime above the door. A familiar buzz flows through my body, and when I turn around to see chocolate-brown eyes and windswept hair, a smile breaks across my face. She looks like a fantasy that just blew through the door.

My fantasy.

A sight for sore eyes.

And a very welcomed surprise.

As quickly as possible, I finish up with the table I'm serving, asking if they need anything else. One lady needs some butter, and another dropped her fork. I try to keep a pleasant look on my face as I tell them I'll be right back, but I want to tell them to get it themselves. My girl just walked through the door.

My Ania.

When I walk back out into the café, I see she's sitting at a small table for two on the opposite side from where she normally sits. She places her bag down by her feet and looks up, finding me across the room, smiling brightly.

"Welcome to The Crescent Moon," I say as I walk up to her table.

"Thank you," she replies, going along with the ruse.

"Can I get you anything? Tea or coffee, perhaps?"

She purses her lips, trying to hide her smile as she looks at the menu. "I think I'll have a hot tea with lemon and honey, please."

I can't hide the smile on my face. It's impossible. Just the fact she's here is huge. I didn't expect it, and it's making my palms kinda sweaty, and the marching band in my chest is in full swing. I want to lean down and kiss the shit out of her, but I can't.

I take the few minutes while I'm getting her tea to calm down and collect myself. I don't need to get fired for indecent exposure right before Christmas. That would suck.

Sliding the steaming cup of tea in front of her, I take the liberty of sitting in the empty chair. "Is someone sitting here?" I ask, keeping up the charade.

"I was hoping you would." Her eyes are hooded as she blows on her tea. It's too much to handle. I discreetly adjust myself and thank God for the tablecloth that's hiding my uncomfortable situation. She has no idea what she's doing to me. When I look back up, she has a sly smile on her face.

Maybe she does.

"So, to what do I owe this pleasure?"

"I was missing you."

The drumming in my chest is louder and more pronounced. "The feeling is mutual."

"Grace left, and I was looking around my mostly empty dorm room and couldn't think of anything to do, so I came here. Besides, I needed to apologize for pushing you so hard yesterday."

I reach across the table and grab her hand. "You don't need to apologize for that. I told you to push me, and you did . . . and I'm glad."

"You're not mad at me?"

"Of course not."

"So, we're good?"

"We're *so* good," I smirk, rubbing circles on the palm of her hand.

She clears her throat, but her eyes stay glued to where our hands are on the table. "How much longer until you get off work?"

I look at the large clock on the wall that reads four o'clock. "I get off at six today, so a couple more hours."

"Mind if I occupy a space?"

"I can't think of anything I want more at the moment. Well, there might be . . ."

"Get back to work." The blush on her cheeks tells me she knows where that thought was going. When I stand up, I lean over and place a chaste kiss on the side of her mouth. Her audible exhale tells me she's thinking the same thing.

I check on her periodically over the next couple of hours. She ordered a sandwich, and for whatever reason, that made me happy. I guess seeing her happy is what makes me happy, knowing she's not here to feel guilty or punish herself . . . or whatever she was doing.

From the first moment I laid eyes on her, all I wanted was for her not to be sad. To think I may be the reason for her happiness is overwhelming. I have so much love for her. It scares me sometimes. Everything is going so well, almost too well, and I feel like I'm waiting for the other shoe to drop . . . something to trip us up. The last few years of my life have been like that. Just when I get to a good spot, something comes along to ruin it. I can't let that happen with Loren. I want her with me always.

Glancing over at her from across the room, a new surge of want and need bubbles up. The last few minutes of my shift can't end fast enough. I want to be near her, touch her, feel her. She sees me and smiles as she slips her book into her bag.

Wyatt must realize my anxious behavior because I notice him smirking at me from where he's standing in the back of the café. He nods his head in the direction of the kitchen, telling me it's okay to leave. I don't waste any time. Ripping my apron off, I hurriedly hang it on the hook and jet out the back door, yelling my goodbyes as I go.

When I round the corner, she's standing there under the streetlamp, by our bench, exactly where I thought she'd be. Her long hair hangs loosely down her back, and her hands grip the straps of her backpack. Everything about this moment is similar to so many moments before, but something is also different. Maybe it's the fact I know I love her, and I know she loves me. I hope she knows just how much I love her.

My dad always told me that the best way to tell someone you love them is by showing them. And the best way I can think to show Loren right now is to let her know I trust her and I want to get better for myself, but also for us.

"Hey."

"Hey," she says, standing on her tiptoes and pulling me closer. She places a searing kiss on my lips and I open my mouth to allow her access, my hands instinctually going for her perfect ass, gripping her cheeks.

"Did you drive?" I ask into her mouth, needing her to say no, because I don't want to let her go.

"No," she says, pulling away to look into my eyes. "I walked. I wanted to be able to walk with you."

I smile at her and take her hand into mine, loving how it fits so perfectly, and we begin to walk in silence, enjoying the cool evening breeze.

When we turn down the block and start heading north, no longer blocked from the crisp air, Loren latches onto my shoulder with her other hand, leaning her head on my arm. I bend my head down and kiss the top of her head, inhaling deeply.

"I've been thinking . . ." I start, swallowing the flood of nervousness I get from what I'm about to agree to, but knowing I need to do this.

Loren tenses a little beside me, before asking, "About what?"

"I'll ride with you . . . out to Kenner," I tell her, forcing the words out of my mouth and forcing my body not to react.

She stops in the middle of the sidewalk, pulling me to a stop with her. "Tripp, I meant what I said at the café. Don't do this if you're not ready. I'm sorry for pushing so hard."

"I meant what I just said too. I want to ride with you. I'm ready."

"I see the nervousness in your eyes. I don't want this to be a setback for you."

"I can't make any promises that it won't be, but I want to try." I frame her face with my hands, tilting it up so that she's looking me in the eye. "I want to do this . . . I want to show you how much I want to get better . . . for you . . . for me . . . for us. Just promise me you won't leave me if things go to shit."

"Never," she says, shaking her head adamantly. "I'm not going anywhere. You believe me, right?" She laughs lightly, but grows more serious when I don't answer right away.

"Yes? No?" I say, smiling. "Of course, I do."

"I love you."

Those words leaving her lips cause me to press mine to hers. "I love you." Our noses touch and her breath is warm on my face, causing the familiar burn to build in my stomach.

"Stay the night with me?"

"Of course."

I feel like sweeping her off her feet and running the two blocks to my house. She laughs when I grab her hand and take off speed walking.

When we finally get inside my apartment, I kick my shoes off at the door and quickly begin peeling off the layers, tossing my jacket on the chair and unbuttoning my flannel. I look up to see Loren mimicking my actions. The need and want on her face are evident. I still don't feel like we're ready for sex, but it doesn't mean we can't be together. It doesn't mean I can't bring her pleasure. I've found various ways to accomplish that, and I'm pleased to know I haven't lost my finesse. The cocky teenager I once was surfaces now and then. It's inside me—part of who I am, and I can't help it. But I'm learning to like the new me . . . a mixture of who I once was and who I'm becoming.

When Loren has her jacket, shoes, and sweater off, she walks over to me, toying with the buttons on my jeans. "I've been thinking about being alone with you since I had to leave last night."

"Me too. I hardly slept."

She giggles, pulling up to kiss my lips. Like out on the street, my hands find her ass, and I pull her up, allowing her to wrap her legs around my waist this time. She groans as I grind my now very erect cock against her. I have an immediate need to consume her in every way possible. Every strip of fabric between us is too much. I need to feel her skin beneath mine, stroke her, bring her pleasure. I want to see her face when she is at the point of complete and utter release.

"Take me to bed."

She doesn't have to tell me twice.

A loud squeal erupts from her as I toss her onto the mattress. She bounces a couple of times before I pounce on her like a predator to his prey. I love seeing her playful like this, and as much as I can see she wants me, I don't feel pressured to be ready to have sex right now. Somehow, we always seem to know what the other needs. It's what gives me hope that we'll make it. Someday, we will be ready. It will be right for both of us, and it might not be perfect, but it'll be perfect for us.

⚜

THE HONK OF LOREN'S CAR makes me want to vomit. I actually did . . . earlier. I thought I had my panicking over with, but now that she's here and expects me to get into the car with her, I'm having second thoughts . . . about everything. Well, everything except that I love Loren, and I want to show her how much by doing this—taking a step, pushing myself. It's been long enough. I know it's all a mental game, and I'm stronger than the fear.

I can do this.

When I finally make it down the steps, I see Loren leaned up against her car, waiting patiently. I also see Ben standing over by the front door of the house, in the wings, just in case. My sister is at work, but she gave me a pep talk before she left. And after a phone call with my mom a few minutes ago, I felt prepared, but now I'm not sure if I am.

Loren must sense my hesitation. She pushes off of the little red car and walks up to me, pulling the lapels of my jacket, forcing me to lean down closer to her.

"We don't have to do this. Ben said he'd drive out to Kenner and pick up the parts for us."

I take a deep breath and dig deep for the resolve I had found earlier.

"I . . . I want to do this." These kind of setbacks and holdups are what affect me the most. They're what keep me from doing the things I want to do. I'm not going to let my past dictate my future. Those are Dr. Abernathy's words—something about taking back control of my life. She said I've been in the back seat since the accident, at the mercy of my injuries and limitations, but it's time for me to move back to the driver's seat. And this is the first step.

Loren's soft lips touch my cheek and then my mouth. "Have I told you how proud I am of you?"

I swallow a lump that appears in my throat. Those words mean everything to me. I want to make her proud. I want to be the best I can be for her. I stare down into her eyes and see the sincerity on her face. "Thank you."

I open the car door and practically jump into the passenger seat. Suddenly, I'm taking the band-aid approach and decide that the faster I do it, the less painful it'll be. Once I'm inside and buckled in, I look over at Loren, who's wearing the cheesiest grin I've ever seen. I try to return it, but I think all I manage is a grimace.

"Are you ready?"

I nod, because I don't trust my voice . . . or opening my mouth. The sick feeling is back, and I'm trying hard to keep that shit down. Throwing up in Loren's car would not be cool. My heart is beating so fast and hard. I feel it in my temples, kinda like when you smash your finger in the door and it throbs. It's a lot like that. I need some fucking air.

Looking down, I see the handle to roll down the window and glance over at Loren for approval.

"Whatever you need to do." She's looking at me with worry but also trying to keep her eyes on the road. It's weird, though, because it's not like I think Loren's going to wreck us or that we're going to be in a wreck, period. I can't really explain where the irrational fear is coming from, but it's real, and I wish beyond anything I could make it stop.

Once the window is down and the cold air is hitting my face, I feel better. The tightness in my throat lessens, and my heartbeat seems to take on a slower rhythm.

"Better?"

"Yes."

We drive like this for what seems like hours, though even on a bad day, I know it only takes about forty minutes to get from my house to Kenner. My dad and I used to come up here looking for parts. I've traveled this road a thousand times.

Loren's hand reaches over the gear shift and latches on to mine. "Wanna hear some music?"

"Sure."

It's when the soothing sounds of Otis Redding fill the car that I finally begin to relax.

Closing my eyes, I enjoy the warmth I feel flowing through my body as the girl I love sings about sitting on the dock of the bay. It reminds me of days in the Impala with my dad, and it makes me hopeful for brighter days to come.

I can do this.

twenty-one

TRIPP

"MERRY CHRISTMAS, BABY," MY MOM says, greeting us at the door and enveloping me in her warm embrace. The sweet aromas filling the house and the gifts around the tree make my heart happy, but the beautiful girl beside me is all the gift I need.

It's only just begun, but this is already shaping up to be the best Christmas I've had in a long time—since my dad passed away. Christmas was always his thing, and after he was gone, it took us a while to get back into the spirit. If it hadn't been for Emmie and Jack, we probably wouldn't have even celebrated Christmas that first year. Which shows it's not about the presents and the commercial hoopla. It's about the people.

"Uncle Tripp!" Jack and Emmie yell, running down the stairs.

"Look!" Emmie squeals, smiling brightly. Her hair's a mess, and her eyes are sleepy, but her face is glowing with excitement. "Look! Santa came!" She's pointing toward the tree where the gifts are spilling out and flooding the living room.

I look over to Loren and see that her smile matches Emmie's. The way she's watching them and taking it all in, I can tell it's something she's never seen before, but she seems to be handling it pretty well so far.

"I got a fire truck!" Jack exclaims, sliding to a screeching halt in front of the tree. "A big, real fire truck! It's red, just like I wanted. And it makes sounds!" He's lying on his stomach in awe at the gifts he sees.

I see my sister look over at Ben and let out an exasperated breath. "Those batteries better die fast," she grits out from behind her smile, trying to keep a good game face on for the kids.

"Coffee, anyone?" my mom asks.

"Yes!" all of the adults reply in unison, still trying to wake up.

For a split second, I allow myself to think about my dad and how he's loving this. I really feel him on days like today. I see him in my sister and especially in Jack, and I know he's with us. Sometimes, I swear I hear his laugh, and I can almost picture him sitting in the big chair on the other side of the tree. He'd be so happy, and he'd love Loren.

I take my spot on the end of the sofa that's closest to the tree and pull Loren onto my lap. "Merry Christmas," I whisper into her ear, kissing her neck. She does a full body shiver and turns her head so our lips meet.

"Merry Christmas, and in case I forget later, thank you for today."

We watch as the kids tear through their presents. Emmie is so happy about the princess dress Loren made her. It's green and pink—her favorite colors. And my sister is going to have a hard time getting the superhero cape off of Jack. Loren even put his initials on the back. "Super Jack," is the most repeated phrase of the morning.

I bought Loren a new journal and had her name engraved on the cover. I'm hoping it will be a happy place for her to write, full of good thoughts.

She gave me a bright, shiny, good-as-new Impala decal for the front fender of my car. It's one of the last pieces we need to finish up the exterior, once it gets its new paint job, which Ben and my sister gifted me for Christmas. After a few tweaks under the hood, it'll be in tip-top shape, and then I don't know what. I guess like with everything else, we'll cross that bridge when we get there.

As I look around the room and see the genuine happiness on everyone's faces, I'm eternally grateful. I'm having one of those moments where I realize how different things could've turned out, but I'm so thankful for how the pieces of our lives fell together. I wish I could save this moment like a photograph and take it out to look at whenever I'm feeling down.

⚜

LOREN'S LAUGH RINGING THROUGH MY apartment is the best sound ever. Well, maybe second to the sounds she makes when she has an orgasm. Her laughs, though. They make me happy. They make me laugh. They can wipe away fears and bad days. They're magic.

The more Loren drinks, the more Loren laughs. And we've drunk half a bottle of Southern Comfort tonight.

It's New Year's Eve. Most people our age are out at big parties or on Bourbon Street, but that's not really our scene, so we decided to stay in and celebrate. Loren's being the DJ right now, and she's playing every girl power rock song she has on her iPod. I don't mind, though. Watching her dance around my apartment in a T-shirt and leg warmers is the best damn way I can think to ring in the New Year.

Except for *one* other thing . . . and that's still on the table.

As in, we discussed it, and we both feel like we're ready, but we don't want to set any sort of timeline. It'll happen when it happens.

Loren's been spending every night with me since Christmas. We came close to having sex last night, but just as we were getting hot and heavy, Ben knocked on the door, asking if we wanted to go to the garage to work on the Impala, to which we said yes.

By the time we got back up to the apartment, we were both too exhausted and pretty much passed out as soon as our heads hit the pillow.

The strands of white lights Loren hung around my apartment before Christmas are the only lights on. She insisted that we needed them because it wasn't Christmas-y without them.

Have I mentioned that I'd give her anything she asked for?

Loren switches the playlist to something we both agree on—one we made together that includes Otis and Ray and a few of our other favorites mixed in here and there. If this were the '80s, this playlist would be our mixtape.

She picks up the bottle of Southern Comfort and two small glasses off of the counter and plops herself in the middle of my bed.

"Wanna play a game?"

"Sure. Whatdya have in mind?" I ask, skimming my hand over her leg warmers and up to her bare knee.

"I ask you a question, and you answer."

The glaze in her eyes is adorable, and the constant smile on her face is contagious. I feel like I've already bared my soul to her. I'm not sure what's left to tell, but I'll play her game.

"So, I can ask you questions too?"

"Of course." She swats at me lazily, the alcohol in full effect. "I'll tell you anything you want to know. I'm an open book." The way she looks at me and slides her hands down the inside of her thighs makes her words have a double meaning, and it goes straight to my dick.

I clear my throat to get myself in check and tell her she can go first.

"Okay, so the deal is, if you refuse to answer, you have to drink. Or . . ." she pauses, holding up a finger in the air. "You can drink first, if that'll help you answer."

"Sounds like a plan."

"So, Tripp?" she starts, crossing her legs in front of her. "How many girls have you slept with?"

What the hell? Damn. She ain't messin' around.

I take a second and think hard, not wanting to give an incorrect answer, because if we're doing this, we might as well have the facts.

"Seven."

Loren's eyes grow two sizes, and she leans forward a little. "Seven? Really?"

"Yep." I sit there and try to gauge her reaction.

"Wow."

"Is that bad?"

"No . . . No, it's not bad. I don't know what I expected. I probably wouldn't like any answer you gave me." Her smile is small and apologetic.

She doesn't ask for an explanation, but I feel like giving her one. "My first was Whitney, of course, and then the other six were pretty much one-night stands when Whitney and I were split up, which was a lot. I know it probably makes me sound like a douchebag, but it is what it is, and I can't take any of it back."

"No, it's fine. I mean, it's not like I'm a virgin or anything."

Of course, she's not, but just hearing that statement leave her mouth makes me understand where she was coming from. The thought of someone else touching her and being with her like that makes me feel insane with jealousy. "How many guys have you been with?"

"One."

Deep down, I think I already knew that, and now, I kinda wish I hadn't asked. She looks sad, and I don't want her to be. This was supposed to be fun. I try to think of some way to lighten the mood back up and take her mind off of wherever it's gone.

"Who's your favorite Ninja Turtle?" I ask, in an effort to change the subject.

She looks up from where she's picking the label off the Southern Comfort bottle and smiles at me with a goofy grin. Soon the grin turns into a full-on belly laugh, and she tosses her head back, exposing her neck.

Perfection.

When she composes herself, her face grows serious again as she contemplates. "I think I like Michelangelo the best. He's such a party animal."

There is nothing sexual about her answer, but God, I want her. I love her so much, and I want to claim her in every way possible.

"Who's your favorite?" she asks.

"Donatello. Hands down. He's the brains of the operation."

"I can see that." She nods her head in agreement, staring across the bed at me. "You're really smart too, you know."

"Thanks."

"I mean it. You don't give yourself enough credit."

"Next question," I tell her because I always get uncomfortable when people give me compliments.

"Okay." She thinks for a minute, tapping her finger on her chin. "This is kind of a cliché question, but where do you see yourself in five years?" she asks, leaning her elbows on her knees and resting her chin in her hands. She looks so young and beautiful. No makeup, her hair a wild mess from the way she was dancing around the apartment earlier. Just Loren—*my Ania.*

"Wherever you are. That's where I want to be."

Her eyes get glassy as her brows draw together. Her face almost looks pained as she says, "God, I want that too."

"Yeah?"

"Yeah. I know they say that when you find *the one,* you'll just know, but I always thought that was some kind of myth or legend. I didn't think it would ever happen to me. And the way we found each other is so crazy . . . I mean, it makes me start to believe in fate and destiny. For the first time in my life, I feel like the universe is on my side. And the scariest part is that I know . . . Like, first hand, I *know* that everything could be taken away from me in the blink of an eye." She pauses for a second, clutching her chest. "But I don't care. I'd rather have you for a little while than not at all. *That's* how I know you're it for me, Tripp Alexander. That's how I know that you're the only one."

I crawl quickly to the middle of the bed and hover over her, pressing my forehead to hers. "I'm not going anywhere. You know that, right? You can't get rid of me."

There are tears on my face, and I'm not sure if they're mine or hers, but I don't care. I capture her lips with my own, putting action behind my words. Loren wraps herself around me, and I fall back into the bed, allowing her to take over and set the pace . . . allowing this to go wherever she wants it to go.

I'm ready.

"I don't want to wait anymore," Loren says, panting as she pulls her shirt forcefully over her head.

"Me neither. I want you . . . this."

"I love you."

"I love you, too . . . so much . . ." My words are broken off by her kiss. Her hands make quick work of my T-shirt and then my pants. There's no awkwardness or question, just raw need and resolve.

Just us.

"You know what I've never done before?" she asks, leaning up and gripping my hands with hers, her hips rolling over my erection with only her panties between us.

I shake my head, unsure of where she's going with the question.

"I've never made love before. Make love to me, Tripp."

Flipping her over, she squeals in delight, and I strip the flimsy piece of fabric off of her, laying her completely bare beneath me. With a stroke of my fingers between her folds, I can tell that she's wet and ready. I don't think either of us could stand to wait another second, or we might combust.

Holding her gaze with my own, I push two fingers inside her, eliciting a moan.

"That feels amazing Tripp, but I want *you*. Please."

Slowly, I line myself up to her entrance and brace myself for what I know is going to be the single most intense experience of my life. I feel it in the air around us . . . It's different. *We're* different. This may not be my first time, but it feels like it.

Pushing in, I feel how tight she is around me, and I have to pause to keep myself from ruining this moment. Her hips buck up and force me in further. A hiss leaves my lips as euphoria floods my body. Loren cries out beneath me, her head thrown back into the pillow, waves of mahogany hair fanned out on either side of her face, and I feel like I've died and gone to heaven.

When I have a second to adjust—to her, to us—I lean back on my thighs and pull Loren up with me, keeping us connected. This position gives me access to the wonderland that is her body—beautiful breasts, curvaceous hips. She is beauty incarnate. And she's mine. With each thrust of my hips, the speed picks up. The flush of her skin is gorgeous, and I can't keep my lips from kissing every inch of her.

Her pleas for release let me know she's close. I want this for her. I want to make her feel good. Reaching between us, I apply pressure on her clit, telling her that I want her to come for me. My name falls from her lips as she falls over the edge. Her walls tighten, and it pulls me over with her—free falling and not caring where I land, as long as I'm with her.

Lying spent next to Loren, our legs and arms tangled together; I look over to the clock and see that it's after midnight.

"Happy New Year, beautiful."

"Happy New Year, my love."

WHEN I WAKE UP DURING the middle of the night, the white lights are still glowing around the room, and Loren has her head on my chest.

For the first time in a long time, I allow myself to think of the future, and I don't have any regrets. I don't wish away the past. As painful as it is to admit, I see now that the past is what led me to her. I want to kiss her and hold her for the rest of my life. We're not promised tomorrow, so I'm going to love her every day like it might be our last.

I think back to Loren's question from earlier, about where I see myself in five years, and my mind begins to wander. I have so much more I could say to her. Like, I hope that in five years Loren's now flat stomach will be round, and she'll be glowing, or maybe there will be a baby asleep somewhere with her brown hair and my green eyes.

Hopefully, we'll have a house and lives of our own. But no matter what, I hope we spend every New Year's Eve just like this.

twenty-two

TRIPP

"TRIPP," MY MOM SIGHS, CUPPING my cheek, "you have no idea how happy and proud I am of you."

"Mom." I shake my head and pull away, trying to hide my embarrassment and accompanying smile. She's always told me she's proud of me, and I know when I succeed, she feels like she's succeeded as well. She's always told me so. But now, it's hard to see what she's so proud of. I got in a car. What's the big deal? It's not as tangible as throwing a touchdown pass.

"You listen here." She places her soft hand on my cheek and forces me to look back at her. "I'm proud." She points to herself, emphasizing her words. "And there's nothing you can do about it." Her hand grips my jaw a little tighter, and a smile breaks across her face before she plants a big kiss on my cheek. "Damn, I made some good-looking kids."

"Damn straight," Ben chimes in, swatting my sister's ass with a dishtowel. "You've got the goods, Mama A."

"At least someone appreciates me," she teases. The truth is we appreciate her more than she'll ever know. We're the pieces; she's the glue. I've never met a stronger woman in my entire life. Loren and Liza come in close seconds, but my mom's amazing.

"I love you, Mom," I whisper, kissing the top of her head as I scoot past her to put some bread in the oven.

"Tripp, Loren's coming for supper, right?" my sister asks as she stirs a pot full of sauce. I don't know why she's asking. It's not like we're not going to have enough food to feed a small army.

"Yeah, she'll be here as soon as her last class is out."

"Okay, good. We'll wait on her, then. The pasta is ready, and the sauce is almost there. Jack! Emmie!" she yells over her shoulder at the whooping hyenas in the next room. "Go wash up! We're eating as soon as Loren gets here!"

"Loren!" Emmie's love affair with my girlfriend has only grown stronger over the last couple of months. She thinks Loren hung the moon.

"Loren!" Ben mocks his mini-me, throwing his hands in the air.

Actually, everyone thinks Loren hung the moon. Me included.

Jack runs into the kitchen, practically flying across the wood floor, his socks acting as skates.

"Hey, Super Jack!" My mom slows his flight, keeping him upright.

"Is Loren here?" he asks, his blue eyes big as saucers.

"Not yet, buddy," I tell him, ruffling his hair.

We all go about setting the table and carrying food into the dining room. Jack and Emmie argue over who's going to sit in the chair beside Loren. My mom finally settles the argument by reminding Emmie she got to sit by Loren earlier in the week when she was here for supper.

"She's the best thing that's happened to this family in a long time," my mom says, not looking up from where she's placing the silverware at each setting.

I look up and see Ben with a big cheesy grin on his face. "She's pretty awesome."

The fact that my family has embraced Loren so fully makes my heart swell. *She's mine.* Sometimes I still have to pinch myself. It's hard to believe she's real, and she's with me . . . and she loves *me*.

"I don't know what I'd do without her," I admit. "I couldn't have done any of the stuff I've been able to do without her."

"Hey," my mom says, getting my attention from across the table. "Loren might be the catalyst, but you've done the work. You don't give yourself enough credit."

"That's what Loren says."

"And that's one of the reasons I love that girl so much." My mom smiles and continues setting the table.

"I'm proud of you too, bro," Ben says quietly, slapping my shoulder.

Just before things can get too sappy, the doorbell rings, saving me.

Loren.

"Loren!" Emmie and Jack yell, running for the door.

We've all told her she doesn't have to knock or ring the doorbell, but she still does.

I hear the door open, and my girl's sweet voice carries through the foyer. "Oh, I must have the wrong address. I'm looking for Jack and Emmie Walker."

"That's us!" they say in unison.

"No. The Jack and Emmie I know are about this high," she says, pausing. "And one's a superhero: Super Jack. And the other is a princess who loves, *loves* the color green. Have you seen them?"

"That's us!" Their screams are louder, and they start talking over each other, both explaining how Loren knows who they are. "You . . . you said," Emmie yells, finally winning the battle for who gets to talk first. "You said a princess doesn't have to have a tiara to be a princess!"

"Oh, that's right! I did say that, didn't I?" Loren says, finally giving in and laughing a little.

"Just like you, Loren! You're a princess, even if you don't wear a tiara!"

"Aww! Emmie, I love you!"

I hear my niece squeal as I peek around the corner and see Loren swinging her around in a big hug.

"What about me?" Jack asks, tugging on Loren's jacket.

"Of course, I love you too, Super Jack!"

Standing in the hallway watching the three of them makes a weird feeling stir in the pit of my stomach. This isn't the first time I've felt it, In fact, every time I watch Loren with Jack and Emmie, it hits me. I start letting myself wonder what it would be like to have a life with Loren, one that includes marriage and children. I want that.

"Hey," she says when she notices me watching. Her smile is so wide it lights up her whole face. "Hey." I take the few steps to her, wrapping my arms around her waist and pulling her close to me.

"Are you guys gonna kiss?" Jack asks, disgusted.

"Yep."

"Cooties!" he yells, covering his eyes.

"You better run if you don't want the cooties to jump off on you," I tell him, giving him fair warning.

We laugh as they both scurry out of the room, screaming for their lives.

"I missed you," I tell her when we're finally alone.

"Right back atcha."

Her lips meet mine, and I feel complete. As I thread my fingers through the soft tendrils of hair that fall down her back, Loren lets out a quiet moan in my mouth, making me want to deepen the kiss and take things further, but I know I'd only be starting something I can't finish.

"Later," I whisper, to which she responds by pressing herself into me, her hands gripping the back of my neck.

When my sister calls her name, Loren laughs and places a soft kiss on my jaw. "Later," she promises.

We all eventually take our seats, Jack beaming with pride as he sits in the seat on the other side of Loren. Somehow, when she started coming over and eating with us on a regular basis, I ended up in dad's old seat. No one has sat here for years. It's kind of weird but also a concrete example of how life goes on.

I look to my left and see Loren helping Jack put pasta on his plate. My mom is assisting Emmie with buttering a roll. Liza is telling Ben that he needs to eat some salad, like he's a little kid. I smirk across the table at him, which earns me a piece of bread thrown toward my head. Mom reprimands us both, and I smile, feeling content.

Loren may not be the sole reason life feels so good right now, but she's definitely part of it. I know it's hard to know what life would be like right now if I hadn't started working at The Crescent Moon. Who knows? Some of this happiness might have found us on its own. But like Loren was saying a couple of weeks ago, the way we met and the fact we're so perfect for each other makes me believe in fate. I have to believe that we'd have met one way or another, that our paths were destined to cross. She needed me, and I needed her.

Right now, watching her smile and interact with my family, there's a flutter of hope in my chest, hope that I've brought as much happiness and goodness into her life as she's brought into mine.

My mom catches my eye and winks at me, as if she's inside my brain and knows what I'm thinking. I return it with a smile, before digging into the delicious food in front of me.

"How are your classes, Loren?" Liza asks, causing everyone to look over at Loren.

She blows out a deep breath and wrinkles her nose, which makes me worry that something is wrong. I expected her to say they were going great. That's what she usually tells me.

"Classes are okay right now, but I think I'm going to try to find a part-time job again. I really need the extra money to get me through the semester."

"Have any idea where you'd want to work?" Ben asks.

"Well, I used to work at the bursar's office, but I was thinking about applying at this bookstore near campus. The lady who runs it is nice, and I like going in there, so I figured it wouldn't be a bad place to work."

I'm trying to keep an open mind as I listen to Loren talk, but I remember what she told me about how things were before. She went to school all day, worked all night, and barely had time to do her class work. I worry for her . . . and for us. If she's working and I'm working, what if we don't have time for each other?

I try to keep a neutral expression on my face, so I don't let on to what I'm thinking inside. I'm not sure if it works, but at least no one says anything. I don't want to have a conversation about Loren working or not working in front of everyone.

Anxiety starts to build inside me because I know if I voice my concerns, she may take it as me trying to tell her what to do. Loren and I haven't ever really had an argument, not since we hashed everything out about the accident.

I know I don't have any right to tell her how she needs to live her life, but I feel like I should have an opinion when it comes to *us*. I war with myself as we all pitch in to clean up after supper. Ben asks me if I'm okay, and I tell him I have a headache. It was a puss way out, but I took it.

When Loren and I say goodnight and leave out the back door, I can tell she's hesitating on whether to come up to my apartment or not. She keeps looking over at her car in the driveway and chewing on her lip.

"Do you have to leave right now?" I ask, hoping I'm reading her wrong.

Her toes kick at the sidewalk, and she drops her head down to her chest. "I really have a lot of homework to do, and Grace picked up a few applications for me today. I'd like to be able to take them back tomorrow."

"Why didn't you tell me about needing a job?"

She shrugs her shoulders, looking off into the distance. "I didn't want to worry you with mundane things like me needing a part-time job."

"Nothing about *you* is mundane." I reach my hand up and brush the hair away from her cheek, tilting her face back toward me so I can see her pretty brown eyes. "I want to know if you get a paper cut, or when someone serves you bad coffee . . . Everything is important to me."

I notice her swallow hard, and her hands are fidgeting. I can tell something is bothering her, and I wish she would just tell me what it is before I go crazy. "Loren?"

"I . . . I just didn't want you worrying or feeling like I was putting my problems off on you."

"Loren," I warn, hoping I don't have to repeat myself. "If you worry, I worry. That's just how it is. We're a package deal."

She stiffens a little at those words, but I chalk it up to her trying to put on a brave face for me, so I continue.

"If money is an issue, why don't you just move in with me?" I ask her with a light laugh, trying to lighten the mood. I know it sounds crazy, and it might not work, even if she was to consider it, but I want her to know she has options. Besides, the idea of Loren in my bed every night sounds fantastic.

I stroke her cheek when a small tear leaks out of the corner of her eye.

"Loren?"

Her gaze is far off, like she's not even standing here in front of me. Her breaths come in short, fast bursts. The color in her face pales, and I know what's happening.

"Loren, baby," I say, trying to soothe her, bringing her closer to me, wrapping my arms around her and trying to shield her—from the world, from her past, from whatever memory is haunting her at the moment. "Just breathe. I've got you."

Her hands grip the sides of my jacket, as if she's hanging on for dear life. She buries her face into my chest, and I worry she's having some sort of breakdown.

I hate seeing her cry; it physically hurts me.

We stand there for a while, her holding on to me and me holding her together.

Soon, her breathing slows, her grip on me loosens, and her body slowly melts into mine.

I rub her back, whispering that it's okay . . . even though I'm not sure it is. It's my turn to be strong enough for both of us.

"What happened?" I ask when I think she's able to tell me.

"I . . . I don't know. One second, it was you, and we were here having this conversation, and the next minute, it wasn't . . . and I wasn't here . . . And you weren't you . . ."

Her voice breaks, and I squeeze her a little tighter. I think I know where this is going, but I want her to have a chance to get it all out. "Where were you, Loren? Who was I?"

"You were *him* . . . PJ. And we were at his house, and he was telling me that I should move in with him. It all felt so real. It was scary. I'm . . . I'm sorry." Her sobs break through at that point, and I let her cry it out.

"You're here with me, and I'm not going anywhere."

"I wish I could believe that," she cries. "I wish I could tell my mind what my heart knows."

"Maybe it would help to say it out loud. Give your fears a voice, and then face them head-on. I'm gonna help you."

She leans her forehead against my chest for a couple of minutes before taking a staggering breath. "I—I love you, Tripp. I love you more than I've ever loved anyone before, but I'm still afraid of putting all of my trust in you. It's not that I don't trust *you*. I guess it's . . . fate or life or whatever I don't trust because I know this can end at any second. I was devastated when PJ died, but if I lost you in *any* way, I don't think I'd survive it. I wouldn't want to."

I sigh heavily, stroking her hair. "We can't worry about things that are out of our control. We can only live the best way we know how. For me, that means spending as much time as I can with you and my family. Nothing else matters. I want you to know, though, if something happens to me . . . like PJ . . . I died the happiest man in the world." I can feel the sobs wracking her body, so I hold her tighter. "I'm not going anywhere, baby. You have to believe in that. I'm not leaving unless you ask me to leave. It's my hope, one day, to be old and gray with you, sitting on our front porch, watching great-grandchildren run around in our front yard. We're forever."

She lets out a small laugh, some of the seriousness finally lifting. When she looks back up at me, her eyes are glistening, but the tears have stopped. Her fingers brush the hair away from my forehead, and she gently caresses my scar. I used to feel self-conscious when she'd touch me there, but now I don't mind. I actually like it.

"Kiss me," she demands, and I do. When I think we've kissed long enough, I kiss her a little longer, promising to do it over and over again—every chance I get.

One thing Loren and I will never do is take what we have for granted. We have PJ to thank for that. His departure from this earth gave each of us a unique perspective, as well as a new beginning.

We can do this.

twenty-three

TRIPP

MARDI GRAS SEASON. IT'S MY favorite time of year. I mean, the more traditional holidays like Thanksgiving and Christmas are great, of course, but you just can't beat the first two months of the year here in New Orleans. Everyone is filled with even more *joie de vivre* than usual, and the traditional Mardi Gras colors of purple, green, and gold cover just about anything that's standing.

My personal favorite is seeing the Mardi Gras trees. Once the parades start, you can see them covered with beads that were thrown, but not caught, by spectators. The beads literally drip off the trees. It's so unusual and beautiful and makes the city even more festive. Unfortunately, the parades haven't started yet, but my second favorite part of Mardi Gras has—King Cakes.

Who makes the best King Cakes in New Orleans is a popular topic for debate around here, and it all depends on your preferences. If you want a fancy King Cake, go to Sucre's. You like your cakes more traditional? Go to Gambino's. But in my opinion, the best bakery is Randazzo's. Their pecan praline King Cake is heaven on your tongue, and I'm not the only one who thinks so. During Mardi Gras season, you can often find lines of customers out the door of their store and around the corner. In fact, that's where Loren and I are right now.

We've been here for about thirty minutes, and I reckon we have at least another thirty to go, but it's worth it. What makes this even more exciting is that this will be Loren's first King Cake from Randazzo's. In fact, it'll be her first *real* King Cake, period, other than the couple she's bought over the years from local grocery stores. That type of King Cake is good too, but it's nothing compared to what we'll be eating soon.

I've been mindlessly tracing the skin on Loren's lower back with my thumb, not really paying attention to anything, so I'm startled when I feel her elbow nudge my ribs.

"What's the matter?" I wrap my arm around her, pulling her close to me. After her breakdown a couple of weeks ago, I find myself even more protective of her. If it bothers her, she hasn't mentioned it.

"There's a guy and a girl over there staring at us." She jerks her head back, and I glance behind her right as she whisper-yells "don't look". I'm about to call her out on her contradiction when my eyes focus on the couple Loren pointed out.

Evan and *Whitney*.

Once they see I've spotted them, they start walking toward us. Evan looks reluctant—remorseful, even—but Whitney still wears the smug I'm-better-than-you look she's always had.

What did I ever see in her?

I don't know what to expect from them, and I can feel my body tense the closer they get to us. Loren must sense my discomfort because she tightens her grip around my waist while watching me, waiting for my answer.

"Remember a while back when you said you'd love to give Whitney a piece of your mind? Well, here's your chance."

"*No way!*" Her eyes narrow, and I'm pretty sure she just cracked the knuckles of her hand resting on my hip. "This should be fun."

"We don't have to talk to them, you know."

Before Loren can respond, Whitney and Evan are standing directly in front of us. I can tell Whitney is expecting some sort of reaction from me, but thankfully, Evan chooses to speak before I vomit all over her shoes, which is the only reaction I can think of at the moment. If memory serves, I'm pretty sure she wouldn't appreciate that.

"Hey, Tripp. How's it going?" he asks, looking around nervously. "Looks like half the city decided to get a King Cake today. Man, this line is insane." Evan was always good at using small talk to deflect awkward situations.

"It's good to see you, Evan." When I say his name, Loren's eyes flash to mine. I realize I only told her Whitney was walking toward us, not Whitney and my ex-best friend. She's obviously surprised to see the two of them together. I'm surprised as well, especially since Evan didn't mention it when we ran into each other a few months back. Naturally, I'd assume their relationship is a new one, but the huge diamond Whitney is flashing as she pretends to inspect her fingernails says otherwise.

"Aren't you going to say hello, Tripp?" Whitney gives me a little pout and flutters her eyelashes.

I can't believe I used to fall for that shit.

I barely nod in her direction, not particularly wanting to give her the time of day, before speaking. "Evan . . . Whitney, this is Loren, my girlfriend."

The word "girlfriend" doesn't begin to adequately describe what Loren means to me, but the less information these two have, the better. I don't feel like I owe them anything. And the protectiveness I felt earlier has multiplied with their arrival. Instinctively, I pull Loren tighter, closer.

"Loren, I used to go to school with Evan and Whitney," I say, making direct eye contact with them both and feeling proud of myself for not cowering away. Loren knows the real truth. She knows just how well I know them, but I'd rather not focus on that. I want them to see I've moved on, and I'm better for it.

Evan seems to take the hint, but of course, Whitney demands more attention.

"Wow, Tripp, way to downplay the last five years!" Whitney laughs haughtily, turning to Loren. "We were *more* than friends back in the day. In fact, I thought we'd be married by now. Isn't that right, Tripp?"

"And now you're engaged to his friend. How charming." Loren speaks with a smile on her face, but disdain drips from her voice, sending her message loud and clear. Whitney's smile fades as she watches Loren glide her hand across my waist, latching on to her other hand and effectively encircling me in her arms.

Is that the female way of staking her claim? Regardless, I love it.

Evan lets out a nervous laugh. "Yeah, can you believe that?" he asks, scratching his head like he still can't believe it himself. "I asked Whitney to marry me over Christmas break, and she said yes."

I can tell he's happy, and I'm glad for him. I guess somewhere deep down inside, I hope Whitney is happy too, but that's about as far as it goes.

"That's great, man. Congratulations," I say, reaching out to shake his hand as the line starts to move.

"Guess we'll see ya around," I say, ending the conversation.

I don't even give them a backward glance as the line moves.

This moment feels like a good representation of my life as a whole.

I feel light and free as another burden I didn't realize I was carrying is lifted. I'm at peace knowing that part of my life, and even more so that part of *me*, is in the past.

"Are you okay?" Loren asks.

"I'm more than okay," I assure her, pulling her even closer. "I didn't expect to see them here, but I think it was good. They reminded me that everything I went through with the two of them eventually led me to you, and I can't find it in me to be mad anymore. We've all moved on and are better for it, I think. I hope so anyway." I lean over to kiss the top of her head as the line moves again. "Sorry, you didn't get much of an opportunity to tell Whitney off."

Loren shrugs. "It's okay. She and I both know I win, but if she would've tried to cut in line with us, I would've definitely kicked her ass."

I bark out a laugh and squeeze her tight. "I love you so much."

⚜

"I CAN'T BELIEVE THE CAR'S almost finished," I tell Ben, leaning over the hood of the Impala. I've just installed new windshield wipers, and now I'm cleaning every window, making them shine. Yesterday, Ben and I replaced the brakes and all of the rubber bushings, so today we're putting on the final touches. It's been a long time coming, but it almost looks brand new, or at least like it did after it was rebuilt the first time, before the wreck.

As I continue to wipe down the outside of the car, Ben slides into the driver's seat, turning the key and listening as it purrs to life. My hand rests on the hood, feeling the vibration from the motor.

"Okay, we just need to let the engine run for about thirty minutes, then change the oil. After that, she should be good to go, brother!" Ben smiles at me and throws a clean rag my way. "Why don't you help me wipe down the inside before we open a beer and celebrate?"

Laughing and without thinking about what I'm doing, I open the passenger's side door and sit down. I reach up with the clean rag and begin to wipe down the dashboard. It's then, when I look up through the windshield, that my body freezes. I haven't been in this seat since the day of the accident, and although it's been my goal to get back in this car, I wasn't prepared to do it today.

My hands clutch the dashboard, with my knuckles white and my palms sweaty, while I try to figure out what to do. My breaths escape in ragged pants, and my head pounds. I lean forward and let my head fall to the leather, concentrating on not passing out. Movement to my left side catches my eye, and I see Ben reach across, placing a hand on my shoulder. He speaks to me, but I can't hear him over the ringing in my ears. I squeeze my eyes shut, trying to block out everything around me.

I can't do this.

Do I sit here, frozen, and wait for the attack to pass, or do I run?

Part of me wishes Loren was here to help because she's the best antidote, but the other part is glad she doesn't have to witness this.

Ben's grip tightening on my shoulder makes me open my eyes and look over at him. When I see him mouth the word "breathe", I nod my head and then force myself to take in a large gulp of air, then let it back out.

After doing this a few times, my body starts to relax, but I have no idea how long it is before I'm able to pry my hands off the dash.

"I'm sorry," are the first words out of my mouth, but Ben rejects them.

"No, Tripp. I'm the one who's sorry. It never even occurred to me that you would react that way, and it should have." He takes a deep breath like he'd been holding it for a while. The concern is written all over his face, and his hand is still resting on my shoulder.

"I didn't think about it either." I laugh without humor behind it, shaking my head. "I don't know if that's good or bad. I mean, I guess it's good that I wasn't thinking too much about it and dreading it like I normally would, right?"

"Of course, that's good. What's also good is that you stayed and worked through it; you didn't give up and shut down. You could've bolted. That's what you would've done a few months ago, and I would've chased your ass down the road." He smirks.

I scowl at him, but he only laughs. I know he's right, though.

"I know you panicked and forgot to breathe, but once I reminded you, it didn't take long for you to calm down. I'd say that was a success." He pats my back roughly.

I reluctantly agree before my eyes widen in surprise. "I'm still here, Ben."

"Well, duh. Were you planning on leaving?"

"No, I mean, I'm still sitting in the car, and I'm okay. I'm really okay." I look at my hands, turning them over, realizing that I'm not even panicking anymore. There're no tremors, no sweat. I'm just sitting here talking to Ben like I would've before all this shit happened—like we have a hundred times before.

I guess I can do this after all.

"What do you say we take this baby for a spin around the block?" Ben asks, his eyebrows rising to his hairline.

I feel the nerves back in my stomach, and my hands are a little sweaty again, but I don't feel like I'm going to throw up or pass out, so I nod my head.

After riding with Loren out to Kenner for parts, I thought this would be easier, but there's something different about being back in the passenger seat of *this* car.

"How about some Otis?" he asks, pulling an old 8-track from under the seat and popping it into the stereo.

I nod again, taking deep breaths and blowing them out.

"Put your seatbelt on," he instructs, doing the same. "We'll turn around whenever you want to. Just say the word. I'll even stop and let you out. We won't go far." He stops for a second, pausing with his hand on the gear shift. "You can do this."

I nod in agreement because I feel like I can. I *want* to.

Ben throws his arm over the seat and cautiously backs out of the garage with a strong hand resting on my shoulder, reminding me that he's here and that I'm not alone.

As Otis croons about love, with the windows rolled down, we cruise slowly down the street. The cool air fills the car, and it's as if I can literally feel the lingering fears flying out the window.

I can do this.

twenty-four

LOREN

CHECKING MY MAKEUP ONE LAST time in the mirror, I also try to check my nerves and leave them right where I'm standing. I don't want anything getting in the way of today. This date has held so many bad memories and moments for Tripp and me, but not today. Today is going to be about us—our love, our lives—and about leaving the past behind.

We considered taking the easy way out and locking ourselves up in Tripp's apartment, blocking out the world and trying to forget this day even exists, but that's not who we are. Neither of us likes to ignore things because we both know that eventually, shit has to be dealt with. Maybe it's from all of the therapy we've had, being forced to face our emotions and fears, but we like to deal with things head on.

After our joint session with Dr. Abernathy last week, she helped us realize that going out and celebrating this day would be the best gift we can give ourselves. It's been a year since I lost PJ and a year since Tripp's life was turned upside down. We deserve this. We deserve each other, and we deserve to be happy.

"You look great," Grace says, standing in the doorway of the bathroom.

"Thanks."

"Hey, tonight's gonna be awesome." She nudges me with her

shoulder as she sidles up beside me at the sink. "I know you're worried and probably feeling sad, but you and Tripp are going to make new memories, and they're gonna be good ones." I smile at her through the mirror, knowing deep down in my heart she's right.

"Thanks, Grace Bug." I lean over and pull her into a hug. I don't know what I would've done without her this past year. It was the Lord's work, putting us in the same dorm room. When I met her, I had no idea what my life was going to be like a few months later.

"What am I going to do when I don't get to see you every day?" she asks, squeezing me back tightly.

"You'll call me. And we'll meet for coffee and library dates."

"You know, if you need me to, I could hold off moving in with Will one more semester."

"No way. You're moving in with Will, and y'all are gonna be happy and get married and have lots of babies who'll call me 'Aunt Loren'." We both laugh at the thought, still holding on to each other, but we know it's true. She and Will are meant to be together. "You're not putting your life on hold for me any longer."

"It was never like that," she whispers into my shoulder.

"Thanks for always being there for me."

"I'm glad you found Tripp."

"Speaking of," I say, realizing I probably need to hurry and get out of here, "I've gotta go. He told me to meet him at our bench at four o'clock." What Grace doesn't know is that I'm going to take Tripp up on his offer to move in with him. I encouraged her to take Will up on his offer of them getting an apartment together because I knew I wanted to move in with Tripp. I haven't told her yet because I think Tripp should be the first to know. Plus, I've been a little hesitant to admit it out loud because honestly, I'm still afraid of the emotions I felt when he originally offered. But I know it's what I want, and I refuse to live my life in fear of the *what ifs*. I don't want to be ten years down the road and look back with regrets.

"Do you know what he has planned for your date?" she asks as I grab my sweater and purse from my desk.

"I have no idea, but I love surprises."

"Have fun," she calls behind me as I make a mad dash for the elevator.

When I get outside, I look at my watch and realize that I only have ten minutes to get to the bench in front of The Crescent Moon—our bench. I find my steps going from a walk to a jog, needing to get there as soon as possible. I haven't seen Tripp since yesterday morning when we met for coffee, and that's too long. I miss him. I always miss him when I don't see him for a day or so, which is all the more reason I should move in with him. At least that way, I know I'll see him when we go to sleep and wake up.

I want his mornings, his nights, and anything he'll give me in between.

I'm ready to spend forever with him. If he doesn't know that by now, he should, but I don't mind telling him every chance I get.

I slow down just before the corner the café sits on, opening my bag and making sure Tripp's gift is still in there. I bought him a book about Greek mythology that he doesn't have. I especially love this book because there's a part in here about the Algea, specifically mentioning *Ania*, the nickname Tripp gave me before we actually met. I know Tripp will love it.

I also marked a page in there where it talks about Adonis. If I'm his Ania, then he's my Adonis. I snicker at that thought, knowing Tripp will shake his head and blush over that, but it's true. He's beautiful and doesn't see himself clearly. I think the old Tripp was over-confident, with his talents and looks being the foundation of that confidence. But this new version is just starting to find his footing, and he's realizing he's so much more than the game-winning quarterback or the teenage heartthrob he once was.

I feel like I came into his life at the perfect time, and not just for the obvious reasons. I'm fortunate enough to watch him be reborn, like a phoenix rising from the ashes.

When I get to the bench, I expect Tripp to be there waiting for me, but he's not. I think about going into the café, but he specifically said the bench, so I sit down and wait. Besides, I don't think I want to tarnish today with thoughts of the past, and I know those are all I would have if

I went in there right now.

He'll be here.

I tell the nagging, annoying voice in the back of my brain to shut the hell up.

He'll be here.

A few minutes later, I'm still sitting on the bench, practically glued to the wood, my hands gripping the edge, when a shiny black car turns slowly around the corner. I do a double take, knowing I must be hallucinating because I could swear that the messy dark head of hair in the driver's seat of that car belongs to my Tripp.

I hate Thursdays.
I hate this café.
I hate coming here.
I hate that PJ left me here.
I hate him sometimes.
I hate myself for hating him.

If my therapist was here, she'd tell me that the fact I can admit those things is progress, and I'd call bullshit. I don't feel like I've made any progress. I feel like I'm good at putting up pretenses, but deep down, I feel stuck. I feel like I'm in that movie, Groundhog Day, where he continuously wakes up and relives the same day over and over. For me, that day is February 14th.

When I slide into my regular booth, I scoot over toward the window, craving the warmth that comes through it. That's why I sit so close. As I sit there, losing myself in my thoughts, I feel a pull deep inside, something urging me to turn around, so I do. And it's as if the world stands still.

There's a mess of dark hair and troubled eyes looking back at me, and I no longer crave the warmth from the sun shining through the window. I crave the warmth that spreads through my body as he looks at me. It's the briefest of moments, but it's profound. In those few seconds of exchanged glances, I feel like I want to know him . . . like there's something pulling me to him.

Awkwardly, he stumbles out the door, and my heart clenches. He's gone, but everything about him is etched into my mind, giving me something to think about other than the darkness and sadness that usually consumes me when I sit in this seat.

Shaking my head to clear it of the sudden flashback from the first day I saw Tripp in the café, I realize I'm not hallucinating or dreaming. Tripp—*my Tripp, my Adonis*—is sitting behind the wheel of his 1967 Impala, and he's smiling . . . *at me.*

He pulls up to the curb, and my heart drops out of my chest. Stepping out, he closes the door behind him and casually leans up against the car. In that instance, I get a glimpse of the old Tripp mixed with the new Tripp. There's an air about him that exudes confidence and sureness.

I can't stop my feet from running to him and jumping into his arms, wrapping my legs around his waist.

"Surprise," he whispers as he holds me close. His lips collide with mine, and I decide right then and there that I don't need another thing in this entire world. I only need him. *Just him.*

And maybe this car. Because damn if it's not sexy, especially with him behind the wheel.

"Best surprise ever," I tell him, kissing his jaw and down his neck, unable to keep the public display of affection at bay. I need him. Want him.

"Wanna take a drive?" he asks, his voice husky and low . . . confident, sexy. He's killing me in the best way.

I nod, my eyes drinking in every inch of him.

He slowly lets my legs back down to the ground, taking my hand and walking me around to the passenger side of the car. When he opens the door for me, the cockiest smirk is on his lips, and I can't help but kiss it.

"Get in the car, or we're never going to make it farther than this corner," he growls.

I do as I'm told and slide into the seat, fastening my seatbelt, eager to go wherever Tripp wants to take me.

Tripp practically runs around the car, hopping into the driver's seat and there's no hesitancy, no nerves. Just him.

My cheeks hurt from smiling so big.

"I'm so proud of you."

He looks over at me before pulling the sunglasses off the top of his head, back down onto his nose. "I couldn't have done this without you."

His hand grabs mine, and he kisses the back of it.

"My *Ania*," he whispers, causing need and want to stir deep inside me. He has no idea what he does to me, the way he makes me feel—it's intense and frightening and wonderful.

"Where are you taking me?" I ask, still trying to wrap my mind around being in this car with Tripp.

"I thought we'd go to Stanley and get some dinner and then maybe drive down to The Fly and watch the sun set over the river," he says, checking his side mirror before changing lanes.

I nod, agreeing in silence, unable to make a coherent sentence because I'm so dumbfounded by what I'm seeing. I realize to everyone else besides me, and his family, that this would seem normal and like nothing spectacular, but it's huge. I can't help staring at him, in awe of him.

We continue driving down the road, the late afternoon sun ahead of us. Tripp throws his arm across the back of the seat, and I melt. I can't take my eyes off of him as he maneuvers through the streets. I'm paying absolutely no attention to where we're going, only to the man sitting beside me.

"How long have you been keeping this a secret from me?" I finally manage to ask.

He glances over at me, his smile reaching up to his eyes that are hidden behind the sunglasses. "Only a week or so," he says, directing his eyes back to the road. "Ben talked me into taking a ride with him, and that's about all it took. I realized I'm not afraid anymore. The panic was there, but I didn't run, and that gave me the boost of confidence I needed. The next day, it was him in the passenger seat. Took me a few days to make it out of the neighborhood, but I did it and I wanted to tell you, but I also wanted to surprise you."

"You did." My smile matches his, and I want to kiss him so bad. I want to show him how much this means to me; how proud I am . . . how much I love him. "I love you."

"I love you too. So much," he says, bringing our hands back up and kissing the back of mine again.

"Happy Valentine's Day, Tripp."

"Happy Valentine's Day, my *Ania*."

epilogue

TRIPP
6 YEARS LATER

"STAY," I PRACTICALLY BEG WHEN I feel Loren slipping out of bed, trying not to wake me, but it's too late. The second her warm body separates from mine, I'm awake. I miss her touch immediately.

"Happy Anniversary, baby." I pull at her T-shirt, trying to keep her in the bed. "Happy Valentine's Day . . . Happy Reveal Day . . ."

"I love you, and yes . . . Happy everything, but I've gotta pee." She giggles, wiggling out of my attempts to hold her there with me. "Either let me go, Mr. Alexander, or you'll be changing wet sheets."

I could hold her forever. I would if she'd let me, but unfortunately nature calls, and it calls damn often these days. "Go, Mrs. Alexander, and then get your fine ass back to this bed. I still have ten minutes before I'm forced to get up."

I watch as Loren sleepily shuffles to the bathroom. From the back, you'd never know she's five months pregnant. *She* thinks she looks like a beached whale, but the truth is, she's never been more beautiful. Her skin glows. Her hair is shinier. Everything I've always loved about her is more pronounced. Not to mention the boobs. The boobs are phenomenal. I have a feeling I'm going to be jealous in a few months.

"What are you smirking about?" she asks as she makes her way back to the bed, snuggling under the covers as I resume my former position of being wrapped around her.

"You." I kiss the top of her head. "And you." I slide down her body and kiss her round belly.

"Baby, you're so sweet. How'd I get so lucky?"

"I'm the lucky one."

"We don't have time to have this debate this morning. There's too much to do before everyone gets here," she tells me, sighing heavily. "But we do have time to kiss. Kiss me."

Gladly. She doesn't have to tell me twice. Shit, she doesn't have to tell me once. I press my lips to hers and kiss her so hard she'll still feel it when we've gone our separate ways for the day. "I'd like to do more than kiss you," I tell her, nibbling down her neck and taking a minute to worship at the altar of pregnant boobs.

"I'd like that too, but there's so much to do." She groans, probably from a combination of her reaction to what I'm currently doing with my tongue and not looking forward to everything she has to accomplish today.

"Don't worry, love. I'll go to the grocery store and stop by the bakery," I tell her, kissing farther down her body. "All you have to do is be your beautiful self."

"Your mom and Liza are supposed to be here at four o'clock to help me cook," she moans, her head pressed back into the pillow as we continue our conversation . . . *both* conversations.

"See? No worries. They won't let you lift a finger."

"I like how you lift *your* fingers." Her hips press up into my hand, putting pressure where she needs it the most until her entire body clenches and a brilliant smile breaks across her beautiful face.

"I love you, and not just because you gave me an orgasm." She chuckles beside me, and I nuzzle her hair, soaking in the last few minutes I'll get for the day, because I know it's going to be busy. We're having our gender reveal party tonight, and everyone will be at our house. The best part is that by the time we're back in this bed tonight, we'll know what we're going to call the little peanut growing inside of Loren.

We were going to leave it a surprise, but our family hounded us until we couldn't stand it any longer. Besides, it'll be nice to be able to plan for the little guy . . . or girl. I don't care which. Although, the thought of having a girl does make me a nervous wreck. But then, I think about her having wavy brown hair and big chocolate eyes, and my heart melts.

A healthy wife and a healthy baby. That's all I care about.

"We're gonna have a baby!" Loren exclaims, her face splitting with the widest, happiest smile I've ever seen.

My heart immediately drops out of my chest and back up again, like when I'm on a rollercoaster.

A baby?

We're gonna have a baby?

Finally, I get my mouth to catch up with my brain and practically scream "We're gonna have a baby!" Inside the confines of the car, all that can be heard are Loren's sniffles and my kisses on every inch of her skin that's exposed. I'm kissing her neck and then her chest, down her arms, her hands, until I'm staring at her flat stomach.

"Hey, peanut," I whisper to the teeny, tiny baby growing in Loren's belly, who might not even have ears yet. "I'm your dad." I want him or her to know I'm out here and that I can't wait until they are too.

Holy shit, I'm gonna be a dad!

"Yes, you are! And you're gonna be the best dad ever."

I look up to meet Loren's tear-filled eyes. "Did I say that out loud?"

She nods, her face a mixture of tears and smiles. "I love you so much."

I grab both sides of her beautiful face and pull it to me, sliding my fingers through her hair and kissing her stupid.

Quickly, our kisses turn into more, and Loren is straddling me in the driver's seat. I chuckle between kisses, thinking that we won't be able to do this much longer, so we better indulge and get as much car sex in before we don't fit like this anymore.

"I want you so much. Like, if I can't have you right now, I might go insane. I want you more than I wanted that pickle with cheese dip earlier."

Loren has had the craziest eating habits lately. I should've known something was going on.

"I want you too, baby. Always," *I tell her, gripping her hips and pulling her against me so she can feel just how much truth is in that statement.*

"You have too many clothes on," *she says, moaning into my mouth.*

I reluctantly take my attention away from her to pull my shirt over my head, tossing it into the passenger seat. "Lean up. Lemme get these off."

Loren braces herself on my shoulders, while I pull her panties down her legs and drop them to the floor board. Since she's wearing a dress, giving me easy access to her fantastic tits, it can stay.

"You're so fucking beautiful," *I tell her, as my mouth worships her.*

"Just fuck me, Mr. Alexander," *she says with a groan.*

"As you wish, Mrs. Alexander."

I unbutton my jeans and pull my excruciatingly hard cock free, lining up and plunging deep into Loren's tight warmth. We both sigh in relief and pleasure, needing to be one and feel each other as we move in unison.

One of her hands pushes against the roof of the car, pressing her harder into me, gaining friction where she needs it. I won't last long. Watching her move above me, combined with her amazing tits bouncing in front of my face, could easily send me over the edge.

"You feel so good, baby."

"Ah, I'm so close."

"Come for me, Loren. Let me feel you."

I slip a hand between us, helping her reach her orgasm. As her legs shake and her body clenches around me, I lose it, thrusting forcefully into her. "Shit! Oh, God. So good, Tripp."

"Fuck!"

"That was . . ." *Loren sighs, leaning forward, resting her head on my chest.*

"It always is. My Ania." *I kiss her hair, inhaling her scent, loving her more than I did an hour ago, if that's possible.* "We're gonna have a baby."

Loren's soft laugh fills the car, and I couldn't be any happier than I am at this moment.

"Tripp," I hear my mom call as she comes in our back door.

"Kitchen, Mama," I call back.

"Hey, baby," she says, planting a kiss on my cheek as she sets a bag of groceries on the counter beside me. "Liza will be here in a few minutes. She stopped by the bakery and picked up the cake."

"Thanks for your help," I say, smiling over at her.

"Of course. I want to! You know that."

"I know, but we appreciate it."

She starts unloading the bags and buzzing around the kitchen and suddenly lets out a squeal. I turn quickly, thinking something's wrong.

"Mom?"

"Sorry! I'm just so excited! I can't wait to find out what we're having." Her face is beaming, and I can't help but return her smile because I'm excited too. And nervous. And anxious. "Aren't you just *dying* to know what it is?"

I laugh, shaking my head, because my whole family acts like they're the ones having the baby. "Yeah, I'm excited."

"I think it's going to be a girl."

"Yeah?"

"Yeah. I've had a few dreams, and they've all been about girls."

"Well, *that* scares the shit out of me."

"Oh, you're gonna be wonderful . . . either way. You're so much like your father," she says, cupping my cheek. "He'd be so damn proud of you."

"Thanks, Mama." Her words mean a lot to me and make me a little sad. I know he's looking down on all of us, and I know he's happy about the baby, but I wish he were physically here to enjoy this with us.

Before I can get too caught up in my melancholy thoughts, the back door opens up again, and a noisy Jack, Emmie, and Liza flood the house.

"Uncle Tripp!" the twins exclaim in unison, both giving the other a glare. It's funny because the older they get, the more they hate when they do things like that. They're the best of friends, but they both crave their independence. However, if anyone, and I mean *anyone*, does something to one of them that the other thinks is unfair or mean, watch out. They're fiercely protective of each other.

"Hey, guys!"

"Where's Loren?" Emmie asks, sticking her head into the living room.

"She's upstairs getting ready."

"I can't wait to find out what the baby is!" she squeals, sounding just like her grandmother.

"It's going to be a boy," Jack says, leaning over the counter.

"It's so not going to be a boy," Emmie retorts, rolling her eyes. "It's going to be a girl. Grandma said so!"

And the fight is on. The two of them are going back and forth about why they think it is or isn't going to be a girl or a boy, depending on who's giving their rebuttal. These kids should be on a debate team.

"Jack, can you get the last two bags out of the car?" my sister asks, defusing the argument. "Emmie, go with him, and help him."

"Sure, Mom," they both say, fighting over who gets the keys to unlock the car.

"I swear, those two are working my nerves today!"

My mom and I both laugh.

"Just wait," Liza says, looking at me pointedly across the counter. "Your time is coming. And remember what Dad always said about paying for our raising?" Her eyebrows shoot up, and she shakes the knife she's using in my direction. And suddenly, I'm scared for my life. "Yeah, well, just think about that, 'cause you've got a lot of raisin' to pay for." She snorts, muttering under her breath.

"Could I get you a glass of wine?" I ask because she looks like she could use it.

Mom, Liza, and I work seamlessly in the kitchen, while the kids take over the television in the living room. Loren eventually makes her way downstairs and starts helping with the salad. And just as we're putting the finishing touches on everything, Ben comes through the back door carrying three large bouquets of flowers.

Always an ass-kisser.

"For you," he says, handing one of them to his wife and planting a kiss on her. "Happy Valentine's Day, my love."

Liza giggles like a schoolgirl, taking the flowers from him. "Aww, baby, you're so sweet. I don't care what Tripp says about you." She shoots me a smirk across the kitchen and winks.

Such a brat.

"And for you," Ben says, handing another bouquet to my mom. "Happy Valentine's Day, Mama A." He kisses her cheek, earning him a big hug from my mom.

"And last but not least . . . For you, mama," he says, handing a big bouquet of blue and pink flowers to Loren. "Since we're still not sure what we're having, I decided to represent both." His smile shows how damn proud of himself he is.

"Why does everyone act like they're the ones having the baby?" I mutter, rolling my eyes. Loren leans into me, kissing my cheek and laughing.

"Thank you, Ben! These are beautiful," she says gratefully, going in search of some vases for all of the flowers.

"I would've bought some for you, Tripp, but I didn't know what color you'd like."

"You're such a suck-up."

"Excuse me? I'm sweet! Ask any of these beautiful ladies!" He motions around the room, and everyone is laughing at his grand gestures.

"Like I said, suck-up."

"Who's a suck-up?" Wyatt asks as he and his wife, Olivia, let themselves in the back door.

"Ben," I murmur.

"I could've told you that."

Olivia heads straight for Loren, rubbing her belly. She's been doing this for the last two months, every time we're all together. She and Wyatt have been trying to have a baby for three years now but still haven't been successful. She thinks rubbing Loren's baby bump is going to bring her some luck.

"Supper is almost ready," my mom announces.

Soon, we're all seated at the dining room table, passing around plates and bowls of delicious food and having loud conversations. Before the baby is big enough to sit at the table, we're going to have to get a bigger one. There's not an empty seat. We have to add an extra seat from the breakfast nook as it is when we're all here, which is often.

On nights that Grace and Will join us, we send Jack and Emmie to the bar to eat.

"So, when do we get to cut the cake?" Jack asks as he's shoveling food into his mouth.

"Manners, Jack!" my sister admonishes.

"Just like his father," I contribute, shaking my head in mock disgust.

"I'm going to have to thoroughly kick your ass later," Ben says, never looking up from his plate.

"Language!" Liza says, slapping her hand down on the table.

"That's a dollar, Dad!" Emmie tells him.

"I said ass! It's in the Bible," Ben says, rolling his eyes in frustration.

"Is it okay for Emmie and Jack to say?" Liza asks, trying to make her point.

"So, when are we cutting the cake?" Ben asks, attempting to take the attention off of himself.

As soon as everyone finishes, we quickly clear the table and bring in the cake. The excitement and anticipation are written all over every face around the table.

A flutter of nerves hits me.

Every ultrasound and doctor's appointment has made it feel more and more real, but *this*?

This makes it so fucking real.

I'm going to be a dad.

"Are we ready?" Loren asks, smiling over at me.

"Ready as we'll ever be," I tell her, meaning that on so many levels.

I look up and see my mom holding her hand over her mouth. Liza is leaning over on Ben's shoulder, while Ben hasn't taken his eyes off the cake. Olivia is holding Wyatt's hands, practically bouncing out of her seat. Emmie has her eyes closed, and her fingers crossed, saying a silent prayer, and Jack is just sitting there, mimicking his dad's stare-down with the cake.

"Go on. Let's see what we're having."

Loren's smile is so wide that it causes her eyes to crinkle at the edges, and they glisten in the warm light.

"I love you," I mouth to her. She leans over and kisses my cheek, whispering it back to me in my ear.

As the knife cuts through the cake, I close my eyes, wanting to stay in the dark for just a few seconds longer.

"It's a girl!" Loren exclaims, placing the first piece of cake on a plate before turning and kissing me soundly. The entire table erupts in cheers and congratulations—hugs, kisses, and tears of joy.

Today is one of the best days of my life. Every *best day* has included Loren, but this one is extra special because now we know that pretty soon, we'll have a sweet baby girl to love.

I hope she looks just like her mama.

Maybe we'll name her *Ania*.

about the authors

IN CASE YOU DIDN'T NOTICE, there are two of us.

We're both from the south, one just a little further than the other.

Jiff was born and raised in Louisiana. She's now living in Texas with her two teenagers and two bulldogs, Georgia Rose and Jake. She loves purple, 80's movies, and geeking out at Comic Cons.

Jenny Kate was born and raised in Oklahoma. She's the mom of a twelve-year-old and two Cavalier King Charles Spaniels, Wrigley and Oliver. She loves Kris Bryant, the Chicago Cubs, and coffee.

Some people think we've been friends forever, but in reality, we've only known each other for five years. Four of those years, we've spent spinning tales and writing words. Our first published book, Finding Focus, was released in November 2015.

If you like romance set in the south, then you'll love our southern fried fiction with heart and soul.

CONNECT WITH US

www.jiffykate.com

or find us on

Facebook—*www.facebook.com/jiffykatewrites*
Twitter—*www.twitter.com/jiffykatewrites*
Instagram—*www.instagram.com/jiffykatewrites*
Goodreads—*www.goodreads.com/jiffykate*
Facebook Reader's Group—Jiffy Kate's Southern Belles

acknowledgements

FIRST AND FOREMOST, WE'D LIKE to thank our families. You're the ones who have to put up with our lack of domesticity while writing words. Thank you for being so understanding and willing to make yourselves meals and play hours of Minecraft and watch dozens of videos on YouTube while we write.

For this story, our team of support started long before these pages were ever published. So, we'd like to thank the people who've been there since the beginning. Our kick-ass beta, Christine, and our amazing pre-readers, Pamela and Rachel, thank y'all so much for your expertise and time.

We're so grateful for our editor, Nichole, at Perfectly Publishable. You're so good at coaching us in the right direction and giving us a pep talk when we need it, and most importantly, you make our words shine.

Christine, our formatter, and the other half of Perfectly Publishable, you're a beam of sunshine. You have been a godsend from the very beginning. We're still in debt to Heather Maven for putting us in contact with you. Thank you for always being so generous with your time and for making our pages pretty.

Jada, thank you for another gorgeous cover!

And vodka. Always vodka. Vodka gets us through the hardest parts.

Also, a special shout-out to Amanda Daniel and MaryLee Teneyuque Huerta, for being some of our first pre-readers when we decided to publish this story. You're awesome! Thank you for your time and feedback.

And there is no better pimp than Lynette Nichols! We're so happy you're our friend and that you love our stories! We love you! Thanks for always being willing to help and read our words and telling everyone about them.

Thank you to THE FANDOM (you know who you are) for accepting and loving this story. It was a risk for us to write TOO and, now because of you, we can take an even bigger risk and put this story out for everyone to read. We're forever grateful for all you've done for us.

If you've made it this far, bless your heart.

We're so thankful for you, our readers. Writing is what we love to do, but having people read our words is what makes it worthwhile. If you loved this book or even liked it a little, we'd love to hear from you! Your reviews make our day.

Until next time,
Jiff and Jenny Kate

Made in the USA
San Bernardino, CA
10 March 2017